Tyler  s his
chest y scene.

His giggling daughter ily? Tyler blinked and refocused his eyes. He a gone close to a month, but certainly he wouldn't have mistaken Lily, the tall, slender, pale-eyed woman who had saved his life and befriended his daughter.

Only, the Lily he viewed today had curves in places he'd have been sure to remember. He closed his eyes momentarily, wondering if this apparition might disappear. But when his eyes scanned over Lily once again from top to bottom, he knew that what he was seeing was real.

A vibrant smile graced Lily's face. Her cheeks, rosy from playful exhilaration, only enhanced the sky-blue of her eyes. Light brown hair, shaken loose from its braid and kissed by the sun, was the color of darkened honey. Silken tresses flowed down her back in long golden waves.

Lily was lovely.

**Harlequin Historicals is delighted
to introduce Charlene Sands
and her terrific debut book**

Lily Gets Her Man
Harlequin Historical #554—March 2001

LILY GETS HER MAN

CHARLENE SANDS

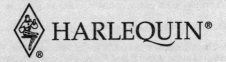

HARLEQUIN®

TORONTO • NEW YORK • LONDON
AMSTERDAM • PARIS • SYDNEY • HAMBURG
STOCKHOLM • ATHENS • TOKYO • MILAN • MADRID
PRAGUE • WARSAW • BUDAPEST • AUCKLAND

ISBN 0-373-29154-X

LILY GETS HER MAN

Visit us at www.eHarlequin.com

Printed in U.S.A.

Please address questions and book requests to:
Harlequin Reader Service
U.S.: 3010 Walden Ave., P.O. Box 1325, Buffalo, NY 14269
Canadian: P.O. Box 609, Fort Erie, Ont. L2A 5X3

To my dear friend Allyson Pearlman,
here's to climbing fences, great childhood memories,
constantly encouraging me to finish the story,
and especially for loving "Lily" as much as I do.

Special thanks to my editor, Patience Smith,
for her kindness, enthusiasm and consistent support.

Chapter One

Sweet Springs, Texas
1880

Lily knew she was being followed.

She recognized the distinct jingle of spurs and the sound of boots as they hit the sidewalk in a slow easy gait. With a nervous hand, she packed the bun knotted at the back of her head tighter. Lily scurried faster on the walkway, heading toward her mercantile store. Tyler Kincaide picked up his pace from behind.

She swallowed hard, keeping up her stride. With just a single glance from the handsome rancher, Lily's brain became muddled and her heart thumped too eagerly in her chest. It was always the same. No matter how many times she called herself a foolish ninny, she couldn't battle the yearnings Tyler Kincaide brought out in her.

Darn the man.

Too tall, too thin and plain, Lily held no notions of attracting the widower, but his unflinching smile made her feel…womanly.

More than womanly. Almost desirable.

Desperate to disappear from his view, she hastened her footsteps. His resounding thumps from behind made her heart pound. A decided stitch in her side ached like the dickens, but she kept up her rapid pace.

Suddenly the toe of her boot caught in a loosened floorboard and Lily desperately struggled for balance. A gasp escaped when she realized she was going down. She landed on the sidewalk with an ungracious plop. When the chorus of spurs ceased their jingling, dire dread surrounded her.

With eyes downcast, she struggled unsuccessfully to right herself, only to fall rather ungraciously again.

"Oh, pooh!" she exclaimed, then wanted to die right on the spot when she heard a deep masculine chuckle.

"Mornin', Miss Lily."

Tyler grinned at her, then offered his hand.

Mortified, she stared at his hand. Strong, large and calloused, Lily couldn't tear her gaze away. How often she'd envisioned Tyler Kincaide putting those hands on her body. How often she'd daydreamed of him, in her dreary room at the boardinghouse, hoping for things that would never be. For the briefest moments in time, Lily wished she were someone else. Someone Tyler Kincaide would want to hold in his arms on a cold, lonely night. But Lily scoffed at the notion. Tyler would never want her and she…she wouldn't know how to entertain such a man. Her experience with the male gender was sorely limited.

"Miss Lily?" he repeated.

A flush of blood singed her cheeks. Wasn't it bad enough she should fall flat on her backside like some pathetic town drunk staggering for balance? Now, wearing a mud-brown dress that should have been thrown into the hearth along with last winter's dry timber, she'd made a fool of herself on the main street of town in front of the most appealing man Lily had ever laid eyes on.

When she didn't readily answer, Tyler crouched down. "Are you hurt?" His dark eyes searched hers.

Lily let out a high-pitched chuckle. "N-no. I hate being clumsy, is all."

Tyler pried up the guilty floorboard. "Seems to me just about anyone might have tripped on this."

This time when he offered his hand, Lily accepted. She tried not to think about how his powerful hand felt as he closed strong fingers over hers. "Thank you."

"Actually, I was coming to see you." He helped her up. "Let's walk the rest of the way to your shop, Miss Lily."

Lily couldn't help smiling. Aside from her father, Tyler Kincaide was the only man to ever call her *Lily*.

Once inside Brody's Mercantile she breathed a secret sigh of relief. Familiar territory. She put on her apron and stood behind the counter. "Have you a need for supplies?"

He nodded slowly. "Some." His eyes scanned her near-empty shelves. "You down on supplies?"

Lily swallowed the lump in her throat. "I'm closing up shop. Since my father died, business has been trailing off, I'm afraid. Folks don't especially like doing business with a woman. And that grand new shop opened up on the other side of town."

"I heard something of it. That's why I'm here. First, let me say I'm sorry things haven't worked out. Jonah was a good man. Me and some of the other townsfolk would've tried to keep your business going if you had a mind to stay on.''

"Thank you, Mr. Kincaide, but that's not possible.'' Pride kept her from explaining that after she'd paid her father's debts, there was very little money left.

Jonah Brody had been a wonderful father and a decent man, but he'd had a weakness for gambling that had cost him his savings. Of course, he hadn't planned on taking sick, leaving his daughter pretty much to fend for herself these past few months. Once he'd realized his blunder, he'd apologized each and every day they'd had together until his passing. Lily had forgiven her ailing father, which had seemed to ease his mind some but still presented her with one monstrous problem. Survival.

"Miss Lily, we've known each other since your daddy opened this store some years back. I've asked you to call me Tyler.'' He removed his black felt hat treating her to a view of dark shaggy hair.

Her cheeks blazed pink. "Oh, well, Ty—Tyler.''

He grinned and her heart did a little flip. "That's better.''

She put her head down, intent on straightening out a crease in her skirt. "Now about those supplies you'll be needing. I'll do my best, but as you can see, I haven't reordered any stock.''

"Appears you have what I need. But, I have a question for you—if you're not opposed to answering.''

"No, Mr. Kin—Tyler. What's your question?''

"What will you be doing, now that you're closing up shop?''

"I—I promised my father I'd look up his brother.

My uncle Jasper lives in Chicago with his family. He'll take me in.''

Lily's promise to her father was to contact her uncle Jasper and make a home back east. It had been the one thing Jonah Brody had really asked of her. Knowing his daughter would be cared for had given the dying man his only real sense of peace. Tearfully Lily had promised as she'd watched her loving father take his last breath. She would keep that promise. But the thought of leaving Brody's Mercantile and Sweet Springs made her stomach clench and her heart hammer almost as much as it did when she gazed into Tyler Kincaide's deep soulful eyes.

She felt at home here, even though she had few friends. She had a mind to keep the store operating—to see if she could make a go of the place on her own. It would be a welcome challenge—the store always turned a profit, but her father's weakness for gambling had kept them pretty much on the brink of poverty.

"I see." Tyler frowned, slapping his hat against his knee. "What if he doesn't?"

She gasped. "I—I haven't given that a thought. He will take me in." Her hand flew to the knot at the back of her head. "I'm...sure he will. I'm paid up at the boardinghouse until the end of the month, then I hope to be heading east."

The door opened and Joellen Withers entered. "Mornin', Joellen," Tyler said with a charming smile.

"Why, Tyler, mornin'," the neighborly woman said, a note of surprise in her voice. "Hello, Lillian."

She walked up to the counter and Lily nodded her greeting. A pair of aged deep-set eyes twinkled when Joellen spoke. "Tyler Kincaide, you're a sight. My

Letty Sue was just saying the other day how she doesn't see much of you anymore.''

"How is Letty Sue?"

The woman placed a gentle hand on his arm. "She'd be a mite happier if you came callin'. She's always had a soft spot for you."

Tyler shook his head and chuckled. "You know, Joellen, your daughter's a beauty. She'll find herself a fine husband real soon."

Joellen Withers put her hands on her hips. "I know. My Letty Sue has more beaus than a cat's got whiskers. But you can't blame me for trying now, Tyler. You and that adorable little girl out there on that ranch. Makes a woman hanker for grandchildren. How is Bethann?"

"Growing faster than a wildflower and just as pretty."

"My, my. I bet she's the image of her mama. Bring her over to the house Sunday. I'll fix fried chicken."

"Will do. Thank you, ma'am." They watched Joellen wander down a near-barren aisle before Tyler turned to Lily. "I have business to tend to over at the bank. How about I come back and we go to supper at Emma's Place? I need to ask you something."

Lily's hand went to her chest. Her breath caught. "Why—I..." She'd never taken supper with a man before. No man had ever asked. And she was more than a little curious. What brought handsome Tyler Kincaide into her mercantile, asking probing questions, inviting her to supper?

"I'll come by for you in two hours." He shoved his hat onto his head, flashing white teeth in a broad smile, and sauntered out the door before Lily could say another word.

* * *

"Howdy, Emma. We'll have two of your daily specials and two lemonades. That is, if Miss Lily agrees." He cast a quick look her way. Lily nodded.

Tyler knew Emma was trying as she might to size things up. Nothing happened in town that Emma Mayfield wasn't privy to and it appeared today would be no exception. "How are you today, Miss Lillian?" Emma asked in a sugary voice.

"Fine. Thank you."

Emma looked from him to Lily before stalking off. It was clear Emma's curiosity was sparked. So was Lily's, judging by the way her pale blue eyes widened every time Tyler uttered a word. And she appeared as skittish as a baby calf searching for his mama, constantly tugging at that damnable knob of hair on her head.

Tyler wanted to ease her nervousness. He'd bet his best Hereford heifer, she'd not had any experience with men. He wished to hell she wouldn't keep looking at him as if he were some two-headed monster. Hell, he wasn't courting her. That's the last thing he'd ever want to do, with any woman. The notion made him shudder. No, he needed Miss Lillian Brody for more practical reasons.

He smiled. "Emma's got about the best food in town."

Stiff-shouldered, Lily placed her hands primly in her lap. Her eyes darted around the room. She did have pretty pale blue eyes, he thought, when they weren't fluttering around like an energetic butterfly near a honeysuckle bush.

"I haven't eaten here since before Father died. We

would come," she added quietly, "every Saturday night."

Tyler leaned back in the chair and stretched his legs. He studied her for a moment. She hadn't had an easy time of it. Tyler remembered Jonah Brody's penchant for gambling. He'd been as good a man as they come, but his weakness for placing a bet was known throughout the town. He'd aim straight for the Golden Garter after supping with his daughter and, word had it, he'd not leave until the wee morning hours, usually with his pockets more threadbare than when he'd first arrived. Tyler had witnessed his run of bad luck a time or two.

Must have been hard for her.

Now he had a chance to help her out. If only she'd accept his offer.

"Do you miss Emma's cooking or are you a good cook yourself?"

She let out a tiny laugh. "Oh, I can cook. Been feeding my father since Mama died, but I don't cook anymore. Mrs. Anderson's meals at the boardinghouse are really quite good. More food than I can bear to eat."

Tyler swept his gaze over her slim body. Somebody ought to put some meat on her bones, he thought. She was far too thin to appear healthy. He glanced away before she figured out what he was thinking. She was so fragile-looking with light skin and the palest blue eyes. But when she smiled, her eyes held warmth that portrayed her heart. She had a childlike vulnerability. But she was no child. If he recalled correctly she was three years shy of his twenty-eight.

"Tell me, Miss Lily, are you happy here in Sweet Springs?"

"Well, yes. I love it here." She eyed him skeptically. "Of course, now that my father's gone, it's…"

"Lonely?"

"Yes, lonely."

Tyler sighed, knowing about the kind of loneliness that can consume a body. He'd felt it, too, since Lizabeth's death. He'd nearly drunk himself into oblivion for months, thinking about how she died. If it weren't for Bethann and the ranch, he might not have survived. But with the help of loyal friends, he'd pulled himself together.

Since Lizabeth's passing, he'd had no use for any female, except the occasional lady at the Golden Garter Saloon. But now he needed a woman. Desperately. And he knew of no better choice than Miss Lillian Brody, a proper lady. "Do you want to go to Chicago?"

Lily crossed her arms over her chest, bringing in loose folds of material enough for Tyler to see she did have some womanly attributes. She straightened in the seat. "Mr. Kincaide, I have little choice. Uncle Jasper is my only family and from what I remember of him, he's a dear man."

"Tyler, remember?" he asked, curling his lips up.

She nodded with a tense smile.

"But, what if you had another choice?"

"A choice? I don't understand."

Judging by the tone of her voice, he'd obviously perplexed her. Leaning in, he rested his elbows on the table, eyes intent on her. "Sorry. I got something to ask you, but first I wanted to know the situation. I have a proposition for you."

Lily's back went rigid. "A proposition?" She swallowed and lowered her voice. "What kind of proposition, exactly, Mr. Kincaide?"

"A very respectable one, Miss Lily."

Emma brought their lemonades, slowly lowering them to the table. She swept her sharp gaze from one to the other. "Thank you kindly, Emma," he said with a quick nod and watched patiently for her to move on.

"I'm just going to come out and say it." Tyler raked a hand through his hair. He was a man who wasn't comfortable with words. He believed actions spoke more clearly. "I need a woman to come out to the ranch to live with me."

Lily gasped, her pale blue eyes going wide. She started to rise. Tyler realized his blunder immediately. He grabbed her arm and held her gently.

"Ah, hell! I said it all wrong. Sit down and let me explain." Lily stared at the arm he held. He released her reluctantly hoping she'd not dash away. "Please."

Lily hesitated, then looked him in the eye. He reassured her with a nod. Frowning, she slowly sat down. Tyler let out a silent sigh of relief. He knew he'd better get to the point quickly. This was too important to him.

"Bethann needs a woman around. That's what I meant to say. She's growing up fast, nearly six years old now."

Lily appeared to regain her composure. At least she wasn't frowning at him now. "I remember her. Adorable pigtails. Green eyes. You brought her to the mercantile a time or two. I snuck her a peppermint candy once."

"Yes. She seemed to like you, too. Fact is, Louisa and Manuel left the ranch to make a home for themselves in New Mexico a while back. I can make do without them, but Bethann needs more. It's almost time for spring roundup. I'm shorthanded as it is. I can't keep being both mother and father to her.''

Anger sparked in her eyes. Tyler couldn't imagine what he'd said this time to insult her.

She bristled and spoke to him as if she were the school marm and he a youngster who wouldn't do his lessons. ''What you need is a wife. And from what I gather, Mr. Kincaide, you could have your pick of any female in the territory.''

So that was it. He slammed his fist on the table, causing Lily to jerk back. ''I don't want a wife,'' he snarled. ''I had a wife. Lizabeth's gone.''

Tyler closed his eyes. Why was it every woman on the good earth saw fit to try to get him married again? It was the very last thing he wanted.

But he did need Lily. For Bethann.

When he reopened his eyes, he was relieved to find sympathy in Lily's expression. ''I'm sorry, Miss Lily. Honest. I have nothing but respect for you. What I'm offering is a job, a respectable position. I'd like to hire you to stay on at the ranch and take care of my daughter.''

Lily let out a compressed breath. ''What you are offering, Mr. Kincaide, is highly improper. I cannot live under the same roof as you or any man without the sanctity of marriage. I'm sorry.''

Lily was a churchgoer. She had high moral standards. That's what he wanted for his daughter. Nearly six years of age, Bethann needed a female's influence. Her wild and precocious ways were starting to nettle at him. Why, his daughter refused to wear a dress most of the time. A young girl's got to learn to wear more than britches.

It wasn't all that unusual for a woman to hire on at a ranch as housekeeper. He had to make Lily understand. "Now, Lily, don't go getting the wrong idea. I wouldn't compromise you."

"I know that." She gave him a sad smile as if to say she knew she wasn't the sort of woman to strike a man's fancy. "All the same, I cannot live under your roof, working for you or not. We'd be alone in that ranch house." Her voice was barely above a whisper. "There'd be talk."

She hoisted her chin and stood with a prideful look on her face. Tyler admired her conviction, even if he didn't agree with her.

"Thank you for the lemonade and the meal. I'm sure it would have been delicious."

Tyler swore under his breath and watched her head for the door. Tarnation! There wasn't another woman here in town he'd trust with Bethann's care. Besides, he wanted no real ties to any women. They would try to drain every last ounce out of him while attempting to retrieve his soul. Only, he had no soul. Bethann, the tiny replica of her mother, had his heart, but his soul had been buried along with Lizabeth nineteen months ago. Somehow he knew Lily would understand.

He'd seen the depth of her understanding in her gentle blue eyes. She'd be good for Bethann. Soft-spoken and kind, Tyler knew of no other woman whom he'd trust with his daughter's care. Whether she admitted it or not, Miss Lillian Brody needed his help and he certainly needed hers.

Damn. The last thing he wanted was a wife.

He stood and called out before she reached the door, "What if I married you?"

Chapter Two

Lily froze. His words stung like shards of ice pelting down her body. Another proposal from Tyler Kincaide! This one even more unfathomable than the first.

In her imaginings as a young girl, when her beau proposed there'd been flowers—daffodils and lilacs—surrounding her. Nightingales would sing out a melodious tune. The moon would shine and the stars twinkle as her gallant man spoke dearly of his love and devotion to her.

Ha! The irony was enough to make her cry. A nearly shouted proposal from across a crowded room. The offense ran too deep, even for her to ignore. If she were a betting woman, she would have laid down her last dollar that Tyler Kincaide didn't know the depth of the insult he'd just bestowed upon her.

She knew what she was. But to have a man admit in one breath he didn't want a wife, then casually throw out a proposal gave her the full measure of her appeal. Absolutely none.

She turned to find him standing before her. All eyes in the supper house were watching, waiting. Lily suppressed a shudder. The humiliation was unbearable, but she kept her head up and looked him square in the eyes.

"No, thank you, Mr. Kincaide." She pushed open the door and stepped out, taking in a steadying breath of crisp air. She heard the familiar jingle of spurs from behind and knew he'd followed her outside.

"Lily, wait."

She stopped short on the sidewalk. Tyler knocked into her. She felt the hard wall of his chest meet with her back before he took hold of her shoulders and turned her.

"What'd I do?"

She had a good mind to tell him, but the warmth of his touch was seeping into her skin. Firm fingers dug in with gentle determination. He was as close as any man had ever been to her, inches away. He was beautiful, magnificent—she'd always known. Lily closed her eyes, relishing the feel of his hands on her before stepping out of his reach.

Then the absurdity of it struck her. She laughed. A good hearty laugh, easing the tension that had her wound tighter than newfangled barbed wire around a fence post. Shaking her head, she said, "I'm sure, Tyler Kincaide, you wouldn't understand."

He glared at her. Lily realized her mistake. She doubted too many women chanced to laugh at Tyler Kincaide.

With arms folded, he rasped, "Explain it to me."

"I don't think I could. Have a good day, Mr. Kincaide." She shrugged and managed to walk gracefully away as if marriage proposals were an everyday occurrence.

But when she heard his string of muttered oaths

from behind, she hiked up her skirts and scampered across the street in a most undignified fashion.

Lily took several deep breaths when she entered the mercantile. Watching the rancher from a distance made her heart swim with delicious thoughts but this time, being so near him, remembering his touch on her skin, unnerved her completely. Why, the very thought of living under his roof, sent uninvited thrills down her spine. How long before she lost her foolish heart to him entirely?

It's a notion you'd better not entertain.

She couldn't be his housekeeper. All sense of in-grained propriety warned her off. And then there was the deathbed promise she'd made to her dear father.

Lily began rearranging the meager supplies on the shelves. Forcing her thoughts to her own dilemma, she considered her options. Contacting her uncle in Chicago was her first priority. Since Uncle Jasper hadn't returned her letters, she'd send him a wire. Today. Time was running out and so was the little bit of money she had tucked away.

The door opened then slammed shut. Lily twirled around. Tyler stood with hands on hips, scowling at her. "We're not through yet."

Her heart fluttered at the sight of him again, but she forced a glare his way. "I'd say we were."

"I didn't get what I came for."

Lily stared at his face, the firm line of his masculine jaw set stubbornly. A small feminine part of her rejoiced. No man had ever pursued her, even if his proposal was quite out of the question.

Tyler thrust a list of needed supplies her way.

She bit her lip, chagrined at her mistake and angry all the same. She picked up the list and began filling the order. She dumped a package of Arbuckle's coffee on the counter and reached for the next item on the list, sugar.

"You know, Lily, you could stand to hear me out."

Lily had heard just about enough. The man's audacity spurred her courage. She set the sack of sugar down and rounded the counter to stand before him, jutting a finger in his chest.

"I know what you want, Tyler Kincaide. You want a woman to come out there and run your house. To school your daughter, cook your meals, clean your clothes, to…to—you know. You can't hire someone, so you figured you'd find some pathetic creature and up and marry her. You, Tyler Kincaide," she said poking her finger one last time into his chest, "want to *get* married, without *being* married!"

Anger flashed in his dark eyes as he pulled her finger off him. His teeth clenched. "I don't want to get married at all. Damn it, Lily." He yanked off his felt hat and rubbed his forehead, squeezing his eyebrows together.

Lily put her hands on her hips. "Do not swear in my presence, Mr. Kincaide!"

Tyler blinked before giving her a long studious look. Then she noticed a gleam in his eyes. Not anger this time. It appeared to be…a spark of admiration?

"Yes, ma'am. I apologize."

He rubbed his chest where she'd jabbed him. Lily blushed. What had come over her? She'd never *attacked* a man before.

"There's many a woman who'd take me up on my offer."

Marrying Tyler Kincaide for the wrong reason would surely cause her nothing but heartache. She had always been honest with herself; Tyler would never come to love someone like her. Her foolish pride wouldn't let her accept anything less. And she hadn't forgotten the sincere promise she'd made to her father to locate Uncle Jasper.

Lily threw her arms up out of frustration. "So why me? I'm sure Letty Sue Withers would love to become your wife. Why not ask her?"

Tyler rested an elbow on his folded arm and scrubbed his jaw. He shook his head. "Couldn't. A woman like that, she'd be—expecting things."

Expecting things? Lily stared at the cleft in his chin momentarily, then lifted her eyes to his in certain understanding. "You mean like..."

His slow nod was affirmation. "I got no room in my heart for anyone but Bethann. It's best you know that right on. You need a place to live. My daughter needs a woman around. If that means taking a wife, so be it.

"I'd respect you, Miss Lily, and I swear, you'd never want for anything. But I was being honest when I said I don't want a wife. I mean in the real sense, that is. So I guess you're right. I'm offering marriage as payment for caring for Bethann and running the house."

That took the starch right out of her. Lily's shoulders fell. "I see."

"You could do worse, Lily," he said softly, laying several coins on the counter. "If things don't work out with your uncle in Chicago, my offer still stands. Think about it." Lily noted his quiet strength as he hoisted the parcels over his shoulder and sauntered out.

She let out a heavy sigh and watched the handsome

man as he strode to his buckboard. He was right about one thing, she *could* do worse. Much worse.

"Papa, Papa!"

Tyler smiled when he heard the small voice call to him. He jumped from the wagon and threw out his arms. Bethann came running into them. He lifted her up as little arms and legs wrapped around him. "Ah, how's my sweetcakes this afternoon?"

"Papa, you left without me. I thought I was goin' to town with you."

"Not this time, darlin'. Papa had some business in town. Next time." He lifted an auburn pigtail and tugged.

"Promise?"

"I promise." Setting her down, he took her hand. "Papa's got to have a talk with you. Come inside."

"Is it about my birthday?"

"Maybe." He sat down in the parlor and lifted her onto his lap. A soft, plump hand went around his neck.

"Do I get my pony, Papa?"

"Now, Bethann, I know you've been wanting a pony. But you're a mite too young yet. A pony needs lots of care."

"Oh, I'd care for it! I'd love it and love it. Just like I love you, Papa." She hugged his neck.

Tyler gave his guileless daughter a sideways glance. How'd she learn to do that so young? Her innocent charm could talk him into just about anything. If this was any indication, he was going to have a high time of it, fending off her beaus ten years from now. "What's your second choice, darlin', if you had to wait a bit for a pony?"

She frowned. Tyler imagined the little wheels in her

head clicking, considering. Then her eyes lit. "A sister, Papa. Rhonda Mae McDowell is getting a sister. She said I couldn't have one, 'cause I don't have a ma."

Tyler suppressed a grimace. Lizabeth would've given him more children by now and their only daughter wouldn't be so lonely. Damn, he knew what Bethann needed. A mother.

Unfortunately, that meant a wife for him.

"Rhonda may be getting a brother for all she knows, darlin'."

Bethann shrugged her small rounded shoulders. "Rhonda Mae said that don't matter. A brother's all right. Long's she can boss him around a time or two."

Tyler chuckled and kissed her cheek. His mind went to the ponies in his remuda. He'd have to pick out the gentlest one of all.

Lily packed the last of her merchandise in a large crate and paid Tommy Mayfield two bits to help her haul it to the new emporium across town. With a little bit of haggling on her part, the new proprietor agreed to buy out what was left on her shelves. It didn't amount to much, but she was grateful for the small profit.

"Here you go, Tommy," she offered. "I don't think they'll be wanting these two broken peppermint sticks, and that licorice whip is all but dried out."

The boy put his hand out. "Yes, ma'am. Thank you."

She watched him take a bite of licorice before heaving the crate in his arms. Tommy was built like his ma, stout and sturdy. And his big eyes rounded in curiosity with the slightest bit of encouragement just like Emma's did.

"You leaving town soon, Miss Lillian?" the boy asked good-naturedly as they strode toward the east end of town.

"I hope so, Tommy. I'm waiting to hear from my uncle in Chicago. I wired him a week ago."

"My ma—well, she says you should take Mr. Kincaide up on his offer. Said he proposed in a most unusual way."

"Yes, that he did," she said with a weary sigh. Emma Mayfield made short work of informing the entire town about Tyler Kincaide's odd proposal. Lily would have known, even if long-winded Micah Pennicott hadn't come into the store days ago, spouting off, pretending an interest in the last book on her shelves. A book of poetry, for land's sake!

She'd have known by the way she was being treated. Amazing, how one gesture changed the town's opinion of her. Instead of sympathetic glances stolen by averted eyes, she was getting long, curious stares, marked surprisingly enough by unbidden respect and slow smiles.

"Are you goin' to marry him?"

"Now, how can I marry him if I'm going to Chicago?"

"No, I don't suppose you can, but my ma says that any gal in her right mind would've took Mr. Kincaide up on his offer. Said he'd be the finest catch in all Texas, and if she weren't already—"

"Uh, Tommy—" Lily's steps faltered, watching the boy move slightly ahead of her, until her unblinking gaze fastened to bright red suspenders hitching up his trousers. "I don't think we should be discussing this, do you?"

Tommy slowed his steps. "No, ma'am."

Lily tousled his hair and the young boy gave her a bright smile. When they reached the new emporium, he set the crate down and proceeded to wander about the store, exclaiming it was three times larger than Miss Lillian's.

Lily, too, looked around, seeing Wilbourne's Emporium with consuming eyes. It was a fine store, enormous in size, housing everything imaginable from ready-to-wear clothes to an array of jars overflowing with candy to the latest dime novels. There were dry goods, canned goods, some new farming tools, yards upon yards of fabrics and bolts of ribbons and fine laces.

Brody's Mercantile might have been this fine, but her father's mind had never been on business. He'd taken the monthly profits from the cash drawer under Lily's protests and instead of investing them in his livelihood, he'd chosen to squander them away at the gaming tables. *"You'll see, my darling girl,"* he'd promised. *"One good night's all I need. We'll be set for life."*

Unfortunately he'd never had one good night.

Lily settled up with the clerk, wishing she could indulge and buy a new dress. One that fit her better, in pretty calico like the one she spied when she entered. She'd have to take in the seams. They didn't make dresses to fit her gangly form, but she couldn't afford the dress anyway. No use hankering for something she couldn't have.

She was about to depart when she heard the sweet

sound of a child's voice. "Papa, do I have to get all gussied up?"

"Bethann, I would think you'd want a new dress for your birthday party."

"But, Papa, I don't need a dress to ride my new pony. My britches'll do."

"Now, darlin', a lady needs to wear dresses from time to time. You can't be wearing them britches every day."

Lily gasped when she recognized the man's voice. She turned to make a quick departure only to find Tyler's eyes on her. She stilled her quickened heart as best she could. He took hold of his daughter's hand and approached her.

"Hello," he said with a grin, then bent his head. "Bethann, you remember Miss Lily Brody, don't you?"

Lily looked down at the little girl. Bethann clung to her daddy's legs. "Uh-huh."

Lily's heart melted at the sight of two chubby arms wrapped around this big, strong man's thighs. Lily bent down. "Hello, Bethann. I remember when you came to my daddy's store."

Eyes, the color of polished jade, widened in recognition. "You gave me a candy."

"That's right, I did."

"My papa's giving me a pony for my birthday. I'm going on six."

Lily chuckled. "A pony? That's wonderful. I know you'll take excellent care of it, too."

"I'm going to love my pony, just like Papa," she offered with a big smile. Then her lips curled downward. "I don't have a ma, so I can't have a sister."

Something tightened in Lily's heart. She'd been an

only child, too, and often longed for a sibling. Now that her father had passed on, she had no one to turn to, except an uncle she hadn't seen in fifteen years. "A pony is the next best thing to a sister, I'd say. And you don't have to share your clothes."

Bethann giggled.

Lily straightened, averting her gaze and smoothing her skirts. She felt Tyler's eyes on her.

"Have you heard from your uncle?" he inquired.

She looked down, clicking the toe of her worn-out boot to the other. "I'm heading to the telegraph office now, to see if he's sent a message."

"So you haven't heard?"

She lifted her chin. "I expect to anyday now."

His brows furrowed as he studied her.

"Papa, I have to go. Hurry, Papa." Lily's gaze fell on the child's frowning face as she shuffled to and fro. She was tugging at her father's pant leg with one hand while the other hand grabbed at her own britches. Lily stifled a chuckle, finding the usually confident man wearing a befuddled expression.

"Uh, okay, darlin'. Just let me—"

"If you'll allow me, I'll take her," Lily offered, this time letting go a full giggle when a look of relief washed over Tyler's face. She put out a hand to Bethann, hoping the child would take it.

"But, Papa—"

"It's all right, Bethann. Miss Lily will take you around back. I'll be waiting right here."

Bethann laced her fingers through Lily's as they strode out. Lily was amazed how much the little one could chatter. She seemed to go on incessantly, without coming up for a breath. And in the span of a few minutes, Lily knew a whole lot more about Tyler,

Bethann and the Circle K Ranch than she had ever expected.

Bethann let go of Lily's hand the minute they reentered the emporium and ran to her father. "Can we invite Miss Lily to my birthday party, Papa?"

Tyler bent down and scooped his daughter up so that two pairs of eyes looked Lily's way. "Why, sure. That's a fine idea. How about it, Miss Lily, would you like to come tomorrow to Bethann's party?"

Flustered, Lily stammered. "Well, I—I have so much to do and I...I have no way out there—"

"Papa can pick you up in the wagon, Miss Lily. Can't you, Papa?" Bethann asked with a hope-filled expression.

"I'll be riding fences in the mornin', but I'm sure ole Wes, or one of the ranch hands can pick her up, darlin'."

"Oh, yippee! You can see my new pony, Miss Lily."

"Well...I—" Lily shrugged in surrender. She didn't want to disappoint the little girl who seemed to crave attention. It was obvious the child was hungry for a female friend. She'd already been advised by Bethann that Rhonda Mae was her only other friend. And she'd be busy when her baby sister arrives. "I'd love to come. Thanks for inviting me."

Both Kincaide heads nodded in approval. But when Lily turned to leave, the older Kincaide stopped her. "Oh, Miss Lily, one more thing."

She whirled around, "Yes?"

"Will you help pick out a new dress for Bethann and doodads to go with it." He scratched his head. "I can't seem to figure 'em all out."

* * *

Lily felt a lightness in her step as she headed for the telegraph office. Helping Bethann choose a new party dress had been fun. She'd felt as if she were dressing up a doll, matching colors to Bethann's auburn hair and dazzling green eyes. They'd decided on an emerald green and white poplin dress. Matching ribbons were purchased as well as new under-drawers and stockings.

Tyler had looked on from a distance. With each choice, Bethann held the article up and waited for her father's approval. He stood with arms folded, casually leaning against the far wall, watching. When he gave his daughter a wide grin of approval, Lily found her heart in her mouth again.

Darn the man.

With just a look, he could turn her insides to plum pudding.

She hastened her steps to the telegraph office. The sooner she rode out on that stage the better. When she arrived, the telegraph operator was frowning. With a shake of his head, he said, "Sorry, Miss Lillian."

Lily's whole body sagged while she tried to suppress tears that were welling up and shuffle her disappointment down. "Nothing for me, Charlie?"

"No, ma'am. Not today."

"You know I'm at Mrs. Anderson's boardinghouse. Please send a message as soon as you hear anything."

The operator complied, smiling pleasantly, looking as if he hadn't heard those very words each day that week. "Yes, ma'am. As soon as it comes in," he promised.

Well, Lily mused, at least he held out some hope. Lily was losing all of hers. And she still had to con-

tend with Bethann's birthday party at the Circle K
Ranch tomorrow. She couldn't disappoint the child,
but it was truly the last place she wanted to be.

A single look from the girl's father did things to her
body she didn't understand.

Things, for the ever-loving life of her, she couldn't
control.

Chapter Three

Wes Farley helped Lily onto the Kincaide buckboard. His leathery hands were gentle on her waist as he lifted her up. She adjusted herself, smoothing out her skirts, making sure her hem covered her ankles. With her tall frame, the dresses were always an inch or two lacking.

"Sure is nice of you, Miss Lillian, comin' to the youngun's birthday celebration and all. That girl needs a female touch, if'n I ever saw it."

Wes ambled around the wagon, hopped on and gave the team of horses a click of the reins. Lily hung on as the wagon lurched forward. "Oh, Wes, that little one didn't give me much choice with those wide eyes and happy smile. I couldn't say no."

"Her pa's got the same problem, I'm 'fraid. That little un can talk her pa into anythin', but don't ya be repeatin' this old fool's notions, ya hear? That boy'd have me set out on my ear. Can't say as I blame him none. He's had a tough time, raising Bethann by himself."

"It's never easy when one tries to do the job of

both parents. Bethann seems like a sweet child, though.''

''That she is, what with havin' a fine ma and pa and all. Got her ma's looks.''

''Did you know her well?''

''Sure 'nough. Ever since Tyler brung her to the ranch, prouder 'an a peacock spreadin' colors. About eight years back as I recall. Benjamin Kincaide, his pa, was alive then. Yep, them were the days.''

''What was she like?''

''Aw, Tyler don't like nobody talkin' about Liza-beth. Saw him fire a hand right on the spot when he brought up her name. She was a fine lady, that Liza-beth was.''

Lily didn't want to pry so she held back the dozens of questions that were popping into her mind. Liza-beth, beautiful, sweet-natured, adored by her man, and Lily, did have one thing in common. Tyler Kincaide had proposed to them both. And there the similarities ended.

Lily knew one proposal was filled with love, desire and want. The other, hers, was derived from certain masculine desperation. She'd be a fool to think of it as more. But in the privacy of her lonely room, where she was sure no one would intrude, Lily did fantasize about Tyler Kincaide. His slow grins and deep-set dusky eyes. What they did to her! The darkened circles under her eyes were evidence enough of her restless nights of fancy. It was daft and as fruitless as a peach tree in the dead of winter.

She'd remembered peering longingly out the window of the mercantile whenever Tyler and his wife rode into town on this very buckboard. Tyler would gaze down at Lizabeth with adoration in his eyes. And

Lizabeth would give him a warm smile, as if they shared a sweet secret that no one else would ever know.

Oh, to have a man look at her like that, she thought with a wistful sigh, then called herself a foolish ninny again. No man would ever look at her like that.

Lily tied the ribbon of her straw hat tighter under her chin. The Texas sun beat down, burning her cheeks. Rivulets of perspiration moistened her best white shirt until she felt a single drop easily make its way down her chest, spreading thin against the waistband of her skirt.

She half listened to the old man ramble on about any which subject, all the while looking out at the scenery. It wasn't often she ventured out of town. She settled back in the seat and decided to enjoy the excursion.

Wildflowers laced the grasslands, a healthy glow of springtime color painting the landscape with vivid hues. And a fragrant pungent scent sweetened the air. This was Lily's favorite time of year. Everything was beginning to bloom in the southernmost tip of the Texas Panhandle.

Nearly an hour later the buckboard pulled to a stop in front of a sprawling ranch house.

"Tyler's checkin' fence posts goin' up on the east end of the property. He's asked fer you to help Bethann put on her new duds fer the party—if'n ya don't mind, Miss Lillian, since you was the one that helped pick 'em out. Party'll start at three this aft'noon."

Lily nodded as she was helped off the wagon. She turned to stare at the Kincaide house. The structure was painted dove gray, but the steps, the window shutters, railings and the door all sparkled milky white. A long, flowing veranda wrapped itself around three sides. Flower beds, long since neglected, graced its perimeter. Lifting her skirts, Lily took the steps tentatively, then twirled around when she heard the clinking of the wagon as it pulled away. "Wes! Wait!"

"I got work to do, Miss Lillian. Ya jus' go inside and make yerself comfy now. Boss's orders. Bethann's prob'ly drivin' Randy plumb crazy in there. You can spell him."

Perplexed, Lily turned to stare at the wide panel door. She hoisted her skirts and moved to the door, but before her hand reached the knob, the door burst open.

"Miss Lily, you came!" Bethann smiled brightly.

A lanky jeans-clad figure lurked behind the doorway. As soon as he saw Lily, tension eased from his face. "Looks like your friend's here, Bethann. I'll be headin' out. Your daddy's expectin' me on the range." The man brushed past Lily with a tip of his hat. "Afternoon, ma'am."

"Her name's Miss Lillian Brody. She's here for my party. You coming, Randy?"

"Sorry, I can't." Randy moved quickly down the steps, as if escaping a terrible fate. "Have a nice time now, Bethann." He was at a complete run when those last words were uttered.

Lily glanced down at Bethann. The child gave her a mischievous smile and Lily couldn't help but chuckle.

Bethann led her into the parlor, then threw herself down onto the settee. "My papa says we can't go out to see my pony till he gets back."

"That's fine, Bethann. We'll wait." Lily looked the child over. Caked-on dirt covered her overalls and seemed to be an extension of her small body. Where did dirt end and little girl begin? Two long braids hanging past her shoulders looked more like seasoned pepper than the ginger color she knew her hair to be. "How'd you get so dirty?"

Bethann shrugged. "I fell."

"Where on earth did you fall?"

"Near the creek."

"The creek? Tell me you weren't out there all by yourself."

"It ain't so far from here. 'Sides, Randy was being an old feather-head."

Lily hid a grin. "It isn't so far from here," she corrected. "Did you sneak out?"

"Randy ain't my papa. I don't have to listen to him. He said to stay put, but I wanted to see the tadpoles."

"Bethann," Lily said sternly, "Randy may not be your papa, but your father gave him the responsibility to watch out for you today. You should've listened to him. You might've been hurt. And nobody would know where you were."

"I almost fell right smack in the water."

Lily hugged the child to her chest. "Bethann, what you did was dangerous. Your papa would be really sad if you were hurt. You don't want to make your papa sad now, do you?"

The little girl's eyes broadened in understanding then she slowly shook her head. Lily hoped she made her point clear enough for Bethann to take heed.

"Bethann, you've got to do something for me. You've got to promise never to run off like that. Your papa needs you around, sweetie, safe and sound."

"I promise. I got to take care of my papa."

Lily watched Bethann's solemn expression. She believed her, for now. "All right then, first I think a bath is in order, then we'll get you dressed for the party."

The words seemed strange coming from Lily's lips. Since when had she been appointed guardian over Bethann? The way she was taking over, a body might think she belonged in this house.

"I hafta take a bath?"

"Of course, you're filthy. Lead the way."

It was almost three when Wes let Joellen and Letty Sue Withers into the house. A clean-scrubbed Bethann was propped on Lily's lap in her new birthday attire. Lily was reading a book of nursery rhymes to her.

The women greeted Lily and wished Bethann a happy birthday before sitting down in the parlor. Shortly after, Rhonda Mae McDowell came prancing in, running over to Bethann. The two girls took to scampering through the house.

Letty Sue did her best to ignore Lily by turning away and engaging her mother in conversation. That suited Lily just fine. But Joellen was a gracious woman and steered the conversation to Lily.

"Lillian, I hear you've sold your goods to Wilbourne's Emporium. Will you be staying in Sweet Springs?"

Lily straightened in her seat. "I hope to be moving on soon. I've an uncle in Chicago. I expect to hear from him any day now."

Joellen nodded, a look of compassion crossed over her features. "I see, dear. Well, I hope it works out for you."

"Yes. Thank you." Lily felt Letty Sue's eyes on her. She wouldn't return her gaze. Instead Lily stared down at her hands.

"Everyone knows why he did it, Lillian," Letty Sue said smugly.

Lily's head shot up to view the young woman sitting forward in the chair. The material of her flowery dress tightened, jutting out her full bosom and cinching in her small waistline.

Lily stiffened. Letty Sue Withers was everything Lily was not. Petite, exceptionally pretty and feminine. Not to mention, five years younger. "Did what?"

Steely blue eyes rounded on her. "Propose. He only wants you for Bethann. The whole town knows it, too. He'd never want you for anything—"

"Now, Letty Sue," Joellen said, her eyes softening on Lily, "a man like Tyler doesn't propose lightly. If he asked her, he meant it."

"But, Mama, he said just the other day, if things were different, he'd be asking me."

Joellen shot her daughter a cautionary glance. "He did no such thing, darling. He merely stated you'd make some man mighty happy when the time comes. Tyler is a gentleman, Letty Sue. Let's not be discussing this any further."

Lily's face heated. She wanted to dash out of the room and pretend she'd never laid eyes on Tyler Kincaide. Because of him, her entire existence had been set out for the town's scrutiny.

Lily had lived in Sweet Springs for ten years and not once in that time had anyone taken much notice. She had few friends. Lily preferred spending her time alone, and while all the other young women were being courted, Lily stayed in her room and read books. She had a love for the written word. She'd read everything from Hawthorne's *The Scarlet Letter* to

Brontë's *Jane Eyre*. And even though she'd read Jules
Verne, his notions of the future gave her pause.

Throughout her younger years, books and periodi-
cals had become a shy awkward girl's closest com-
panions. She stole a quick glance at Letty Sue. Lily
doubted she'd known a lonely day in her life. No,
Letty Sue Withers thrived on being the center of attention.

Joellen's gentle voice broke into her thoughts.
"Please pay her no mind, Lily. I'm sure it's none of
our business. We came for Bethann's birthday celebration, not to make you at all uncomfortable."

Lily forced a small smile and glanced at the clock.
It was three-fifteen.

A clean-shaven Wes came in with the food he pre-
pared. The amiable cook headed for the kitchen. The
ladies joined him, helping set out chicken, dumplings,
boiled potatoes, a berry pie and a chocolate cake. He
poured each of them a cool glass of lemonade from a
large pitcher.

"Boss should've been back by now. Can't see him
bein' late for the little un's big day."

"Maybe someone should ride out and fetch him,"
Letty Sue suggested with a sugary smile.

Wes scratched his head. "If'n he's not back directly, I'll ride on out to find him. Prob'ly lost track
a time."

Bethann raced into the room with Rhonda Mae in
hand. "Oh, boy! Look at all these fixins. When's my
party gonna start, Uncle Wes?"

Wes laid a gentle hand on Bethann's shoulder.
"Soon as your papa gets on home."

"But I want to see my pony!"

Letty Sue smiled prettily at the child. "Bethann, I'd

love for you to show me your pony. When your papa comes home, we'll all three go see it." When the youngster nodded, Letty Sue raised victorious eyes to Lily.

Lily did her best to ignore her, focusing instead on the dilapidated flower garden outside. She longed for a garden of her own. Her mind conjured up images of how she'd plant those beds, which flowers would thrive best on what particular exposure. She envisioned sinking her hands in the ground, tilling the soil, nurturing the tiny stalks until beautiful flowers bloomed.

The gunman snaked his body forward. Hidden behind a crop of ironwoods on the rise, he took aim. Three long days he'd been staked out, waiting. Hoping to find his prey alone on the range. A shadowy target, at long last, came into view.

The beauty of it was beyond comprehension. He'd plotted and planned, and now his scheme was upon him. He licked his lips in anticipation. The man was getting no better than he deserved. Hell and damnation wouldn't be justice enough for him.

But now, the rider was within range. "Hell is too good for you, Tyler Kincaide." The gunman smirked into the scope of the Winchester rifle before squeezing the trigger. When the unwitting rider slumped in the saddle, the gunman leaned back against a tree, took a sound swill of whiskey and let out a satisfied laugh.

Lily was sure she wouldn't be seeing the ranch hand who'd watched Bethann earlier anytime soon, but there he was knocking on the door, calling for Wes to come quick.

A look of confusion crossed over the spindly man's features before he stepped outside. Lily heard words whispered urgently, then the two men raced to the bunkhouse.

Lily paced, wringing out her hands. Judging from the desperate sound of the ranch hand's voice and the fact that old Wes probably hadn't moved faster in the past decade, Lily knew something was definitely up. And it wasn't good.

"Where'd Uncle Wes go in such a fast hurry, Miss Lily?"

"I'm not sure, Bethann. Maybe, there's a problem with one of the animals," Lily said, hoping it was true.

"Where's Papa anyhows?"

A sudden sharp pang of realization seized Lily. When the clock chimed four, she knew the trouble had to be about Tyler. He hadn't come home. She closed her eyes, silently praying for Bethann's sake, he wasn't the reason for all the commotion. But in her heart, she knew differently.

"Your papa'll be here shortly, Bethann," Letty Sue said, oblivious to the problem and to Bethann's distress. "My, it's stuffy in here. Won't you take a walk with me?" She held out her hand for Bethann.

Bethann looked at Lily. With a nod she said, "You go on. I promise to come get you when your papa gets back. Maybe you can take Letty Sue down to the creek. But don't get too close to the water."

Letty Sue's eyes focused on her mother. "Momma?"

"Don't mind if I do," Joellen replied, bringing herself up from the parlor chair. "I could use some fresh air, too, darling."

Lily waved as she watched them trek behind the house.

Wes came in minutes later. "Where's Bethann?"

Lily didn't like the anxious look on Wes's face. "She's out taking a walk with Joellen and Letty Sue."

He let out an audible sigh and shook his head. "That's good, I reckon. Tyler's been shot real bad. Don't want the child seeing her pa that way."

"Shot!" Lily took a quick, sharp breath. "What happened?"

"Don't rightly know. He come home slumped acrossed his horse. Good thing that ole cattle pony a his knew where his oats come from. I sent Randy on out for the doc."

"I think I'd better take a look. Doc Ramsey may not get here in time."

Wes eyed her warily. "You know about doctorin'?"

"Some. Now, we're wasting time. Take me to Mr. Kincaide."

The bunkhouse was dimly lit, but as soon as Lily walked in, her eyes riveted to the crimson streak of blood oozing from Tyler's shoulder. His shirt was saturated and the vital juices were beginning to seep onto the narrow cot. Lily rushed to his side.

He was unconscious and so very still. She bent her head down to listen and heard his faint breathing. "First, we've got to stop the bleeding. Then we'll clean him up and get him into the house. Wes, please get me some fresh linens and a pitcher of water."

Lily chewed on her lower lip, evoking a memory of the wounded rebel soldiers her father had patched up during the war. She'd been very young, but she'd never forgotten them.

"Butternuts" her father said they were called. The Confederate gray uniforms in short supply, these men wore dyed cinnamon-hued wool made from butternut extract. The dye might have faded from wear, but the name endured—soldiers who'd given their last breath for the Confederacy.

She'd helped her father tend them; bringing in water, cleaning the wounds, changing their bandages, until the only cloths left in the house were the few clothes they'd salvaged and the ones on their backs. She'd brought spoonfuls of cush, a weakened stew, to their trembling mouths while her mother had hummed the tune to "Dixie," lulling them into peaceful oblivion. Lily remembered the men whose lives they'd saved, but more so, she was haunted by the stark faces of the frightened boys who'd died. Lily shook the memory clear. Tyler couldn't die. He couldn't. Beth-ann needed him.

But there was so much blood.

Gingerly, she unbuttoned his shirt. She heard him groan when she lifted him slightly to peel away the garment.

Wes hurriedly placed the items on the table next to the bed. Lily tore several small strips and dipped them into the water. She washed away as much blood as possible, then took a thin band of material and wound it tightly around Tyler's shoulder. Blood continued to ooze out. She knew he'd never survive if she didn't stop the bleeding.

"Wes, bring me your flat-iron griddle." When Wes didn't respond, she looked up. He hesitated, giving her a sour look. "You'll see. Please, just get it. And hurry!"

Lily took five layers of linen, ripped them into squares and set them on Tyler's shoulder. When Wes handed her the griddle, she placed it over the cloth. "I hope this does it. The pressure should help stop the bleeding."

"That boy gonna be able to breathe?" The old man eyed the heavy griddle.

"It's not directly over his heart, and if we don't do something quick, he'd not be breathing soon, anyway."

Wes flinched. Moisture touched the corners of his eyes. "He'll be a breathin'."

Lily took a second to give Wes a reassuring smile. "I think he'll make it, too. The blood isn't soaking up the cloth as much anymore. All the same we'll leave the griddle on until Doc Ramsey gets here."

"Sure is a good thing you was here, Miss Lillian."

Lily looked down at her patient. His face was pale, an ashen gray, and his broad chest was moving up and down in small shallow bursts. Lily took a clean cloth and wiped down his sweat-stained face. "Maybe it *was* a good thing I came to the ranch today, Wes."

"You'll be a stayin'?"

Wes asked with such a hopeful expression, Lily hadn't the heart to deny him. Besides, she couldn't leave the ranch until she was sure Tyler would be all right and Bethann was cared for.

Maybe it was Tyler's halfhearted proposal just days ago, or maybe it was her own unyielding sense of responsibility, but Lily felt obligated to take hold of the situation. Tyler needed her help.

She shrugged off the repercussions. Her reputation would probably be ruined. Tongues in Sweet Springs could wag all they liked. In a short time, she'd be heading east to make a fresh start with her only remaining family member. With a sigh, she answered, "I'll be staying."

Chapter Four

Letty Sue fainted dead away.

Doc Ramsey had urged everyone to stay clear of his patient while he removed the bullet. Lily had been at the doctor's side assisting when Letty Sue burst through the door, insisting on seeing Tyler.

She took a long look at the unconscious man, then at his bloodstained shirt heaped in a pile by the narrow cot. Once-pristine white cloth dripping with Tyler's life juices draped a stool in the corner. It was all Letty Sue saw before she dropped rather unceremoniously onto the floor.

Doc Ramsey stole a glance her way and rolled his eyes. He asked Wes to fetch her ma. Lily reminded Wes to keep Bethann and Rhonda Mae in the house until Lily could look after them.

Minutes later Joellen rushed in and brought her daughter to, then guided her outside away from another scene that might threaten her sensibilities.

Doc Ramsey shook his head. "I'm not sure how much blood he's lost, but he's a strong man. And you did him a good turn by stopping the drainage like you did. It might've saved his life."

Lily wavered. "Then...he'll live?"

"God willin'. He'll need constant care for several days. And most likely, he'll develop a fever. Tyler won't be splittin' logs for a spell." The doctor grinned. "I've known this boy a long time. He'll be madder'n a hornet when he comes to."

"I'll put up with his anger, Doc, as long as he wakes up."

Doc Ramsey peered down at her through his spectacles. "Miss Lillian, are you going to tend him?"

Did she have a choice? Joellen had taken Letty Sue home. Wes was hopeless. His wrinkled skin had become almost as pale as Tyler's from watching the doctor administer to the man. For a moment there Lily thought Wes was about to meet with the bunkhouse floor himself. Pride and a healthy dose of masculine ego were probably all that kept the dear man upright.

"I'll tend him."

The doctor gave her a fatherly look, one filled with admiration and gratitude. "Best thing for him. We better move him into the house. I'll fetch a ranch hand or two."

Lily left the men to their task. She had other concerns. Bethann being first and foremost. When she entered the house, Bethann was sitting on the sofa, sobbing. Rhonda Mae was holding her hand, trying to console her.

"How's...my...papa?" she asked between sobs. "Uncle Wes says I—I can't see him right now."

Lily seated herself next to Bethann, wrapping an arm about her shoulders. "Your papa's been hurt, but Doc Ramsey thinks he's going to be just fine. He's going to need us to take care of him. Could you do that, Bethann? Could you help me care for your papa?''

The little girl's head bobbed up and down. Lily put gentle pressure on her shoulder. "That's what I thought. You'll make your papa proud, being so brave. Now, you girls must be hungry. Let's rustle up something to eat, then we'll have a piece of chocolate cake. Wes will be hitching up the wagon soon to take Rhonda Mae home.''

Bethann folded her arms across her chest and pouted. "I'm not hungry. 'Sides, I don't want my party till Papa gets better.''

Lily stood up and reached for her hand. "Bethann, you need to eat. Remember, your papa needs you strong so you can help tend him. We won't have your party until your papa's better, I promise.''

The little girl nodded. She jumped off the sofa and took Lily's hand. Lily led the girls into the kitchen.

Lily'd had a full day. After feeding both girls, seeing Rhonda Mae off, tucking Bethann into bed and having Wes give her a quick tour of the house, she was near exhaustion. The night was just beginning. Doc Ramsey said he expected the low-grade fever Tyler developed to spike during the night.

Tyler had briefly come to several times, mumbling incoherently, then drifted off again.

Lily took a cloth to wipe her brow. She was perspiring, as much from the sight of Tyler Kincaide sprawled out near-naked on the bed as from the accumulated heat of the day. Wes had the good sense to throw a sheet over Tyler's lower body, but his manly form was still visible through the thin material.

Lily's eyes roamed over Tyler's face, being able to

leisurely look her fill. She felt guilty—as if she were trespassing over his tempting features and knowing well and good Tyler would never know.

He was calm and relaxed as he slumbered, showing the early signs of a stubble beard. Dark shaggy hair was pushed off his face in an effort to keep him cool. His jawline was well defined and Lily knew from experience how well it'd set in a stubborn stance.

Even in his weakened state, his broad well-muscled chest exuded a certain undeniable strength. The crisp dark hairs tapered down his torso in a vee past his navel and tucked under the sheets. Lily allowed her gaze to wander beyond those sheets, momentarily, imagining the hidden secrets that lay there. She swallowed hard, wondering if there'd ever be another man on this earth who'd create such stirrings in her. In all her twenty-five years, Tyler Kincaide was the sole proprietor of her errant and lusty thoughts.

She shook her head, attempting to shake off her rampant musings and looked over his bedroom. The man was large, but his oak-carved bed was massive. A matching armoire sat against the far wall. Two chairs, one wing-backed, one spindled, were the only other furniture. There were two windows, one facing east and one west.

Sunrises and sunsets.

Lily pulled the softly worn, blue velvet wing chair close to the bed and sat down. Dipping a clean cloth into a porcelain bowl, she carefully wrung it out before gently swabbing Tyler's chest. Her fingers grazed over his warmed skin and Lily's heart thumped so loudly, she feared the man would awaken from the hubbub. One look at his peaceful expression told her she was being a foolish ninny again.

Gingerly she wiped down his face, keeping the cool cloth pressed onto his cheeks. She gave in to the urge to run her fingers through the soft silkiness of his hair, knowing if she'd lived a thousand lifetimes, she'd probably not get another chance. At least not with this man.

She sighed and rested back in the chair. Fighting a losing battle, her eyelids slid closed.

Lily woke to the sound of Tyler's moaning. She blinked her eyes open, confused to find herself slumped cozily in an oversize chair. Another moan brought her to attention and she remembered where she was.

A hand to Tyler's forehead revealed a burning fever. Sweat poured from his body as his agitated movements shuffled him to and fro. He murmured incoherently. Lily pressed her hands on his chest and lowered him down, soothing him with soft words. She dampened her rags and set about cooling his heated flesh. She dabbed at his neck, shoulders and chest.

The sheet covering him had been kicked aside. He was bared to her. There was no help for it. Lily tried not to gape at him, but the realization that she was alone with a naked man in his bedroom had not escaped her. The fact that he was unconscious mattered not at all.

She gritted her teeth and quickly placed a cloth over his privates. Swallowing hard, she admonished herself. He was her patient. She couldn't think of him any other way. Not if she hoped to see him through this ordeal. She'd deal with her own sensibilities another time. Right now, Tyler needed her help. She administered to him until the wee hours of the morning.

Yellow rays of sunlight warmed Lily's face. A yawn

stole from her mouth as she threw her arms over her
head and stretched out lazily in the bed.

The bed?

She bolted upright and glanced at the slumbering
man beside her. Her thoughts raced wildly, remembering last night. Tyler'd called out Lizabeth's name.
He'd taken hold of Lily's hand in his delirium and
brought her down next to him on the bed. Only at her
acquiescence did he finally calm.

She looked down at the naked man. Steady breaths
escaped his lips and his chest rose and fell in a normal
rhythm. She replaced the sheet, covering him to his
waist and laid a hand on his forehead. He was cool.

Thank heaven.

Lily glanced at the clothes tossed against the winged
chair. Her clothes. She must have shed them in her
exhaustion. She'd slept with Tyler last night in her
petticoats and chemise! She rose and dashed to the
chair. Grappling with her skirt, she quickly donned it.

A low raspy voice startled her. "What'd you do to
me last night, sugar? I feel like hell."

Lily whirled around. Tyler's eyes, constricted and
confused, were following her movements. When he
tried to raise up on his elbows, pain contorted his face
and his eyes slammed shut.

"Hush now." Lily moved to his side and bent to
ease him down. She adjusted his pillow and re-covered
his body with the flimsy sheet.

Tyler lifted heavy lids and let out a groan. His body
was one solid ache. Trying to focus, a woman came
into view. He didn't recognize her as being a regular
at the Golden Garter, but his brain, at the moment,
was addled. She bent over him. His gaze met with the
sheer material of a thin cotton chemise. A small but

perfectly rounded bosom appeared before him. He found that even through the pain, his body tightened. The "lady" must have been a real hellcat, he thought, if he's reacting to her again already.

"Get me my pants and we'll settle up. I've got to go."

Again he tried to rise, but searing pain brought his head back down against the pillow. He gritted his teeth. "Damn it all!"

"Do not swear, please," the soft voice said.

Tyler blinked, and for the first time swept his gaze across the room.

His room.

He took a good look at the half-dressed woman whose voice he'd just recognized, not believing his eyes. "Lily?"

"Ah, hell, Lily! I don't want none of Wes's soup. Stuff's worse than horse manure. Everybody knows Wes can't cook."

Lily scooted the chair closer to the bed and sat facing him, balancing a tray on her lap. "Tyler Kincaide, I've asked you time and again not to swear in my presence. And Wes is a fine cook. He got up extra early to prepare this soup. You must have some."

Tight-lipped, Tyler turned his head away.

Lily let out a long audible breath. "For Bethann, if not yourself."

He shot her a look. "You don't play fair."

Lily lifted the spoon to his mouth. Like a small child accepting an awful elixir, Tyler swallowed the liquid. "That's better. You need to keep your strength up. Sheriff Singleton is riding out. He has some questions for you."

"Well, hell." He scowled. "I don't have answers."

"You don't remember anything?"

Tyler shook his head, then cast her a lecherous grin. "I do remember you tending me…half naked."

Lily's cheeks heated. The man was as impossible as Doc Ramsey said he'd be. "I explained about that. I meant about the shooting."

"Oh, that." Tyler closed his eyes. "I was riding out the east pasture, inspecting the fences." He opened his eyes. "Don't remember a thing after that."

"Who'd want to shoot you?"

"Damned if I know." He slid her a menacing look.

Lily remembered reading the new barbed-wire for fencing was being called by some "The Devil's Hatband." There were rumblings in town when her father had displayed a sample of Glidden's twisted oval on the shelves at Brody's. "Are some of the other ranchers opposed to putting up fences?"

Tyler, deep in thought, shook his head. "Don't think so. We held a meeting about a year ago. Most of us open rangers agreed to putting up fences to keep rustling down. Makes roundup easier. I put in my order for barbed-wire six months ago. Most of the others did the same. Far as I know, we're all in agreement."

Lily nodded. She had racked her brain trying to think of who'd want Tyler Kincaide dead. She'd heard of range wars in other territories over this very issue. But now it didn't sound as if Tyler's progressive ranching ideas were the cause of his shooting.

This was all so unsettling. Tyler'd lapsed in and out of exhausted sleep all day and night yesterday. No one had been able to ask any questions, much less get any answers. Now, it seemed, there may be no answers. Tyler hadn't a clue as to who'd shot him.

"Did Wes order the hands to stand guard around the ranch, like I asked?"

"Yes. Randy is keeping an eye on the house, the barn and the corrals. Others are taking turns searching your land."

"Bethann?"

"She's fine. She came in yesterday while you were asleep. She helped me...tend you."

Lily had sat with him, tended his bandages, and cared for Bethann. When Tyler was in a peaceful sleep, Lily had brought the little girl in to see her papa. Bethann, courageous to a fault, held back her tears and kissed her father's cheek. Lily allowed her to take a cloth and gently dab at her papa's chest. The gesture brought a prideful smile to Bethann's face and a swift tugging at Lily's heart.

"Was she scared?"

"Your daughter is a brave little girl. She was, at first, but Wes and I have kept her busy."

"I don't want her left alone for a minute."

Lily nodded. "I won't leave her."

Tyler, as if just realizing Lily'd spent several days on the ranch, stared at her. "Appreciate that, Miss Lily."

Lily made a move to get up. Tyler grabbed her wrist. His work-roughened hands were sure but gentle. And he turned serious eyes toward her. "What about you, Lily? What'll you do now?"

"I promised Doc Ramsey I'd stay until you recovered." She hoisted her chin. "That's what I intend to do."

He let go of her wrist. "I see. Then you're on the next stage back east?"

Lily shrugged. "Finish your soup, Mr. Kincaide."

Chapter Five

Lily waited outside the bedroom while Sheriff Singleton questioned Tyler. She sensed the lawman's displeasure the second he stepped out of the room. Scratching his head, he called her over. "He doesn't remember seeing or hearing a thing. It's good he's set up a watch around the place."

"Do you think there's danger?"

"Don't rightly know. Maybe. Whoever shot him left him for dead. Didn't steal anything. I'm hoping the culprit rode on out of our territory. Don't want more bloodshed," the sheriff declared. "I'll ride out and have a look-see. Could be Tyler foiled an attempt to rustle cattle. It ain't uncommon in these parts to see renegade rustlers." The sheriff placed his weathered hat on his head. "You let me know if Mr. Kincaide remembers anything."

Lily walked the man to the door. "I'll do that."

He stopped in midstride. "Oh, Miss Lillian, I almost forgot. This here wire came for you today. Charlie over at the telegraph office asked me to give it to you."

Lily's heart skipped a beat. A wire from Uncle Jasper! She took the proffered paper, cushioning it in her hand as if it were the finest Austrian crystal. She stared down at the paper. "Thank you, Sheriff. I appreciate it."

He tipped his hat, then faltered. "You, uh, gonna stay on at the ranch?"

"I promised to stay on until Ty—Mr. Kincaide doesn't need my help any longer."

The sheriff ran his fingers along the lapels of his vest nervously. "It's not anybody's business but yours, since you've been tendin' an injured man and all, but—"

"But?" Lily leaned in, coaxing his confession.

"Well, there's been talk. Folks don't think it fittin', you being the only woman out here with Mr. Kincaide and his men." He cleared his throat. "Thought you should know."

Lily expected as much, but for some unnamed reason she felt disappointment of a town who would judge her so harshly. "Some folks are mean-spirited, Sheriff. I couldn't leave Bethann alone, now could I? With her daddy bleeding so terribly, we didn't know if he'd see another day."

"No, don't suppose you could've. I heard tell you saved his life."

"I don't know about that for sure. Mr. Kincaide's young and strong. I'm glad I could help. Now, Sheriff, I really must see to Bethann."

"I'll check back with you in a week or two."

Lily watched the stout man mount his horse and ride out. Turning, she hurried back into the house. In the privacy of the room she'd been using, she clutched the paper in her hand and opened it slowly.

Miss Brody,
Jasper Eliot Brody no longer resides in Chicago.
He left word at my office, he's heading west.
Made mention of business in Cheyenne. Wish
you luck locating him.

Constable M. R. Bradshaw.

Deflated, Lily slumped onto the bed. This was not
the news she'd anticipated. Her biggest fear was
whether Jasper Brody would take her in. Now her
problem was twofold, first locating the man, then hoping he'd allow her into his life.

She could send a letter to Cheyenne to track her
uncle down. There'd be no telling if he'd arrived yet,
but she could leave word to relay her message as soon
as he did. Maybe, with luck, he'd already be settled.

Jasper Brody fought for the north during the war.
Her father never forgave him for turning Yankee and
spoke little of him. She'd known he held a respectable
job in Chicago. Lily had always liked Uncle Jasper.
He was a kind, loving man. He was…family. The only
family she had left.

Lily remembered the last time Uncle Jasper came
to visit their farm. It was right after the war. Their
home was all but destroyed. The farm was in sham-
bles. Her father begrudgingly allowed his brother to
stay for two days. But his bitterness wouldn't allow
reconciliation.

When Lily's mother received a small inheritance,
she'd offered the money to her proud husband to help
replant the crops, restore the house and put more than
meager rations of food on the table. But her father had
had other ideas. Disheartened by the devastation surrounding him, he'd set his mind on a new life; they'd

move off their farm and open Brody Mercantile, a small shop in the growing ranching town of Sweet Springs. It had been a good move. Her father had been happy until he'd lost his wife. Then came the gambling.

But Jonah had abruptly changed his mind about his brother. Lily now believed her father had known he was dying months earlier and had made his peace with him. She remembered a letter coming from Chicago. Her father had never spoken of it, but since that time Jonah had mellowed on the subject and his deathbed plea for her to locate Jasper had come straight from her father's heart.

She choked back a sob. She missed her father. He was a sweet loving man, even if he did have a fondness for the gaming tables that had put her into this predicament. She'd made him a promise—one she'd sworn to keep. She had to continue her search for her uncle.

A tapping at her door startled Lily. Folding the letter and tucking it safely into her pocket, she rose from the bed to open the door slowly. A pouting face stared up at her. "Come in, Bethann."

Bethann strolled in and plunked herself down on the bed. "Papa says I can't leave the house." The little girl dangled her legs off the edge. She swung them to and fro.

"That's right. Remember, we talked about it yesterday."

The girl hopped down from the bed. She wandered over to the dresser, touching everything. "I got nothin' to do."

"Well—" Lily rubbed her chin "—I can think up

a list of chores we can do. Dusting, washing, sweeping…''

Lily stopped abruptly when the child's face contorted in fear. ''Or…'' Lily reached into her reticule and brought out a rag doll. ''I can give you your birthday present.'' She held out the doll. ''Happy birthday, Bethann.''

''Th-that's for me?'' Bethann looked at the small rag doll as if she'd been given a fifty-dollar gold piece.

Lily placed it into her hands. ''I made this for you days ago. I'm sorry, I forgot to give it to you.''

''She's beautiful.'' Bethann hugged the doll to her chest. ''What's her name?''

Lily smoothed away several wayward strands of Bethann's hair, wondering how the child managed to always look so disheveled. She'd bathed and dressed her just hours ago. ''That's for you to decide. She's yours now.''

''Thank you, Miss Lily. I love her!'' Bethann plopped a wet kiss on Lily's cheek.

''Oh, Bethann, I hoped you would.''

The scraps of calico sewed over cotton batting with button eyes and strands of yarn for hair, was nothing special, but Lily remembered how much her dolls had meant to her. Growing up without sisters and brothers was lonesome. Her dolls had always given her comfort.

''She's got funny hair.''

Lily laughed. ''I unraveled the yarn and brushed it with melted wax so the hair would stay curly.''

''Can you do that with my hair?''

''Dear heavens, no! But if you want curly hair, I do know a trick or two.''

''You do?'' Bethann looked at Lily in disbelief.

"Yes."

"Can we curl your hair, too?"

"I suppose."

She began an inspection of Lily's hair. "How long's your hair?"

"Very long."

"Why'd you keep it trussed up all's the time?"

"To keep it out of my way." To make her point, Lily pushed back a few more of Bethann's strays. "Now, sweetie, are you gonna name her or do we call her Funny Hair?"

Bethann giggled, then a frown stole over her face. "Can't rightly think of a name."

"Play with her a while. Get to know her. A name will pop into your head. You'll see."

Bethann smiled, giving Lily a big hug before leaving the room.

Lily finished her chores early, read Bethann a bedtime story before tucking her in, and thought to check on Tyler one more time. He was improving, albeit slowly. It was hard to believe she'd been here five days. Her decision, once made, rolled over and over in her mind until she was sure it was the only solution. She needed to discuss it with Tyler, but wouldn't approach him until he felt much better.

She tiptoed out of the child's room, making her way down the long hallway. Tyler's room was at the far end. Not wanting to wake him if he'd fallen asleep, she quietly turned the knob and let herself in.

The gun was cocked and ready. And staring her in the face. She screamed.

"Ah, hell, woman! You'll wake the dead!"

"T-Tyler Kincaide, d-don't you point that thing at

me! You about shocked ten years off my life.'' Lily
slumped against the door.

"Well, then, don't go sneaking up on a body in the
dark!'' Tyler lowered his guard and his gun. He leaned
back against the bed until his head met with the pillow.

"I didn't want to wake you. I was being considerate.''

"Considerate, ha! Don't you believe in knockin'?''
Lily bristled. "Oh! I've already explained, I didn't
want to disturb you. Who gave you the gun, anyway?''

"Wes. My orders. I am the boss of this ranch, Lily,
and I'm no sittin' duck. Someone wants me or one of
my own, they'll have a fight on their hands.''

Lily nodded. "I understand, but you could've pulled
out your stitches, moving fast like that. Let me take a
look.''

Sitting on the bed, she unbuttoned his shirt and
glanced at the bandages. When she leaned in to take
a better look, she felt the pins in her hair being tugged
out. Her long tresses fell onto her back.

"What're you doing?'' she said, slapping at Tyler's
hand, knocking loose the pins he held.

"Just curious, is all. Doesn't that knot hurt your
head?''

"I'm used to it. Keeps the hair out of my way.''

"You have pretty hair.''

"It's dirt brown and too thick.''

Lily closed her eyes when Tyler's hand touched one
of the strands, sifting it through his fingers. "Feels like
silk,'' he whispered.

Lily's eyes snapped open. Nothing about her was
soft or feminine. Tyler had to be teasing. And here she

sat, like a foolish ninny, on his bed with the soft glow of moonlight streaming in, almost believing him.

She bolted up. "The stitches are intact, for now. God willing and no more of your quick moves and you'll be good as new in a week or two."

"Then, where will you be, *Miss Lily?*"

Lily clasped her hands together and studied the floor for several moments. Her heart thudded heavily in her chest. Lily was forced to make a choice. Taking a deep breath, she met his questioning gaze straight-on. "I've decided to take you up on your proposal."

Chapter Six

Tyler's mouth gaped open. His surprised expression must have jolted her because she backed up a step after making her declaration. He let his eyes roam over her, taking in her long form as she stood over him. He gave her credit for not turning away. Her gaze stayed fastened to his.

Marriage.

So it came down to that. Tyler resigned himself to it. It was best for Bethann. He'd seen over the days how Lily and his daughter got on. Bethann was already acting more the lady. She'd bound into his room along with the scrappy piece of calico she calls Miss Daisy, named no doubt after Lily, forever going on about how a lady does this and that.

With eagerness in her eyes, Bethann announced that Lily wanted to make her and Miss Daisy matching dresses. His daughter asked for permission, as if he hadn't wanted the very thing for Bethann from the start.

And Lily managed to get her to do some chores. Easy ones, but Tyler was impressed. Under Lily's watchful eye, Bethann brought him his supper one day. She carried the tray to his room, carefully balancing it with her small hands, then set out the napkin on his lap. She boasted how she dusted the parlor and helped Lily with the wash.

Tyler was astonished—and grateful. He believed in the discipline, never quite knowing how to extract it from his impish child. He always believed in doing your fair share. It was what ranch life was all about.

An errant thought filtered in his mind. Lizabeth. Ranch life had been hard on her. In the end, it killed her. He never should've brought her here. God knows, if he hadn't, she'd be alive today.

So now he was to take another wife. For Bethann, for the ranch. Tyler would be decent to her, but he'd not love her. He couldn't. This time, marriage held no special meaning to him. It was a means to an end. So be it.

Tyler searched Lily's face. She was a good woman. She'd saved his life. She deserved more than he could give. But he knew if she wasn't in a desperate situation, she wouldn't agree to his proposal.

"I'll send for the preacher tomorrow." He'd tried to keep the regret out of his voice and honestly didn't know if he'd managed.

"No!"

Tyler winced at her sharp tone. "Lily, I'm not one for going to church, but if you want a church wed—"

"No, you don't understand. I don't want to get married. I meant I'd take you up on your job proposal. That is, if the offer still stands?"

"Y-yes. I, uh—" Tyler was baffled. Was this the same woman who made short work of telling him how improper living on the ranch without benefit of marriage would be?

"Good." She breathed out a heavy sigh. "I'm asking thirty dollars a month. And I want to plant a garden."

Tyler let it all sink in. He wasn't getting married, but rather hiring an employee. He should be rejoicing. But it didn't set right with him. Why was Lily doing this?

"I'll pay you forty and you can have your garden."

Her expression changed from courageous to plain curious. He'd offered her the same pay as his ranch hands.

"And what would you expect for your forty dollars a month, Mr. Kincaide?" He imagined the bristles on the back of her neck going up. She folded her arms across her chest and waited.

"You'll do the household chores, keep the place clean, cook the meals, but more than anything, I want you to care for my daughter. She's most important. There'll be times she'll get stubborn. She won't want to do as she's told. Got a wild streak in her that needs taming."

"I've seen it. I think I can manage her. She's a sweet child who needs guidance, is all."

"She's the only thing that makes life worth living. That and the ranch."

Lily nodded. "I understand." She hesitated, staring into his eyes. "Is that *all* you'll be expecting?"

Even in the darkened room, Tyler saw a pink blush rise to her face, bringing a rosy hue to her cheeks. And the color brought out the blue in her pale eyes, making them look like a cloudless spring sky. Her silky waist-length hair draped over her shoulders. Tyler blinked, remembering his stolen glance days ago after the shooting, of two small, well-rounded breasts hidden beneath a thin cotton chemise. His body hardened at the thought.

"'Less there's anything more you might want to give, Lily," he said softly.

"No." It was her flat-out answer. Tyler knew as much. He sighed inwardly. What was he thinking? Lily, always the proper lady.

But for the briefest moment she seemed...

Nah! Tyler wasn't going to let his imaginings get the best of him. It was probably time to visit the ladies at the Golden Garter. He'd harbor no such illusions about Miss Lillian Brody.

He was her employer now. It'd be best to remember that. He had nothing to offer her but a roof over her head and a paycheck at the end of the month. "Why'd you change your mind, anyway?"

Lily's shoulders slumped. She seemed nervous, as if she were debating about telling him something. "My uncle moved west. It'll be a while before I can locate him."

"So you're still planning on leaving?"

"Yes, in time. I don't know when I'll find him."

"I need to know you'll be here till after we drive the cattle north. Cattle drive starts at the end of summer."

"That's six months from now."

Tyler fixed her an icy stare. "I can't take Bethann with me." The thought made him shudder. He'd tried that years ago with Lizabeth. The results were disastrous. "Do I have your word?"

"I've lived without seeing Uncle Jasper for fifteen years," she said, letting out a heavy sigh, "I suppose I can wait six more months."

With a nod, which was also a quick dismissal, he said, "It's settled then."

"I can get myself to the tub, Lily," Tyler barked as they made their way down the hall.

Lily wished it were true so she wouldn't have his arms wound around her as she supported his weight. His body, naked from the waist up, brushed against her time and again. Her foolish fantasies took flight, playing havoc with her mind. The man was injured. She was leading him to a tub of hot water. So why was she imagining his arms around her for other, more appealing reasons?

Maybe because she might have married the man today. Her heart skipped a beat when he'd offered to get the preacher yesterday. One beat, then reason set in. She couldn't marry a man who didn't want her, didn't love her. She'd rather die an old maid than have him feel shackled to her.

Married to Tyler Kincaide?

The thought was as silly as he was, thinking he could make it to the tub by himself. The washroom was just steps away but today was his first day up. She'd watched as he tried to make it out the door of his room. His face grew sallow. Knowing his fierce pride kept Lily away, but when she saw him sway she raced over to lend him support.

"Hush now, Tyler. If you injure yourself, it'll be another week before you're good to anyone."

He grunted, but she felt his resistance fade away as he leaned a bit more heavily on her. When they reached the washroom, Lily turned the knob and with both their weights pushed against the door to open it. Together they moved to the tub. That's when Lily floundered. They both stared down at the tub, Tyler with an eager gleam in his eyes. Lily knew she couldn't leave him to his own devices. He'd never make it alone.

She pulled a large towel out of a cabinet and handed it to him. "Wrap this around your waist. Then, uh, you know."

Tyler grinned. She was mortified, but couldn't do a single thing about it. She turned around, hearing him grunt and groan himself out of his pants. Serves him right for wearing skintight trousers in the first place!

She heard his pants hit the floor, then a splash of water pooled by her feet.

"You can turn around now," he said, amused. "I'm all the way in. Feels better than a whore in—uh—"

Lily snapped her head around, furious.

"Sorry, Lily." He managed an apologetic smile and sank farther into the water. "This feels so damn good, is all. I've felt like a cow stuck in a mud heap for days now."

She put both hands on her hips. "Smelled like one, too."

"Now, Lily. Don't be getting mean. I said I was sorry. Come here and wash my back. I can't lift my arm any farther than this."

He lifted his left arm out of the water midway to demonstrate, then let it plop back down.

Lily took a bar of soap and a washrag then kneeled down next to the tub. "Just this once, Tyler Kincaide. And we'll never speak of it again."

"Wash my hair, too, and I swear I won't recollect a blasted thing."

Lily held her breath. Maybe he'd forget, but she was certain she'd remember the sight of this man, taking up the entire length and width of the porcelain tub, for the rest of her pitiful life. She'd close her eyes and see him there, naked, in all his magnificence, until her dying day. The image would haunt her. There would be no help for it.

She soaped up his back and neck with vigor, trying to erase the image from her mind. When he yelped, she slowed her pace.

Tyler gave her a sideways glance. "Lily, I know you got a gentle touch. Use it."

"I'm not accustomed to bathing men, Mr. Kincaide, and you darn well know it."

"You were gentle as a lamb when you were nursing me the other night."

"That was different."

"Why?"

"'Cause you couldn't—you wouldn't, I mean you weren't… Oh, hush now."

Tyler chuckled.

Lily remembered the feel of his warm flesh beneath her fingers as she'd cut away his bandages yesterday. Gingerly, she'd traced the outline of the wound, healing nicely now, under Tyler's watchful gaze. She'd felt heat rise to her face as he studied her tending to his wound.

And now, bathing the man. Heavens! She thought her cheeks would stain pink from all the color they've received since she came to the ranch. It was scandalous, her touching him like this. Yet his helplessness called to her. She felt compelled to answer—to see to this strong man's needs while in this weakened state.

She threaded her fingers into his dampened hair. Sunlight poured into the room, glistening on the wet strands, until they shone a brilliant blue-black. Using

the bar soap, she lathered his hair, massaging his scalp,
which garnered an appreciative groan from him.

Lily smiled.

This is what it must be like to be married, she
thought. This intimacy. This peace. Harmony in silence.

Regret of what will never be made Lily break the
silence. "I'm planning on going to town tomorrow. I
need to pick up my things at the boardinghouse."

"Have Randy or Wes drive you in."

"Bethann wants to come."

"No."

Lily stopped massaging his head. "Why not?"

"I don't want her leaving the ranch without me.
And I don't think I'll be in any shape to take you."

"But she's wanting a new dress. I promised her she
could come along to pick out the material."

Lily took up a bucket of rinse water.

"You'll do fine to pick out the colors. Something
bright and cheerful-like. And pick out some new material for yourself. Those drab colors you wear are
downright...discouraging."

The nerve of the man! She might not have a good
deal of experience with men, but any woman would
recognize an insult as blatant as that one. Appalled,
she attested, "Well, a lady is not supposed to do any
encouraging, Mr. Kincaide."

"Ah, come on, Lily. I only meant that...well, I'm
sick to death of all those gray and browns you wear."

Lily doused the bucket of water over his head. A
good portion hit its mark, the rest splattered onto the
floor.

"Hey! Tarnation, Lily, what was that for?"

Lily wanted to stomp right out of the room. The
man was so infuriating! Instead, to her chagrin, Tyler

Kincaide brought himself up out of the water and turned to face her.

Beautiful, came to mind first, before mortification set in. His longish hair was slicked back. Droplets of water rained down his shoulders onto his broad, muscled chest. She dared not view any lower, but an instant flash of memory reminded her of what he looked like below the waist. She'd seen him days ago, unconscious. Oh, Lord!

Lily closed her eyes and turned away.

"Hand me the damn towel, Lily."

Lily did as she was told, groping for the towel then shoving it at him. He snatched it away and cursed vividly.

She heard him rustling around behind her and realized he must be struggling to put on his pants.

"Are you okay?"

"Fine," he snapped.

"Are you—"

"For heaven's sake, Lily, the wall can't be that interesting. Turn around."

Lily turned around slowly but she let out a quick gasp when she saw Tyler's face had become as white as winter's first snowfall. The bath and all it took getting him in and out had drained all his strength. She rushed to his side.

"Put your arms around me, Tyler. I'll get you back to bed."

He threw all of his weight against her, but Lily kept her balance by spreading her feet wide. If she hadn't they both would have gone down.

He grunted as they moved toward his room. "Best offer I've had in a month of Sundays, *Miss Lily.*"

Lily knew for a fact, he was not amused.

* * *

Stubbornness is what some might call it, but Tyler knew it was fierce determination that caused him to pry himself up from the bed and put on his pants. That and the sound of amiable chatter coming from the kitchen. It'd been a quiet day yesterday, with Lily in town. The only company he'd had was Bethann. And she had decided to whine about not being allowed to go along with Lily. Tyler'd finally had to feign fatigue to get his six-year-old to leave him be. He hated disappointing the child, but her safety had to be his first priority. She was of no mind to understand.

And now the sounds from the kitchen beckoned him. He lifted his left arm into the sleeve of his shirt. Sweat poured out of him and he winced from the pain it caused. But he'd be damned to spend one more wasted day in bed. He finished dressing, leaving his shirt dangling open, his feet bare, and headed to the kitchen.

Bethann was giggling, Wes was bringing in a bucket of milk, Randy was making cow eyes at Lily. And Lily, her face smudged with flour, was smiling, offering the smitten cowpuncher a handful of biscuits.

"Mornin'," he said, his eyes connecting with each of the four people in the room. He wasn't sure which was most surprised to see him. A prickling of red color crept up Randy's neck, as though he'd been caught with his hand in the cookie jar. Wes grinned and Lily looked shocked.

She'd been avoiding him since the day she'd bathed him, sending in Bethann or Wes with his tray of food, and checking on him under the cover of darkness once she thought he was asleep. He never was, but he hadn't let on.

"Papa!" Bethann ran to him, grabbing him fiercely around the legs. Tyler planted his feet more solidly on the ground to keep from toppling over. "You're better."

He stroked the top of Bethann's hair. "Seems I am. A bit."

He glanced at Lily. She bit her lip then turned around.

Randy headed for the door. Lifting the biscuits up in his own defense, he said, "Miss Lillian's biscuits are the best in the territory. No offense, Wes."

Wes nodded. "I'll be agreeing with ya. I ain't fool 'nough to think my cookin's better than this here young lady's. She's proved herself a mighty fine cook."

"Thank you, Wes." Lily set out plates for breakfast.

"Good to see you up, boss." Randy exited the door before Tyler could reply. Wes was two steps behind him.

"You mind the lady now, son, and don't be doing nothin' but restin' today."

Tyler grimaced. He hated being confined. He hated taking orders from, well, it seemed as though everybody on the ranch had something to say.

"Papa, can I visit my pony today?"

"Sure, darlin'. Later. Right now, I'm anxious to try these here biscuits that got ole Randy so fired up."

He watched Lily flinch at his words. Leisurely, he moved himself away from the door frame and took a seat at the table. Lily flitted around the kitchen like a butterfly, pouring the coffee, filling his plate with food, washing the dishes then shooing Bethann out to clean up her room. Never once did she look at him.

"Lily, sit down."

He knew it sounded more a command than a request, because Lily stopped in midstride, tossed the dishrag aside and took a seat to face him. But it was as if she didn't know where to look. Her eyes wouldn't meet his, and when they flickered below his collar, he realized she was uncomfortable looking at him half-dressed. Finally she seemed to choose a spot over his left ear to set her gaze.

"You got everything done in town, yesterday?"

"Yes."

"Gonna plant your garden?"

"Yes."

"Buy the material you needed?"

"Yes."

"Lily!" he howled. "What in tarnation is wrong?"

That startled her enough for her to cast wide, innocent eyes his way.

"Mr. Kincaide, I—"

"Damn it, it's Tyler."

"I don't think this is going to work out, after all," she blurted.

She was acting strange, averting her eyes again. He softened his voice. "What's not going to work out?"

"This…arrangement," she confessed, her pale blue eyes lifting to his. He held her gaze.

"Why not?"

She closed her eyes briefly, as if searching for the courage to explain. "W-when you walked in just now, it struck me. Up until now, I was nursing a sick man."

"I never thanked you. You saved my life."

Her smile was shaky. "But seeing you like this, having breakfast together, made me realize—"

"That we're living together?" he said softly.

"Yes," she replied, letting out a long breath. "It suddenly dawned on me. I can't do this."

"If it's marriage you're wanting, I've already agreed—"

"No! I, uh, I do appreciate the offer. I can't."

"I promised I wouldn't compromise you, Lily. You know that. I'm sorry about the scene in the washroom. I've got a temper. If that's what's got you thinking about leaving, don't. You have my word, it won't happen again."

Tyler knew she was an innocent. He'd let his anger over being injured and helpless, as well as her soaking his head, sway his better judgment. She'd never been with a man and he'd deliberately exposed himself to teach her a lesson. She was no bawdy-house woman to toy with. She was his housekeeper and a true lady.

Lily appeared deep in thought. Tyler couldn't tell for sure what she was thinking. Hell, he needed her. Already, in the span of a week's time, his household had come to depend on her. "You need time to find your uncle."

"True."

"And Bethann has taken a shine to you, Lily."

Lily grimaced. "Now who's not playing fair?"

"You keep the place orderly. You're a fine cook."

"Thank you."

"Lily, we need you 'round here."

She nodded.

"So, you'll stay?"

She took her own sweet time to respond, but then she smiled a true, unabashed smile for him. Tyler felt an unfamiliar squeezing in his chest.

"Yes, I'll stay."

* * *

He sat in the corner of the saloon, his hat riding low
on his forehead, sipping whiskey, relying on dim light-
ing and dark shadows to hide him from view. Amazing
how much information one can pick up from boisterous ranch hands on payday. Kincaide survived the
shooting, he heard one man say, due to the ministra-
tions of his new housekeeper. Hell, how many lives
did that man have? he thought bitterly.

He'd have been here sooner but landing in prison
had thwarted his plans. The "lady" got what she deserved though, thinking she could sift through his belongings as if she'd had the right. He chuckled silently.
She'd not be earning another red cent in her sordid
profession again.

Kincaide, too, would get his due.

And Lizabeth's death would finally be avenged.

He'd bide his time until the perfect opportunity presented itself.

Chapter Seven

Lily wrapped her hands around a stubborn weed and tugged. There was no budging it. She stared at the unwelcome plant, determined to pluck it up from the ground.

"I'm a good sight smarter than you," she said with a snarl, hoping the tone of her voice would somehow pop the obstinate weed from the soil. She gripped its thick base, feeling a slight give. Lily pulled even harder. But the plant, as if in response to her declaration, seemed to take root, causing Lily's hand to slip. She fell back with a thud and landed on her bottom. "Damn it all!"

"Swearing...*Miss Lily?*" Tyler came up behind her and crouched down. With a quick tug, he uprooted the weed and handed her the ugly twisted plant.

"I'm picking up your bad habits, Mr. Kincaide."

He smiled wide, flashing straight white teeth. Lily was becoming accustomed to the rapid pounding of her heart whenever the man was near.

Tyler reached for her hands, turning them to view her calloused palms. "You're working hard. I'll have one of the men shovel up the rest of the weeds."

Lily's eyes met with his and lingered. His touch always turned her mind to mush. "Uh—no. Thank you."

He let go of her hands and Lily was able to release the breath she'd been holding. "Why not?"

She shrugged. "I don't know. I guess I want the garden all to myself. When each root takes hold, each flower blooms, I want to know it's because of me. Silly, isn't it?"

"Nothing silly about seeing something through on your own, Lily."

"I've always dreamed of having a garden." She lifted her eyes to his. "Thank you."

Tyler stared at her, then nodded. His gaze went to the upturned soil. "What'd you decide to plant?"

Lily smiled and looked over the plot of land. She pointed to the front of the house. "In this bed, I'm planting a flower garden. The flowers will need the protection of the house from the north and west winds. And the foundation will radiate heat and warm the soil here."

He glanced at her and she smiled. "On the west side, corn and sunflowers, on the north, carrots, radishes and turnips."

"You sharing your crop?"

"Of course," she said with a chuckle. "Couldn't possibly eat them all myself."

"Bethann won't eat vegetables."

"I bet she'll eat these."

Tyler grinned. "That I'd like to see."

Lily noticed the color had come back to Tyler's face. He seemed stronger each day. He moved about more easily now and she hadn't noticed pain contort his features when he lifted his arm. The last time Doc

Ramsey had come out to the ranch, he'd said the wound was healing nicely.

He'd also said Sheriff Singleton had no further information about the shooting. They may never find out who shot Tyler. Or why.

Lily plucked out another weed, watching Tyler walk over to where Bethann was playing with her doll. He scooped his daughter up and nuzzled a kiss onto her neck, causing Bethann to let out a string of sweet giggles.

Lily sighed. Tyler was lucky to be alive. And she was lucky to have found this home. Temporarily. But as she viewed the handsome man walk his daughter to her pony, she prayed she'd be lucky enough not to fall in love with him.

After dinner that evening Lily poured Tyler a cup of coffee after sending Bethann to her room to get undressed.

"I want to learn to shoot," she said decidedly.

"Huh?"

"I said, I'd like to learn how to shoot a gun, Tyler."

Tyler cringed. Lily had that determined look in her eyes again, but her request startled him. Not that women didn't take up arms. Many did. Somehow he hadn't pictured Lily holstering a gun.

"I heard what you said, Lily. Why?"

"For protection, of course."

Tyler gulped down more of the steaming liquid than he intended. The coffee burned his tongue. "But there's more than enough men around here who know how to shoot. Damn good, too. You'll be protected."

"I don't want to rely on a man for protection."

Tyler let out an audible sigh. He looked into his coffee cup. "Now, Lily. I don't know."

"Tyler, you're leaving for spring roundup next week. No one knows who shot you or why. I think with Bethann and me staying here by ourselves, I should learn."

"I've told you, I'll leave a hand here to watch things. You won't be alone."

"Will he be sleeping in the house?"

Tyler pushed the coffee cup away and stood up. "Hell no!"

Lily cast him a smug expression. She put her hands on her hips and stood her ground. "There, you see. We will be alone. Who'll be staying on?"

"Does it matter?" he asked. Tyler knew it did. He'd have to leave his most trusted hand on the ranch. With two females alone, no telling what could occur. But Tyler was curious. Was Lily hoping for someone special to stay on while he and the others were gone?

"No, as long as he's good with a gun, I suppose."

"He will be. Don't worry. I wouldn't leave the ranch unless I thought it was safe."

"I still think I should learn."

"Lily, a gun's a dangerous weapon." Tyler caught Lily rolling her blue eyes.

"I'm a fast learner, Tyler."

"I'll have to think about it."

"You know, I don't need your permission. I have every right to learn."

"And if I refuse to teach you?"

Lily hesitated. "Uh—well, Randy said he'd show me."

Tyler raised his voice. "Randy?" He put both hands

in his back pockets and gave Lily a long, searching look. "Be ready at sunup tomorrow morning."

Lily stared at the horse Tyler had saddled and readied for her. "Can't we take the buckboard?"

Tyler shifted in his saddle. "No. Not where we're going."

"I can't ride."

"What do you mean, you can't ride? You grew up on a farm, didn't you?"

"Yes, but all we had was one plow horse and my daddy's old mare. My mom and I used the buggy mostly."

"I got work to do later this morning. No time to teach you to ride today." Tyler leaned down and put out his hand. "Think you can climb on up."

"You mean, you want us *both* to ride on your horse?" Lily shuddered at the thought. It was highly improper. They'd be so close.

"Can't think of another way to get you where we're going. Now, you want to learn to shoot or not?"

Lily glanced warily at his extended hand. "I—I'll try." He lowered his hand further and she took hold.

"Put your leg in the stirrup and throw your leg over."

Lily tried, several times. It was awkward. Her long legs weren't cooperating. "I can't do it."

Tyler dismounted. He took her foot and placed it in the stirrup, then grabbed her other leg to help guide it up. When she faltered, his hand cupped her bottom and he scooted her up onto the saddle. "Sorry, Lily. It was the only way."

Lily blushed down to her toes and wondered if it was truly the only way. But those thoughts diminished and more powerful thoughts took hold when she realized Tyler had mounted and was seated directly behind her.

"Hold on here." He wrapped his arms around her and covered her hands over the saddle horn. With a click of his heels Blaze took off in a fast walk. The other horse followed them to the barn. Tyler called for Wes to unsaddle the gelding and to make sure Bethann was looked after.

After several quiet minutes on the trail, Tyler asked, "Lily, you okay?"

"Mmm, fine," she said, lying through her teeth. How could she be okay with Tyler's arms around her? His thighs were pressing into hers and he was breathing in her ear. She thanked goodness her long-sleeved shirt covered rising goose bumps all along her arms. She kept herself board-stiff so that no more of him would touch her.

Every once in a while Tyler would break the silence of the ride to make a disgruntled sound. After the third time Lily gave in to her curiosity. "Is there something wrong?"

"That knot of hair keeps poking me in the face." He unfastened her hairpins and let her hair loose. "Better," he said, his breath caressing her neck.

"H-how far are we going?" Lily prayed Tyler couldn't feel her trembling.

"Past the creek a little ways. There's some rocks up there. We'll use them for targets."

She nodded numbly. Lily breathed a secret sigh of relief when Tyler brought Blaze to a halt and dismounted. He put his hands on her waist and helped her down. Heat flamed her body where he had touched, but Lily knew she couldn't let him see how he'd affected her. She became aware of another ache, too. Her backside smarted like the dickens. A lady had no call to sit astride a saddle wearing a dress. More than anything Lily wanted to rub the soreness away. It was a most unladylike thing to do.

She did it, anyway, and heard Tyler's muffled chuckle from behind.

With a smile on her lips, she surveyed the area Tyler chose for target practice. The ground was carpeted with a vivid array of wildflowers and off in the distance a rocky hillside.

Tyler tethered his horse to a tree and threw his saddlebags over his shoulder, motioning for Lily to follow.

"It's so peaceful here," Lily said, trying to match his stride. "Seems a shame to disturb the silence."

"I used to come up here a lot. Lizabeth liked it."

It was the first time he'd offered anything about his wife. "I think Bethann would, too. Has she been here?"

"Just as a baby."

Tyler put his head down and said nothing more until they reached the hillside. He unholstered his gun. "What do you know about guns, Lily?"

"When you shoot one, someone usually gets hurt." Lily glanced at his mending shoulder.

He looked at her in understanding. "This here's a Colt .45. Ranchers use them for killing an injured animal or…uh, turning a stampede." For a brief moment anguish marked his expression. He shook it off quickly, giving Lily a determined look.

"Some people call them peacemakers." He slapped the gun into his other hand and opened the chamber. "Bullets go in here, six in all." Then he snapped the chamber closed and gave it a spin. "Always keep your fingers off the trigger, unless you've marked your target."

Tyler lifted the gun and took aim at the rocks. "You need to be sure. Aiming doesn't come easy to everyone. You'll use both hands and squeeze the trigger with your pointer finger. Expect a shock when the gun goes off. If you're not used to it, the retort can scare you."

Tyler stood behind her. Wrapping his arms around her body, he put the gun in her hands and covered his palms over them. "How's it feel?"

Lily would have said "wonderful" except she knew he was talking about the gun. "Heavier than I thought."

"You'll get used to the weight. Takes practice, is all. Okay, ready to shoot?"

She nodded, and held her breath.

"Relax, Lily. You're too wound up."

"I'll try." Lily lowered her shoulders and let out a breath. Taking up a gun was a necessity. She didn't much like it. Guns always made her nervous.

"Okay, we're shooting at the small rock between those two boulders. Hold the gun out, follow the site…that's it. Gently, like a mama would hug her baby, squeeze the trigger."

Lily did as she was told. The gun went off. She backed up right into Tyler's chest. "Oh, my!"

Tyler grabbed her arms. "You all right?"

She nodded, but didn't move a muscle. He took the gun out of her hands and rubbed her arms. "Loosen up, honey. You've got to be sure and confident when you carry a gun. Being alert's good, but your nerves can trip you up. I knew a man, jittery as a colt facing off a rattler, shot his big toe off, then got so darn confounded, shot up the barber shop on accident. Lucky for the townsfolk, the shop was closed at the time.''

Honey? The word warmed her as no wool blanket could on a blustery cold night. Lily was so entranced by the endearment, she'd only heard part of his story. Something about a colt in a barber shop.

''Th-that's nice, Tyler.''

''Lily?''

''Hmm?''

''Want to try again? You hit the rock on the far left side. Pretty good for a beginner.''

''But you were holding the gun with me.''

''Try it again, alone this time.''

Lily turned to face him. He nodded and gave her a reassuring look. ''You can do it.''

Lily turned around again. She stared off into the distance, found her target and took aim. She shot off close to twenty rounds, she surmised. She'd missed the rock on the first two attempts. With Tyler's patience and guidance, she'd managed to hit the mark every time after that.

He was standing so near, occasionally he'd place his hands on her waist to position her. Lily's heart thumped wildly—from his close proximity and from the thrilling power she'd felt handling the gun. She was a fast learner. Tyler had complimented her on her progress. He encouraged her and never lost his patience.

''Time to take a break. I packed us a snack. Got a jug of lemonade, too.''

Lily followed Tyler to where Blaze was tethered. He brought out the food and laid a gray wool blanket out on the ground. Lily sat down several feet away from Tyler. He handed her a biscuit and a chunk of cheese. His eyes were on her as she took a bite.

"Your hair looks mighty pretty blowing in the breeze," Tyler said softly.

"Thank you." Lily refused the rush of blood threatening to rise to her face. Someday soon she'd get used to being near Tyler.

"Smells nice, too, like springtime flowers."

Lily fingered her hair. "It's lilac soap. Came from New York."

"You don't say? Who brought it to you?"

"No one. I ordered some from a catalog."

His gaze lingered on her hair, then he cleared his throat. "You did real good today. We'll have another lesson before I leave on roundup."

"How long will you be gone?"

"Usually takes about three to four weeks. I think you'll do fine with Bethann."

But would she do fine without him? The thought of him leaving brought certain trepidation—she'd miss him. And certain relief—at least she'd be able to put two thoughts together without her mind getting all muddled up. Having Tyler underfoot made her dizzy with desire. There was no help for it.

"Bethann's a wonderful child. For the most part, she minds me. She finally named her pony. She told me last night. Pint-Size." Lily chuckled. "Because it was the smallest one in the herd."

"Pint-Size?" Tyler laughed, too. "'Xcept that yearling'll grow bigger than ole Blaze here."

Their gazes locked. Lily saw the reflection of her amusement in Tyler's smiling eyes. Her smile faltered when she noticed his eyes travel down to stare at her mouth. Several seconds went by before Tyler looked away. He lifted a blade of grass, perusing it with great interest.

"Tomorrow morning, I promised to take Bethann for a ride. You might as well come along. I've got a mare that's lady-broke in the stable. Real gentle horse."

"I think I'd like that, Tyler, but I'm warning you— I may not take to riding."

Tyler stretched out his legs on the tall grass and leaned his head against the tree. "Lily, there ain't much, I've noticed, you don't take to."

"Really?"

"Yep. That's the reason I wanted to hire you. I knew you'd make a darn good—" Tyler paused and glanced away. Damn, he'd put his foot in it this time.

"Housekeeper?" Lily said quietly.

Tyler searched Lily's face. She was his house-keeper, but why'd he feel as though he'd somehow insulted her? Maybe because he knew she was much more. She brought order to his house, but with that also a sense of harmony. The house was alive again with conversation and laughter. He'd walk in after a long day on the range to the warming scents of a meal cooking, his daughter reciting the alphabet and a shy greeting from Lily.

She made his house a home again.

"You know you've won my men over with those biscuits and cakes you're always sending to the bunk-house."

"They work hard."

"Yeah, and there isn't a one of them that wouldn't take a bullet for you, Lily."

That made Lily smile. "You know someone plowed up the rest of the weeds in the garden."

Tyler arched his brows. "Really now. Were you disappointed?" Tyler hoped not. After he'd seen the abuse her hands were taking trying with all her might to yank out those weeds, he stole out of the house early one morning and shoveled up the ground.

"No. It was a sweet gesture. None of the men owned up to doing it, though." When Lily glanced his way, he gave her an innocent look. "I don't suppose you know who did it?"

"Don't suppose I do."

Lily sighed and began putting the food away. "I'll be happy when I see those roots take hold. Radishes are fast growers. They'll be breaking through the soil soon enough."

Reluctant to leave the tranquillity, Tyler took a long look at the lush surroundings, then glimpsed the woman he enjoyed spending the morning with, before standing up. He reached down to take her hand. "Lily, I've got to be getting back. There's a pile of paperwork I've got to do today."

Lily took his hand and stood. They faced each other. Lily's pale blue eyes gleamed as she took in the scenery. "I'd like to come here again."

Her thick hair, lifted by a breeze, shone in the sunlight. It didn't matter that her gray dress hung loosely about her body or that her complexion was too wan to be considered comely. Tyler was unwilling to release her hand.

Together, hand in hand, they walked to his horse and mounted, leaving the solitude of the lush meadow behind.

* * *

Later that day Lily cut out the pattern to the new dress she planned on sewing. The blue and green calico print would be trimmed with white lace. It was a frivolous notion, but she always wanted a dress adorned with lace or ruffles. This one would have both.

Lily wondered when her practical nature turned fanciful. She'd never done much of anything in her life that wasn't entirely sensible. Out of necessity she'd always had to make do. Her father's gambling ways had assured her a life of meager belongings. She'd stopped blaming him a long time ago and accepted her fate. She was a plain-looking woman, too tall and slender to bring on much notice. She wasn't a woman inclined to fancy things.

But now she had cash in her pocket, friends on the ranch and a home she could temporarily call home. She felt fortunate and decided to indulge herself a bit.

On her last trip to town she'd not only purchased several yards of various colored calicos to make new dresses for both Bethann and herself, she'd surrendered to a dire yearning and bought yardage of cornflower-blue satin. Years ago she'd seen a dress in Godey's Lady Book she'd never forgotten. The lines of the dress were soft and feminine, flowing over the woman's body like a gentle caress. She'd memorized the pattern. One day, Lily vowed, she would make that dress for herself.

She'd put it on in the privacy of her room and twirl around, glancing at herself in the mirror from time to time. It would be a vivid reminder…she was a woman.

If only Tyler would see her as a woman. He knew she was a lady. Admittedly, that's the reason he wanted her to stay on at the ranch, for Bethann's sake.

But to be looked upon as a woman by Tyler would surely be a dream come true.

This morning when he'd held her hand, for just one moment Lily imagined him wanting her—the way a man wants a woman. Silly. Tyler had proven himself to be a gentleman in her presence. Taking her hand meant nothing to him but a simple way of offering his assistance. Before helping her mount his horse, he'd gently squeezed her hand and glanced at her lips. Lily's lips parted in wonderment. What would it feel like being kissed by Tyler Kincaide? She banished the ridiculous thought.

No one had ever kissed her before, except Jimmy McMurphy back behind the schoolhouse when she was twelve years old. But that really didn't count, because once he'd stolen a quick kiss, he'd dashed off as though his britches were on fire. Lily remembered rubbing the moistness off her lips, thinking kissing wasn't pleasant at all.

Somehow she knew kissing Tyler Kincaide would be different. The thought alone made her heart flutter.

Lily folded the material and pattern she'd cut out, putting them away in a drawer. She'd been inside thinking fanciful thoughts too long. She needed to clear her head. Leaving her room, she stepped outside and took a deep breath. She stretched her arms over her head and straightened her stiff body. The air was fresh and clean. An early afternoon drizzle stamped down much of the Texas dust circulating about. The rain had also softened the soil—an invitation to plant her garden too enticing to resist.

Joellen Withers had sent a large pot filled with flower bulbs, ready for transplanting, back with Wes the other afternoon. Wes must have spouted off about

Lily's garden and Joellen, generous to a fault, had surprised her. In turn, Lily baked the Withers family two fresh fruit pies and had a ranch hand deliver them. She'd wanted to present them in person to the thoughtful woman, but with Tyler leaving on roundup in a few days, there was too much to do at the ranch. Besides, Lily mused, the idea of having to be cordial to Letty Sue was not at all appealing.

"Aft'noon, Miss Lillian." Randy tipped his hat and stepped a foot on the porch.

"Hello, Randy."

"Nice day, ain't it?" He removed his hat, fingering the brim.

"Hmm, yes. The rain's cleared out all the bugs and dust."

"I wanted to thank you for sending over those molasses cookies. They hardly made their way 'round the bunkhouse."

Lily chuckled. "Nothing better for a woman to hear than her food's in demand. I'm glad you enjoyed them."

"Uh, we did. Excuse me, Miss Lillian, but I got something I want to ask you, so I'm just gonna come right out and say it."

Lily turned a serious eye on Randy. She could tell he was nervous. With a wide smile, she coaxed softly, "Go on."

He put his head down. Lily thought he'd wear out the rim of his hat from all the rubbing he was doing. "It's just that, some of the boys said...well, they said you're the boss's woman. Said I'd be crazy to even ask."

Of all the things she'd expected him to say, this was not within a realm of possibility. Randy stared at her, a red blush colored his face. She cleared her throat and made her declaration. "I'm Mr. Kincaide's housekeeper. I'm Bethann's teacher and...friend. And no, I'm not his woman, Randy."

"That's what I told the boys. I was sure of it, Miss Lillian." The tight lines in Randy's young face relaxed.

"Why?"

"Well, ma'am, there's a barn dance next month and if no one's asked you yet, I'd be honored if you'd attend with me."

"Me?" Lily's voice squeaked in astonishment. "I'm truly sorry. I couldn't possibly go."

Randy put his head down. "I see."

"No!" she said emphatically. Randy's feeling were hurt. She couldn't have that. "You don't understand. It's just that I...well, I don't know how to dance."

His head shot up. "Y-you don't?"

Lily laughed. "No. I'm afraid I don't."

"I could teach you."

His hopeful expression softened Lily's heart. She braced both hands on her hips. "And how does a strapping, big cowboy like you know so much about dancing?"

"I got me five older sisters. Every time one of 'em wanted to try out a new step or two, guess who they picked? I'm pretty good 'cause I got loads of practice. I'd be happy to teach you."

The enthusiasm in his voice was contagious. Lily would love to learn how to dance. "We'll give it a try. If I don't trip you up or worse, I might just go with you."

With a nod, he agreed. "Howdy, boss," Randy said,

taking his smiling eyes off Lily to greet Tyler who had just come from the corral.

"Randy, you look happier than a cat that's tipped over the milk bucket." Tyler gave Lily a questioning look.

"Randy's agreed to teach me how to dance," Lily said cheerfully. "I've never learned."

Tyler pushed his hat farther back on his head. "And why do you need to learn?"

"Uh—well…" Lily looked from Randy to a frowning Tyler. She said very slowly. "If I learn then I can go to the barn dance."

Tyler folded his arms across his middle and shot Randy a menacing look. "A dance? When?"

"The Hendersons are having the annual barn dance up at their place next month," Randy offered. He looked to Lily. "They always throw a big wingding after roundup."

"Never cared for the dang things myself." Tyler stared at his ranch hand.

Randy gave his boss a wide grin, then excused himself to do his daily chores. Lily stepped down from the veranda, having to pass by Tyler to head for the barn. "Excuse me," she said when he blocked her path. The man didn't budge from the spot. He stood there with hands on hips, staring at her. She had to sidestep around him to make her way. What's gotten into him? When she returned with her gardening tools he was crouching, looking at the upturned soil.

"What're you going to plant today?"

Lily kneeled down next to him. "Joellen sent a batch of potted flower bulbs. I thought they'd be pretty here, right by the steps. Daffodils, tulips, and of course, lilies."

"Will they grow here?"

"They won't have a choice." Lily smiled sweetly.

Tyler knew she'd succeed. She'd nurture her garden until every last flower took hold. She looked so serene tending to her plants, taking her small shovel and tilling the soil. Her long braid fell off one shoulder, the tip of the plait landing in the dirt. Without thinking, he lifted her hair. In his large calloused hand, the silky tresses seemed to glide over his fingers like a soft kiss. When Lily glanced at him, he smiled. "Keeps getting in your way."

"I should put it up."

"Looks better down."

Lily gave him a shy smile and resumed planting her flowers. She handled each plant as if it were a precious jewel. Her fingers lovingly guided the bulbs into the ground, then she smoothed the dirt evenly around. With one final pat, she gave a satisfied grin toward the newly planted soil and stood up.

Bethann ran straight into her arms, sobbing. "Bethann, what's the matter?" Lily hugged her tight, pressing her lips to his daughter's forehead.

"I—I can't...find...Miss Daisy."

"Oh, sweetie, we'll find her. Don't worry." Lily's words soothed her. She stopped crying.

"You...promise?"

"I do. She's got to be around here someplace. I bet she's taking a nap in a secret hiding place. Let's sit down here on the steps and try to remember the last time we saw Miss Daisy."

Tyler stroked the top of Bethann's head gently. "If anyone can help find Miss Daisy, it's Lily. Now, darlin', I've got to get back to work. Remember, tomorrow you're going to get to ride your new pony."

Bethann gave him a shaky smile as she pulled Lily tighter. "Only if I find Miss Daisy, Papa."

"That's right." Tyler's gaze found Lily's. "See you both at dinner."

Tyler walked to the corral and met up with Wes. His old friend was pacing back and forth. "Tyler, this 'ere filly is too cankerous! Nearly cut my hand to shreds with all her blame movin' an' ashufflin'. I been tryin' to shod her for pert near a hour. Hammer'd in my own dang finger!"

Tyler looked at Wes's hand. The old man was losing his eyesight, but he'd not be fool enough to bring up the subject. "You got to soothe her first, Wes. This filly's high-strung."

Wes sat down on a barrel. "What woman ain't?"

Tyler laughed and stroked the horse, cooing soft words into her ear. He picked up the shoe and bent to lift the filly's hoof. "Ain't that the truth."

"You talkin' about that sweet thing, Miss Lillian? Ain't nothin' high-strung about her."

"I was talking about Bethann!" He took the hammer to the horseshoe.

"Humph!" Wes grunted, eyeing Tyler. "Randy's got him a hankering for yore hired help. He's a wantin' to stay put on the ranch to watch ov'r the ladies during roundup."

Tyler stopped shoeing the horse to glance at Wes. "Can't spare him. He's my best cowpuncher. I'm leaving Jose here."

Wes let out a long chuckle. "Jose? Well don't that beat all. Interestin' how you see fit leavin' the only *married* cowpoke you got to watch ov'r the ranch."

"Dang it, Wes! What're you getting at?"

"Miss Lily Brody, boss."

"What about her?"

"Ain't no use denying you got feelin's for her. Plain as that ole felt hat on yore head!"

"I got no feelings for no woman, Wes." Tyler jammed the hammer handle into Wes's hand and stalked off, the sound of the old man's laughter buzzing in his head.

Chapter Eight

"Papa says I look like my ma. Said she was the pertiest woman he'd ever seen." Bethann sat on her knees and stared into the hearth. A small fire lingered.

Lily began brushing the girl's wet hair. "From what I remember of your ma, she was very beautiful. And I think you're going be just as lovely."

Tyler peeked through the doorway, watching his daughter climb onto Lily's lap and hug her doll to her chest. He wasn't surprised to learn Lily had taken Bethann's hand and gone searching for the doll as soon as he'd left them. They found the doll lodged under the horse trough. It must have fallen over from the fence post where Bethann had left her. "I don't remember my ma that very much."

"I'm sure your ma is watching down on you from heaven." Lily put her arms around her and gave a tight squeeze. "She's most likely very proud of you, sweetheart. You're developing into quite a lady."

"I don't always want to be a lady."

"I know. And you don't have to be…well, not all the time."

"You always are. My papa says you're a right fine lady and I should listen to you."

"Oh, but sometimes…I wish—"

"What's all this wishing about?" Tyler asked.

Startled, Lily looked up. Tyler leaned against the door. Apparently she didn't realize he'd been there.

"Girl talk." Lily shot Bethann a conspiratorial grin.

Tyler glanced at his daughter held in Lily's welcoming arms. "Time for bed, darlin'. Remember, I'm gonna show you how to feed Pint-Size in the morning before our ride."

"Can Lily come, Papa?"

"I've asked her to." He looked at Lily for confirmation. "Have you changed your mind?"

"I would like to learn if you have the time."

With a nod he said, "We'll leave after breakfast." Tyler reached down and scooped Bethann out of Lily's arms. The back of his hand brushed against Lily's breast. It was accidental but the feel of her soft skin giving way from his touch sent a surge of heat through his body. He hadn't made that kind of contact with a good woman since his marriage to Lizabeth. Of course there'd been the "ladies" at the local saloon. But it wasn't the same. Just knowing of Lily's innocence made the touching more enticing and, of course, wrong. But, he reminded himself, he hadn't planned on touching her that way. It really had been an accident.

Tyler stole a look at Lily. Her eyes went wide. He thought better than to apologize. That would only make the situation more awkward. He chose to pretend nothing had happened. "If you'll turn down her bed, I'll tuck her in."

Bethann wrapped both her chubby arms around Tyler's neck as Lily led the way to the bedroom. Lily pulled a multicolored quilt down neatly and gave a pat. Tyler set his daughter down and lifted the covers to her chin. He kissed her forehead before leaving. With arms folded, Tyler leaned against the door and watched as Lily and Bethann said their nightly prayers. It was a ritual Lily had instituted. One of many. A young girl needed some sense of stability in her life. Tyler had simply muddled through, hoping he was doing right by his daughter, but never really knowing for sure. Now, he felt justified having Lily here for Bethann. She'd already done wonders with his waif of a child.

With all the prayers recited, Tyler made a quick retreat. He'd grinned when he'd heard his name mentioned a time or two during the reciting of those prayers. His daughter had a good heart, asking the Lord to keep her Papa safe and happy. He'd always felt a sense of safety in Sweet Springs, until the shooting. Now his guard was up. He'd not let any harm come to those he loved.

As for happy, hell—Tyler Kincaide had known happiness in the arms of his wife. After her death, nothing seemed to matter except Bethann and the ranch. Sweet of Bethann to pray for him, though.

Tyler paused in the darkened hallway, deciding to wait for Lily. Only a flicker of light streamed in from the half crescent moon, but Tyler caught the scent of Lily's hair and knew she was inches from him. He looked into questioning clear blue eyes. "I've got to say you're doing a fine job with Bethann. She seems more agreeable. She minds you."

"Thank you," Lily replied in a hushed tone. "She's a special child. And she's very bright."

Tyler nodded. "You're good for her."

Tyler's eyes had adjusted somewhat to the dim light in time to see Lily's cheeks turn pink. "I, uh, have grown quite fond of her."

"I'm glad you're staying on a while, Lily."

Lily gave him a halfhearted smile. He knew she had very little choice in the matter. Sweet Springs wasn't exactly a boon of opportunity for unmarried women. What scant jobs there were would hardly suit a woman like Lily. She wasn't one to do menial labor and, of course, a job in the saloons was out of the question. Tyler was glad he was able to help her out and equally glad that his precocious daughter was in her care. He admired Lily's intelligence.

He'd offered her marriage—an easy way out for most women, but not Lily. She, too, saw the futility of entering into a loveless, business-like marriage. But Tyler admitted he did like having Lily around and hoped she'd stay as long as possible...for Bethann. "Any news from your uncle?"

"Nothing yet, but I do have a letter I'd like to post. Maybe Wes could take it with him on his next trip to town?"

"Sure thing."

"Thank you, Tyler. Well, I'd better be getting to bed, unless I can offer you a cup of coffee?"

"No, thanks. You don't have to be waiting on me, Lily. Appreciate the thought. It's right kind of you." Tyler hesitated, lingering in the hallway. He was blocking her from going to her room. What he couldn't figure out was, why? They both should be getting to bed, but there was this gnawing ache in the pit of his stomach. With brutal honesty, he recognized it as loneliness. When Lily was around, he realized he felt far less lonely.

She cleared her throat and repeated, "Well, then, I'd better be getting to bed. Good night, Tyler."

Tyler had no choice but to move out of her way to let her pass. "Uh-huh. 'Night, Lily." He watched as she entered her room, then his body sagged and he slumped against the wall. Thumping his head three deliberate times, he hoped he'd knock some sense into his skull. What in tarnation was happening? He'd never given in to his feelings of loneliness before. He'd simply gritted his teeth, dug in and rode out the storm.

Just because he liked Lily, didn't mean he could rely on her to ease his lonely days. He wouldn't even give credence to her easing his lonely nights. That wasn't ever going to happen. She'd made that clear from the start and he, too, had given his word.

So why was he standing in the dark, wishing he'd accepted Lily's offer of coffee? He could be sitting in his kitchen watching her busy about the cookstove, fussing over him. He'd ask her to share a cup and they'd talk quietly. Every once in a while she'd lift clear blue timid eyes his way and the sharp pang of loneliness would ebb some.

Lily woke earlier than usual. The sun hadn't made its grand entrance to welcome the day yet. She rose slowly, letting the crisp air awaken her senses, then crossed the room and took her robe from the peg on the door. Shivering slightly, she wrapped herself into the warmth of her robe.

A flicker of movement caught her eye as she glanced toward her window. The sound of distant hooves whispering and soft nickering filled the air as she moved closer to her window. Lifting the curtain to the side, she took a better look. From inside the crowded corral Tyler strode with even steps and rope in hand, stalking a chestnut gelding, one of many in his string. With quiet strength, he moved through flowing manes and flaring nostrils in a fluid grace compared only to the horses themselves. He seemed one with them. The other horses sidestepped out of his way, swishing tails and lifting heads as they snorted at the disruption.

Lily held her breath and watched man against animal. With the ease of an experienced horseman, Tyler shook out a broad loop in his rope. Dust rose up as a gust of wind caught and held in the air. The horse Tyler stalked eyed his approach and whirled away, finding a corner of the corral. The white-socked gelding tensed, his hind quarters stood firm as he met Tyler head-on. Lily heard Tyler's deep voice soothing the horse, although she wasn't able to hear the actual words he'd spoken to the tentative animal.

With swift, smooth agility, Tyler cast his rope. His wrist turned downward at the moment of release and the open loop fell softly on target. With a yank, Tyler threw his weight on the rope as the loop tightened around the horse's neck. The horse eyed Tyler, then dropped his head in resignation. Tyler pulled the horse close, stroked his coarse mane and led him into the barn.

Lily sighed and turned away from the window. Her heart skipped a beat every time she viewed the man. Tyler wasn't only handsome in his own right, he was a decent man and a good father to Bethann. Lily once again pondered what it would be like to have Tyler Kincaide view her as a woman.

Silly.

But it was true. Lily longed for more in life. She wanted to love a man with her whole heart. She wanted a family. Children to raise. She wanted to know the feeling of putting a twinkle in a man's eye. To make him smile right before his lips touched hers.

That would never happen with Tyler.

Lily glanced at the letter that was ready to post, sitting on her pinewood dresser. Another letter to yet another town, hoping to find her uncle. This one was addressed to the sheriff of Dodge City. She'd post one each week until she received news of Uncle Jasper's whereabouts. Her uncle would provide the family Lily yearned for. He'd take her in. And she'd finally have a real home.

But sadness surrounded her heart thinking of leaving the Circle K. How could she leave Bethann? She'd already come to love the child. Bethann, the precious, adorably mischievous little girl.

With a deep sigh, she dressed quickly, choosing a light brown skirt, long-sleeved blouse and a stiff suede vest. She pulled on her dark worn leather boots. The air would be crisp this morning when they set out on their ride.

Lily made a breakfast of biscuits, eggs, slab bacon and coffee. She didn't have to wake Bethann. The child was awake, dressed and eager to ride her new horse. Lily asked her to set out the plates on the table.

Bethann made a face, but did as she was told. The girl was learning to help more and more around the house. Lily would give her simple chores to do and was proud of the child when she accomplished the task without too much fuss.

Tyler came into the kitchen, put his hat on the peg next to the door, gave Lily a quick smile and sat down to breakfast. The adults listened to Bethann's excited chatter. Occasionally, Lily would shift her eyes from Bethann to catch Tyler's loving gaze on his daughter. When breakfast was finished, Bethann offered to help Lily with the cleanup. Tyler patted his child's head, giving her a prideful look, and said he'd meet up with them in the barn.

Minutes later Lily and Bethann walked hand in hand over to the barn. Tyler was in the tack room. He came out wearing a wide smile. "You two ladies ready?"

Bethann bobbed her head up and down. "We're sure as anythin' ready, Papa."

Tyler glanced at Lily. She took in a deep breath. "I think so."

Tilting his head, Tyler studied Lily's face. "You catch on to things real quick. You'll do fine."

Lily doubted that. The reassuring look Tyler gave her didn't help. She'd always been wary of riding.

"I had Wes make up a mounting block. It'll be easier to hoist yourself onto the saddle. But right now, it's feeding time."

He showed Bethann where the barrel of oats was stored. "See those oats, darlin'? After Pint-Size eats her share of hay, she can have some oats. Horses eat more than you can figure. They need gallons of water, too. We can't have them filling up on oats. The oats come last. Think of it as dessert." He winked at his daughter. She giggled.

"They need salt every day, too. We've got scattered

salt blocks out in the pasture and in the corral. From time to time they stop and get their fill.''

''How much hay do I feed her, Papa?''

''We'll lead her over to the rack here, let her eat some. Don't hurry your horse when you set her to feed. They eat slow like, take their time. Remember, they can graze on the land when we stop for a rest later.''

Tyler led Pint-Size out of her stall by the reins. ''Careful, darlin'. Don't ever get directly behind a horse. Never know when they turn skittish. Might just rear up and kick. Now, come here and touch her coat. Easy like.''

Tyler lifted Bethann up to let her stroke the animal's shining coat. Chubby hands glided up and down. Bethann wore a beautiful awe-filled smile. ''Papa, she likes it.''

''Sure she does, haven't seen a lady yet that—'' Tyler's face reddened, he choked back a cough, set his daughter down and glanced at Lily. She chuckled. ''I mean, horses like to be groomed.

''I've chosen a gentle mare for you, Lily. She's been fed and saddled.'' Tyler untied a dappled gray from the barn stall post and brought her to face Lily. ''This is Pearl.''

Lily looked at her foe and shivered. True, the horse appeared gentle, but Lily's doubts had more to do with her own ability than the horse's sweet nature. ''Pearl.''

''Lily?''

She shifted her attention to Tyler. He was giving her a strange look. ''Want to try to mount her?''

''Go on, Miss Lily,'' Bethann coaxed with her wide-eyed innocence. The child had dauntless faith in her. Lily didn't want to let Bethann down.

"Sure. I'll try."

Lily listened to Tyler's instructions for mounting. He was giving the lesson to both she and Bethann. "Always from the left, grip the mane with your left hand, put your foot in the stirrup and hold on to the cantle with your right hand for support. Then spring up and throw your right leg over the horse, settle yourself quickly in the center so the horse doesn't lose his balance or get confused."

Lily blinked. It seemed too much to remember. That and fear of looking the fool made her cringe.

Tyler led Pearl out to the side of the barn where Wes set up the mounting block. Lily watched Tyler position the horse. He gave her a nod. "Go ahead now, Lily. Step on up. I've got Pearl. She's isn't going anywhere."

"My skirts?"

Tyler scratched his head and looked from her waist to the hem of her skirts, then back up again. "I know. We'll have to get you some riding gear, but lots of women can ride wearing a skirt." He cleared his throat. "Proper riding skirts, that is."

Lily's mouth went dry from his perusal of her body. She nodded. "Then, I guess I'm ready."

Lily put the toe of her boot into the stirrup, grabbed at Pearl's speckled mane and raised up. She threw her right leg up, but it caught in the folds of her skirts. She heard Tyler barking orders, but it was no use. She lost her balance, swayed too far right, felt her boot release from the stirrup as she toppled up and over the horse, landing with a thud on the hard dirt.

Tyler rushed over to her. "Lily! Are you hurt?"

Lily untwisted her long legs and sat in a heap, her skirts making a wide circle around her. The horse snickered and turned her head to give Lily a long look. Lily only imagined she saw sympathy in Pearl's round brown eyes.

Tyler crouched down. "Lily, say something."

Lily looked around. Wes had an arm on Bethann. Both had the most startled looks on their faces. Tyler was equally stunned. Then the absurdity of it struck her. She began to chuckle. Tyler narrowed his eyes on her, concern rapidly changing to confusion.

Lily's rump was sore, her legs ached and her pride was all but gone. She shook her head and laughter emerged, full and deep. She threw her head back and gave in to it, her eyes fixed on Tyler's. Soon, the confusion marking his handsome features changed once again. Lines around his eyes crinkled, his lips curved up and amusement sparked in his dark irises. Within seconds, his mouth opened and laughter poured out in a deep low rumble. Such a wonderful sound.

Their eyes locked as they continued to laugh. Lily's shoulders shook, her body trembled. At one point tears welled up and threatened to flow. Then, when one sole drop escaped down her cheek, Tyler reached out with his finger to brush it away.

His touch, sure and gentle, seared her skin. She grew quiet, as did Tyler. His eyes roamed over her face. She felt tenderness in his searching gaze almost as if he were truly touching her again. Lily's gaze dropped to his lips. His smile straightened to a fine line.

Wes and Bethann came running over. Bethann giggled. "I thought you was hurt, but then you laughed. You ain't hurt, are you, Miss Lily?"

Lily tore her gaze from Tyler. The moment was

gone. She glanced up at Bethann and Wes. "Just my pride, sweetie."

Tyler stood up and offered her a hand. She took it without looking at him. Brushing off her skirts and stomping the dirt from her boots, she said, "Well, as you can see, I'm not much of a rider."

"Aw, missy, you ain't so bad. Just takes a little practice," Wes offered kindly. "Sure glad you ain't hurt."

"What do you say, Lily? Want to try again?" Tyler moved to the mounting block. This time he offered his hand. "I won't let you go, till I'm sure you're on."

Lily ignored the stiffness in her joints. She walked over to the mounting block. "I'm willing if you are."

Tyler gave her a look of approval. "Take my hand."

Two hours later Tyler, Lily and Bethann reined in their mounts by the creek where it wound around a crop of ironwoods. They set their horses to drink and stretched their legs. Lily prided herself on only falling off Pearl three times. Each time, no matter the pain, she managed to get back up, determined to complete the ride.

Bethann did marvelously well for her first time, or so her proud father announced. Pint-Size seemed to take to the little rider on his back. But the child was tuckered out.

Bethann rolled out a blanket and laid herself down before Lily could even offer her a cup of lemonade. Within minutes the little girl was napping under the shade of an ancient ironwood. Tyler bent to comb a few stray strands of hair off her face, brushing a soft kiss on her forehead.

He leaned back against a tree and watched the creek

waters. Lily, too, stared at the creek. The water raced by, heightened by a recent rain, looking refreshing and more inviting than Lily wanted to admit. Besides the fact she thought the scrapes on her legs might need cleansing from the last fall she took. She'd landed on thorny underbrush and was sure she was bleeding a little.

She poured Tyler a cup of lemonade, trying to forget the slashes on her legs, and walked over to him. He accepted the tin and motioned for them to sit down on a nearby blanket he'd rolled out. Lily spoke quietly, "Bethann is exhausted. She's quite a little rider."

Tyler glanced at his sleeping daughter. "That she is. I'm real proud of her. She did fine today."

Lily sighed. "It's easier to learn when you're young."

Tyler shot her a look. "You did fine, too, Lily."

"Did not, but thanks for trying."

Tyler shifted to give her his full attention. "I mean it, Lily. Not too many women would've taken the kind of punishment you did today. But you got right back on that horse and kept trying."

Lily's chuckle was one of wry condemnation. "Shows you what I know." Absently she rubbed her leg through her skirts. The scrape just above the knee burned now, and she felt some oozing. Lily winced, then hid her pain by plastering on a smile.

She cringed when Tyler noticed. He sat up to stare at her leg. "Lily, you did get hurt. Look at your skirt."

When Lily did, she gasped. Her brown skirt showed signs of seepage. The red patch had made its way through three layers of petticoats. "Oh, dear."

Tyler moved to her side. "Let me take a look."

"No, I'll...I'll be fine." Lily jutted her chin up. "Thank you, anyway."

Tyler ran a hand through his hair. "Lily, your leg needs tending. Look, the bleeding's getting worse." And it was. The stain on her skirt had grown larger. She could only imagine what the gash looked like. Her leg was on fire. "Tarnation, Lily. I want to help."

His eyes pleaded and his face took on stubborn determination. Lily knew she'd not win this argument. "All right, Tyler," she responded softly.

"Lean yourself up against the tree." Tyler moved the wool blanket to the base of the tree trunk. Lily positioned herself, resting her head against the thick bark and laying her legs straight out. Tyler sat down next to her. Slowly he lifted her leg, placing it over his thighs. With sure fingers, he inched her skirt up. Lily kept a hand on her other leg, so she could retain some degree of modesty.

Tyler lifted her skirt nearly to her waist and Lily blushed. He looked at the wide gash on her leg, shook his head and cursed.

"Tyler, please don't—"

"Sorry, Lily. I'm just surprised to see how bad this is. If I don't take care of it right away, it could get worse. There's dirt in there. I've got to clean it. Stay still. I've got what I need in my saddlebags."

Lily closed her eyes and tried to forget the feel of Tyler's hands on her bare leg. He'd been gentle, but the roughness of his hands contrasted sharply with her smooth white skin. No man had ever touched her there. She thrilled at the sensation of being held so tenderly by him. It almost made up for the humiliating position she was in and the fiery pain shooting through her leg.

He came back with a jug of creek water, a clean bandanna and a small round covered container. When he sat down, he took her leg in his hands again. "This is going to sting." His eyes filled with concern. "Ready?"

Lily nodded. Tyler washed out the slight hole in her leg, rinsing the bandanna several times by pouring clean creek water over the stretch of material. He tipped the washed-out lemonade jug onto the open wound and let the water run down her leg. Blood oozed out for several minutes. Then it stopped.

All the while, Lily bit down on her lower lip. The pain wasn't unbearable. In fact, as soon as Tyler started tending to her wound, she began to feel much better. Once he was done, she felt her shoulders relax and most of the tension ebb from her body.

"I think it's clean enough." Tyler cast her a worried look. "You okay?"

"I'm fine. It feels much better. Thank you." Lily tried to remove her leg from his grasp, but he held firm. She shot him a startled look.

"I'm not through yet." He smiled. "I keep a salve for injuries in my saddlebags. Never know when one of the hands is in need. 'Specially since we've been using barbed-wire for fencing." He held up the gray container for her to see. "Stuff's made from aloe vera, grows down south a'ways. I have a batch sent up from San Antonio every year."

Lily tried to remove her leg once again. Tyler wasn't letting go. "It helps the healing. Takes the sting out, too. I'll just rub some on. Sit still, woman. You're about as bad a patient as I am."

Lily chuckled and gave up her leg. "No one is as bad as you."

Tyler grinned. He opened the jar and dipped two fingers in. "Steady now."

The ointment felt cool and soothing. But Lily's blood heated when Tyler laid his palm full-out on her leg and began stroking. His fingers seemed to linger as they grazed her skin. One hand cupped her leg from underneath, while the other rubbed, massaged and nearly drove her to distraction. Lily gave in to the feeling. She rested her head against the tree, unable to watch Tyler's powerful hands stroke her so tenderly a moment longer. But closing her eyes only made the sensations come more to life.

Her leg tingled while her pulse accelerated. Could he hear the rapid thumping of her heart? Sweet heaven.

"How does this feel?" he asked.

There was a deeper, huskier tone to his voice. Lily couldn't answer him, her throat tightened. "Mmm."

Tyler still held her leg, but there was silence. When Lily opened her eyes, she found Tyler leaning back on his haunches, watching her. His eyes seemed darker and his expression looked...well, Lily had never seen that expression on his face before.

While she was gathering her thoughts, Tyler took out a small knife from his back pocket, lifted a clean section of her petticoats and paused. "Sorry, but the wound needs dressing." He proceeded to cut a strip of cloth from her petticoat. Again, his hands were gliding along her leg. Carefully he tied the cloth not too snugly around the wound. "There, that should do."

Lily sat there staring at the newly dressed wound, at Tyler's hands on her leg, then up at the man who caused such stirrings in her heart. Tyler's lips curved up and he reached for her skirt. Lily hadn't realized she'd been clinging to the folds bunched up high on her thigh until Tyler's hand brushed hers. She released her hold, blushed and watched as he settled her skirts back down to her boots.

"Th-thank you," she said numbly.

Tyler stood and looked down at her. "It's a shame such a pretty leg had to get injured." He turned and walked to the creek.

Tyler had an itch that needed scratching, was all. He couldn't recall how long it had been since he'd driven himself deep inside a woman and eased the stiff ache that had settled between his legs. He thought of Renee, the accommodating "lady" at the Golden Garter who'd done just fine relaxing his pent-up tension from time to time. Yes, the good-looking redhead was just what he needed. Soon.

He glanced at the nape of Lily's long, sleek neck and noticed fine curling wisps of hair clinging to a drop of moisture there. He couldn't help noticing. She sat sidesaddle on his horse, nearly across his lap. He'd insisted it was the only safe way to get her home. Now, as his arm brushed along the side of her breast while he held the reins, he wondered at the wisdom in doing so.

The woman couldn't ride Pearl back to the ranch— not with that leg all bound up. One more fall could open the wound further, before it had a chance to heal.

Lily shifted in the saddle, pressing her hip against Tyler's groin. He held back a groan. "You uncomfortable, Lily?" He sure as hell was.

"Tyler, this is silly. I can ride my own horse."

"Lily, we've been through this already. You can't

ride Pearl back to the ranch. You couldn't take another fall.''

"Are you saying you'd think I'd fall again?" Lily turned slightly in his arms to look at him. She was a tall woman. Their eyes were nearly level.

"I'm saying we don't want to tempt fate." He smiled.

Lily's eyes flashed. She pursed her lips. "I told you I couldn't ride. Look at Bethann. She's doing great."

Tyler turned his head. Bethann was several steps behind them strapped into the saddle. Wes had cooked up the device to insure the little one's safety.

"Yep, she is, but she's also nearly hog-tied to the horse."

"Maybe I should tie myself to Pearl," Lily said wistfully.

Tyler chuckled. "You'll get there, Lily. Be patient. Ain't seen a thing yet you haven't taken to. Seems riding will just take some time, is all."

She shifted position again, this time her long braid whipped around her shoulder to rest over her left breast. The tip of the braid landed on Tyler's wrist and tickled him. He sucked in a breath.

The soft hair gliding over his lower arm brought his thoughts back to the mounting tension, the warmth spreading between his legs. And the need. Damn. It'd be another hour until they reached the Circle K. Another hour to think about the soft, milky-white skin he'd caressed just a short time ago.

When he'd lifted Lily's slender leg to tend to her injury, he'd been surprised at how shapely her limbs were. Under all those skirts, he'd expected stick-thin legs. Bird legs. Instead he found beautiful thighs, just the right size for a woman of Lily's height.

He'd applied the salve to the wound, but instead of stopping there, he'd massaged her leg, spreading the thick ointment all over the other small scratches. He'd taken his time and enjoyed the feel of her. Delicate, smooth, creamy.

And when he'd glanced at Lily, she hadn't seemed to mind. She'd had her eyes closed, a slight smile graced her face. She let out a tiny sigh, a sexy little moan of contentment that startled Tyler. She probably hadn't even realized she'd made a sound at all.

A deep hunger washed over him. A yearning he hadn't felt since Lizabeth was alive. Putting that look of contentment on Lily's face stirred something inside Tyler. She'd never been with a man. Her innocence made her all the more appealing.

He'd stopped rubbing then and quickly squashed any fool ideas that triggered in his mind. Tyler had taken that trail once before, with Lizabeth. She'd been an innocent when he'd married her. Now she was gone. He'd not be crazy enough to fall for another woman. One good woman in a man's life was all anyone could hope for. He'd had his chance. He wasn't expecting another. Didn't want another.

No, what he needed was a long tall swig of whiskey and a turn at Renee at the Golden Garter Saloon. That would do him just fine.

The man strode to the Springtime Hotel with purpose. It was time to make his presence known in town. Enough time had passed now, since the shooting. Besides, sleeping way out in that cold abandoned line shack, hiding out, took its toll to his backside, reminding him too much of the time he'd spent in prison. He was accustomed to the finer side of life.

But it had been worth the effort. He'd watched Kincaide and waited. And found the man's weak link.

The woman.

Charming her would be easy, especially with Kincaide on roundup with most of his men. He'd get close to both woman and child.

Soon he'd have all he came for.

Maybe more.

"I'd like a room, please."

"Yes, sir." The amiable hotel clerk scurried behind the desk to retrieve his ledger. "Just getting into town?"

He smiled. "That's right, just this morning."

The clerk handed him a key and slid the ledger around.

"Sign here."

He signed his name.

He had officially come to town.

Chapter Nine

Lily leaned up against the back of the barn, letting the sunshine warm her. She watched and listened as the slim young ranch hand gave her instructions on how to do the polka. "It ain't hard, Miss Lillian. With your long legs you'll be graceful as a…a mustang." Randy gulped air and looked worried that he'd insulted her.

Lily reassured him with a smile. "Why, thank you. That's kind of you to say."

Randy took a step forward, obviously satisfied he hadn't blundered, and held up his arms. "Want to try?"

Lily's leg was healing nicely. Tyler had made sure she didn't do any heavy housework these past two days. All telltale signs of the injury were just about gone.

She stepped closer and placed her hands in his. Randy's neck reddened, but he looked her straight in the eyes. "It'd be better with music—to get the rhythm and all, but my whistling will have to do. If you don't mind?"

"I don't mind, Randy. That'd be nice."

"Fine, then follow my lead. I'll go slow at first, but the polka is a very fast dance. When you get the hang of it, we'll speed things up a bit."

Lily followed Randy's footsteps easily. Randy commented on how quickly she caught on. Soon they were spinning about. Randy twirled her so fast, her skirts lifted and her boots kicked up dust. Excitement whirled around in her head. Her body flowed and swayed along with her partner. She threw her head back and laughed. Dancing was easy. And fun.

There was a lightness in her step and a sense of carefree abandon. Her feet shuffled about, following Randy's lead. He smiled warmly and nodded his head in approval.

"This is wonderful!" she exclaimed when they stopped to take a breath. "I never thought it would be so easy to learn. You're a good teacher, Randy."

Randy blushed. "You think so? I've had loads of practice."

"Yes, I do think so. You practiced with your sisters?"

"Yes, ma'am. I guess I had no choice as I think back on it. My ma had five girls to marry off and said the best way to get a man's attention was to be graceful."

Lily sighed, wondering if Randy's mother's advice was true. It sure couldn't hurt. Lily had always felt awkward with her long arms and legs. As a young girl she was always tripping over herself. Too tall and gangly, it took a while for the rest of her body to catch up. To this day, she still wondered if it had.

"I suppose you did quite a bit of dancing."

"Boy, ain't that the truth. I picked up all the steps over the years. There isn't a one I don't know."

"Will you teach me another? I mean, after I get better with the polka."

"It'd be my honor. And I don't suppose a lady could get much better with the polka, Miss Lillian. I'll be happy to teach you a waltz next time."

"A waltz." Lily sighed. "Oh, I've always wanted to learn to waltz. Do they waltz at barn dances?"

Randy's lips curved up. "If the fiddler and his band can't play a waltz, they'd be chased out of town by all the womenfolk. The ladies of Sweet Springs look forward to these dances. Let's just say, they'd better play a waltz or two."

Lily chuckled. "Oh, that's good."

Randy lifted his hat from the fence post and walked back over to where Lily was standing. He shifted his stance more than once. Staring at the rim of his hat, he raised shy eyes to her. "Then you'll be wanting to go to the Henderson's barn dance?"

With me, Lily thought he meant to say, but was too timid. Lily liked Randy but she didn't want to mislead him. She just didn't feel any stirrings when he held her. Not that she'd had much experience with men. The only man she could compare him to was Tyler. With Tyler, her heart did somersaults.

She didn't hold any fool notion that Tyler would want her, but at least now she understood what she should feel when the right man did come into her life. If he ever did.

"Randy, I'd love to go with you." Randy looked so hopeful Lily hated to disappoint him, but knew she had to be fair. "As a friend."

"A friend?" he squeaked out.

Lily locked eyes with him. "Yes, I think of you as

a good friend. You and Wes and the boys have made me feel very welcome on the ranch.''

He scratched his head and eyed her. Lily hoped she hadn't offended him. In a light tone he said, ''It's nice having a woman on the ranch. Been a long time.''

Lily nodded her understanding. But she wasn't Tyler's wife or his woman. She was the housekeeper and nanny, living on the ranch temporarily. ''I'm glad to be here, too. Do you suppose we can have another lesson after roundup?''

Randy smiled wide, showing a mouthful of white, slightly off-center teeth. ''Sure thing.''

Lily patted his arm in friendship. ''Thank you, Randy. And I'll be making those molasses cookies again. I'll save a big batch for you and the boys. You can take them with you on roundup.''

''Appreciate that, Miss Lillian.'' Randy nodded and tipped his straw hat. ''Goodbye.''

Lily walked back to the ranch house with a barely contained grin. She'd learned how to polka. The steps had been so easy. Is that all there was to dancing? It sure was easier than learning how to ride a horse. And much safer.

Tyler came home early in the afternoon, having accomplished all of the day's chores in a rush. He stomped dirt off his boots on the back porch, shook the day's supply of dust out from his shirt and vest, then entered into the kitchen. The room was neat and tidy. All remnants of breakfast had been cleaned away.

Freshly baked corn bread cooled by the window. Tyler breathed in the scent, enjoying the sweet aroma. A small smile curved his lips. Lily baked something delicious each day. Sometimes cakes, sometimes fresh fruit pies, but more often than not, she baked cookies.

The ranch hands loved Lily's cookies.

How many times in the past few weeks had he come in from a tough day out on the range to find Lily completely absorbed in her task? Her face would be smudged with flour, her hands deep in the mixture she was concocting. She'd give him a cursory glance, a brief smile or a nod and resume the job at hand.

Many times Tyler had a mind to walk over to her, brush stray strands of hair off her forehead and wipe the smudges from her face. But he'd never given in to those urges. No. To do that would seem far too...familiar.

He remembered doing so with Lizabeth. But instead of wiping her smudges away, he saw fit to kiss at them. Soon Lizabeth would forget all about baking when Tyler took her into his arms. They'd spend the rest of the night in the bedroom, never once minding that they hadn't eaten dinner.

Tyler glanced at the corn bread one more time, wondering what the very proper Miss Lillian Brody would do if he ever saw fit to kiss her floured cheeks.

Probably hit him over the head with the rolling pin.

Where was she, anyway? "Lily," he called. When she didn't answer, he went searching. The house seemed so quiet. He knocked softly on Lily's bedroom door, thinking she might be resting. No answer.

He strolled over to Bethann's door and knocked. His mischievous daughter came up from behind him. "Hi, Papa."

Tyler jumped. "Bethann, where have you been?"

"Papa, I was...I was watching Lily do somethin' is all." A frown pulled her lips down.

Tyler had been witness to that particular expression on his daughter's face before. And it usually meant trouble. "Bethann?" He tried to keep warning out of his voice.

"Miss Lily said I could come watch. Only, only…" Tears misted in Bethann's eyes.

Tyler crouched down and took his daughter in his arms. "It's all right, Bethann. Tell Papa."

Bethann sobered. "You promise not to get mad?"

"I promise. Now where's Lily and what did you do?"

Bethann put her head down. With a pout she replied, "I spied on her."

"What!"

"Well, not 'xactly. She said I could come after I finished my chores. But I…I wanted to see."

Tyler was almost afraid to ask what his daughter had witnessed. "For heaven's sake, Bethann. What did you see?"

"Miss Lily's dancing lessons," Bethann whispered. "And…Randy was a holdin' her in his arms, Papa."

Tyler's shoulders went rigid. "I see. Where were you?"

"I…was watchin' from the loft."

Tyler sucked in a big breath. He shook his head. "Bethann, you don't go spying on people. Lily said you could come watch. Why did you hide?"

"Papa, I didn't finish my chores like Miss Lily asked," she admitted guiltily. "I was in the barn checkin' on Pint-Size. I fed her a carrot. But then I heard Miss Lily's voice so's I climbed up the ladder to git a better look. Miss Lily was being twirled around again and again. She was smiling, Papa. And laughing. She told Randy she liked dancing with him."

Tyler cleared his throat. A stab of something un-named shot through his gut. "What else did you see?"

"Miss Lily looked happy."

Happy? Tyler couldn't say Lily was ever really happy. She seemed content at times. Satisfied, as if that was all she expected in life. She'd taken to the ranch, made friends of the hands. She held a special place in Wes's heart. The old man always praised her. Bethann adored her. Randy was clearly smitten.

Tyler frowned, thinking of Lily in Randy's arms. He liked Randy, all right, but Lily was naive when it came to men and their needs. A man, any man, might take advantage. Except, of course, Tyler. He knew bet-ter. But as head of the ranch Lily was under his pro-tection. He'd best keep an eye out for that cowpuncher where Lily was concerned.

But Tyler felt something was missing in Lily's life. Her smile was never quite broad enough, her eyes could sparkle more. Missing her uncle, was Tyler's bet. And having a real family. She'd told him so on more than one occasion, how she longed for a family to call her own. She never spoke much of her uncle Jasper and his family. Was he married? Did he have children? Tyler wondered if he should ask Lily about the uncle she desperately searched for.

Tyler took his daughter by the hand. He sat down on the horsehair sofa in the parlor and set her on his lap. "I told you I wouldn't get angry, but I do think you should apologize to Miss Lily."

Bethann bobbed her head slowly. Her eyes grew wide. "'Cause I was bad?"

"No, you weren't bad, sweetcakes, but what you did was wrong. First, you lied about doing your chores, then you spied on Miss Lily while she was dancing. It's not right to watch or listen in on people.''

"It's not pole-ite."

Tyler chuckled. "That's right, it's not polite."

"Miss Lily said a gentleman should always be pole-ite to a lady."

"That's true, too."

"How?"

Tyler scratched his head and wondered how he'd gotten into such a serious conversation with his six-year-old. "Well, let's see. A man's got to treat a lady kindly. Show her respect."

Bethann nodded. "You mean like when Randy tipped his hat to Miss Lily?"

"Did he now?"

"Sure did. I think he likes her, Papa."

"Miss Lily is a likable sort of woman. You like her. Wes likes her."

"Do you like Miss Lily, Papa?"

Tyler lifted Bethann off his lap, setting her feet firmly on the ground. His inquisitive daughter gave him a questioning look. It wasn't her fault she was so curious. Or that her questions were making him uncomfortable. Tyler didn't like talking about his feelings. "I suppose I like Miss Lily just fine, darlin'."

"Then why don't you teach her dancin'?"

Tyler tapped his finger to Bethann's nose. "'Cause I'm too busy teaching her how to shoot a gun and ride a cow pony, that's why."

"Is that pole-ite?"

Tyler laughed and hugged his daughter. "Don't suppose learning those things are as much fun as dancing, but they're necessary. And I'm always polite to Miss Lily. She's a real lady."

"Like my ma?"

Thoughts of Lizabeth's sweet smile flashed through Tyler's mind. Lizabeth had brought fun and laughter to his ranch house in the beginning. It wasn't her fault she wasn't suited to ranch living. Not all women were. Tyler recognized it to be a hard life. Yet he'd tried to make Lizabeth comfortable every way he could. Lily, on the other hand, took to the ranch easily, as she did most things, except of course, learning how to ride. "Yeah, sweetcakes, like your ma."

"Papa, you look sad."

Tyler wiped the unintentional frown from his face. Maybe it was wrong of him, but he never wanted Bethann touched by his sorrow. He gave her a wide grin. "Do not. Let's find Miss Lily. You've got something to say to her."

"What do you want to say, Bethann?"

Tyler glanced up to find Lily approaching. He stood behind his daughter, bracing her shoulders. With a gentle squeeze, he coaxed her. "Go on, Bethann. Tell her what you did." Tyler met Lily's gaze. She gave him a reassuring nod.

Lily bent down to face Bethann. "You can tell me anything, sweetie. You know that."

"I'm sorry for spyin' on you."

Tyler mentally commended Lily for keeping her expression bland. If it weren't for the slight raise of an eyebrow, no one would've guessed Lily was surprised. But Tyler knew she was.

"When did you...spy on me?"

"When you was dancin' with Randy."

Tyler watched a deep red flush of blood crawl up Lily's throat to singe her cheeks. "I see. Where were you?"

"In the barn. I was tryin' to do my chores like you asked, but I heared you laughing so I...I climbed up to the hayloft and watched."

"Bethann, I told you after your chores, you could come watch." Lily lifted her eyes to Tyler. "We wouldn't have minded." She returned her gaze to his daughter. "Randy might have shown you a step or two. But it takes a big girl to come to me to apologize. I accept your apology, Bethann. Next time, please ask. We won't mind a bit if you watched."

Bethann threw her arms around Lily. "I'm sorry. I won't do it ever again."

Lily patted Bethann on the back, hugging her close. "I know you won't. I trust you."

"I trust you, too," Bethann added in earnest.

Lily broke out into a wide smile. Something twisted in Tyler's gut. The woman was good for his child. He hoped that admiration was all he felt for Lily. Nothing good could come of developing feelings for the woman.

But he'd noticed when she walked into the room, her face held a warm glow. There was a bright crystal-like gleam in her eyes. She'd obviously enjoyed her dance lesson. Or maybe it was Randy who'd put that look on her face.

"Bethann, you go on now. Finish up your chores. We'll see you at dinner. I've got something to say to Miss Lily myself."

Obediently, Bethann left the room.

Lily stood to face Tyler. He smiled at her. "She's a handful, Lily."

Lily shrugged her shoulders and chuckled. "I know. Makes life interesting. I haven't been bored since coming to live here."

Tyler scratched his nose. "Uh, I hope she didn't...I mean...she didn't see anything she shouldn't have."

Lily's eyes grew wide. She took a step back. "I'm not sure I want to know what you mean by that."

Tyler frowned. Damn it, he wasn't good with words. Never had been. "I'm asking you, in private... Randy—"

"Was a perfect gentleman, unlike you, thinking impure thoughts!"

"Now, Lily, a man's got to know. I mean, with you living with...living under my roof and all."

"What I do is none of your business. If you can't trust me to behave properly—"

"Damn it, Lily. It's not you I'm worried about! I mean, I am worried about your reputation, it's just—"

"Ha! You're not serious! My reputation is as good as ruined, living here with you like this. You know it. The town knows it. You didn't seem to mind when you asked me to move out here."

"Lily, that's not what I mean. And I offered marriage. You refused." Lily shot him a look that told him exactly what she thought of his marriage proposal.

Tyler grabbed hold of her arms. He looked her directly in the eyes. Sparks of blue blazed hot and fiery. He'd made her angry. That wasn't his intent, but slowly his temperature began to rise. Once provoked, Tyler wasn't known for his patience. "Listen," he ordered, relieved when she didn't pull away from his touch. "I just want you to know that I'm here if you ever need help. If anyone ever shows you any disrespect, they'll have to answer to me. You got that?" He gave her arms a gentle squeeze.

Damn fool woman didn't know about men and their *impure* thoughts.

Numbly, she nodded and took in a breath. "Yes, I understand. Now, please release me. I have chores to do."

Tyler forced himself to not thrust her arms when he released her. Hell, she was infuriating. All he wanted to do was to assure her she'd be safe under his protection, married or not. But he'd made a mess of things, and for the life of him, he didn't know why it mattered so much.

Lily fumed. She marched out to the barn. Throwing open a hatch from the storage cabinet, she plucked out her gardening tools. Strands of hair fell onto her face as she gathered up her gloves. She blew at the wayward tresses in short gusts, but that did little good. Annoyingly, they just returned to the same spot on her face.

Before donning her gardening gloves, she lifted her braid high on her head, tucking in loose tendrils, and created a haphazard bun at the nape of her neck. She looked around for something to hold her thick mane of hair in place. When she spotted a tin of long, albeit, rusty nails, she knew they would do the trick.

Unmindful to her appearance, she shoved at the bun with the nails until it was secured. Satisfied, she bent to retrieve her gardening tools. "Looks prettier down," she mimicked. Oh, that Tyler Kincaide! He was as arrogant as the day was long. And to think she'd actually *wanted* to please him. She'd kept her hair down in a long plait just because he'd commented a time or two on her hair.

Silly woman.

Heavens! Tyler actually thought Randy made overtures to her. Randy, the bashful young fellow nice enough to give her dancing lessons. And did Tyler also think she accepted those fictitious advances eagerly? Did he think she was so desperate she'd jump at the first young man who showed her the least bit of attention?

Oh, lordy! She'd sure like to know what's buzzing in Tyler's bumblehead.

She placed her utensils in a basket and headed for the side of the house. Weeds were taking over her short corn stalks. And she had radishes to pick. They had popped up from the ground, large and round and pinkish red. It did her heart good to see the hearty vegetables. Seeing her efforts come to life helped lessen the anger that simmered inside like a hot brew.

She started on the weeds first. A healthy dose of that anger was all she would need to tear up the stubborn vines that crept along the rows, choking the precious plants. Just as Lily was about to bend her body to the task, she glanced up to find Tyler watching her from the veranda. He stood leaning on the railing with arms folded, his expression grim. She gave him an equally discouraging look then bent to work at the weeds, one by one.

Let him look, she thought, not caring that her hair was untidy, her skirt was too short or that her face was probably dirt-smudged. No, she didn't give two hoots.

Until she saw Letty Sue Withers drive up in her buggy.

Chapter Ten

Tyler hid his grimace when he saw Letty Sue on his property. Her sugary-sweet smile had no effect on him. He supposed that fact bothered the spoiled girl, but he didn't have time for her antics. He was already raising one child.

Still, she was Joellen's only child and the Withers had been family friends for years. Tyler was too much of a gentleman to not treat Joellen's daughter kindly.

Tyler glimpsed Lily tending her garden one last time before descending the stairs to greet his visitor.

"Afternoon, Letty Sue."

"It's a beautiful afternoon, Tyler. Don't you agree?"

"Sure do. I'm hoping this weather holds up for roundup. Be nice not to chase down those calves in the mud."

"Yes, well, that's why I'm here. Mama has sent over some pies and baked goods for you to take along." She shifted in the buggy. Tyler reached up, took her around the waist as he helped her down. She placed her hands on his shoulders, allowing them to linger a moment longer than necessary and batted her eyes.

Tyler took a step back and glanced around. Three of his ranch hands had come out of the barn, two out from the corral, and one stood in the doorway to the bunkhouse to catch a view of Letty Sue. Whenever she showed up, his men acted as if they'd never seen a beautiful woman before.

"That's very thoughtful of your mama. You tell her I said so, Letty Sue, when you head on home."

Her rosy lips turned down slightly. She cast him a very feminine expectant look. "I was hoping to wrangle an invitation for tea, Tyler. Since I drove the buggy all the way out here. Mama sent your favorite, cranberry loaf cake. You do have time, don't you?"

He didn't, but he couldn't very well refuse. "I reckon I can make the time. Let me see if Miss Lily will join us."

Letty Sue stopped him with a gentle tug of his shirt-sleeve. "Heaven's no. I wouldn't dream of taking Lily away from her work. I saw her tending to her plants when I arrived." She crinkled her delicate nose. "Besides, she'll need a bath before she'll be able to sit down to tea. I'll be glad to serve you."

The look she shot Tyler then would have stopped a gunslinger at twenty paces. Her deep blue eyes flashed heat and her mouth parted slightly. The woman was a temptress. Tyler was sure one day she'd either end up in a wagonload of trouble or land herself a fine husband. He hoped the latter, more for Joellen's sake than her daughter's.

But he wouldn't be the one to warn her off. He'd tried talking to Lily about sensitive matters, and look at the mess he'd made. "Fine then, let's find out if

Joellen's cranberry cake is as delicious as I remember.''

Letty Sue loped an arm through his. Discreetly, Tyler glanced Lily's way as they strode up the steps. She was head-deep in her garden and hadn't paid the two of them any mind at all.

"Damn it, Lily, careful with that thing!" Tyler barked.

Lily put the Colt .45 down at her side. She'd carried the gun all the way from the house. They'd walked several miles, following a bend in the creek, for another shooting lesson. Tyler refused to let her ride Pearl until he came back from roundup. So now her feet ached and she was more than a little perturbed with the man. "Tyler, I've asked you time and again not to swear in a lady's presence. What kind of an example are you setting for your daughter?"

"Ah, he—heck, Lily. You were pointing that gun directly at me. Was I supposed to ask politely for you not to shoot my face off?"

Lily put her chin up. "I was admiring the beautiful carving on the handle. You were the one who walked into my line of vision. And I do have some sense in my head, Tyler. I wasn't about to pull the trigger."

"Glad to hear it."

Lily folded her arms across her middle. She was being difficult. She had deliberately ignored Tyler as they walked all the way up here. He'd been pigheaded about Pearl and her not getting injured, insisting the walk would be refreshing. So she hadn't spoken a word to him, except to answer his questions with quick replies or grunts. The more stubborn she became, the more he tried to get her to talk. After a time, Lily found the game quite amusing.

Tyler had actually been charming.

Several times she'd almost laughed out loud as he tried coaxing her into conversation with little gibes.

"I bet you wanted to," she heard him say.

"Uh, what?" Lily met his eyes directly. They twinkled and Lily's heart flip-flopped. She wondered that if her attraction to him wasn't the real reason she was behaving like a shrew. Seeing him arm-in-arm with Letty Sue yesterday had disturbed her more than she'd like to admit. Lily had glanced up to view them briefly. They'd made a fine-looking couple as they entered the ranch house together. It was a shocking reminder of all Lily would never have.

"You looked as if you'd have enjoyed taking a shot at me."

Lily sighed. Her shoulders fell. "I guess I'm a bit angry with you."

Tyler looked surprised. "Now that's honest. Why?"

Lily holstered the peacemaker. She walked over to the creek and sat down on a thick patch of grass. "I'm...not sure."

"Was it because I wouldn't let you ride today?" He sat down cross-legged next to her.

Lily stared at the creek waters rushing down, hitting a fallen ironwood branch and splashing over it. She felt Tyler's eyes on her as she continued to look out over the creek. "My leg is fine now, Tyler. I think I would have ridden better today."

"Can't chance it, Lily."

"Am I that...inept?"

"'Course not. It's just that...well, your leg looked pretty bad the other day, and—" Lily turned to him just as he swallowed hard. "I don't want to see you hurt again."

Lily stared into the darkest brown eyes she'd ever seen and wondered if Tyler truly cared about her. Was he beginning to feel stirrings in his heart, the same stirrings she'd always had for him? "Thank you."

Tyler reached over to take her chin in his hand. His eyes searched hers. The skin where he touched her tingled with warmth. His fingers were work-rough against her smooth skin. He smelled of leather and dust and lye soap. Pure man. Lily's heart raced. She hoped to the Almighty, Tyler couldn't read the hunger in her eyes. He'd see what she wanted and be appalled.

She jerked her head away, afraid of what her expression revealed. She pondered if a silly woman could actually *die* from mortification. Because that would surely happen if Tyler knew what she'd been thinking. And for the first time since he'd spoken of it, she was glad tomorrow he'd be leaving for three weeks on roundup.

"I want you to promise me, while I'm gone, you won't ride Pearl unless it's a necessity. I'm leaving Jose Morales behind. He's a good man. He'll tend to your needs and watch out for you and Bethann while we're gone. He's going to make a trip into town from time to time. You can give him a list of supplies you think you'll need."

"Do I have a choice?" Lily's voice was soft because she knew Tyler wasn't just asking but giving an order.

"I'm counting on you to care for Bethann. You can't do that if you're laid up. Do I have your promise?"

Lily got the full picture now. Tyler didn't really care

for her, he was concerned for Bethann. He needed Lily
healthy so his daughter would be well cared for. Well,
he needn't worry. Lily would always put Bethann first.
She wasn't sure how or when it happened but Lily had
fallen in love with the little girl. "I promise. But you
don't have to worry about Bethann. We'll be just
fine."

Lily bounded up. She took several steps to the right
and turned quickly, pointing the gun at the bottles Tyler had lined up across the creek in a dry bed. The
ground on the other side of the creek was elevated,
and Tyler had set one bottle on each of five small
rocks, thirty feet away. With one eye closed, Lily took
aim and managed to hit four of the five bottles. One
bottle actually flipped up having been hit where its
bottom met the rock. The bottle didn't shatter until it
came crashing down to the ground.

Tyler let out a low whistle. Lily turned to him and
smiled. "Not bad," he said, but Lily heard admiration
in his voice. "You must have a good teacher."

"He'll do," Lily said with a shrug of one shoulder.
She was still angry with him and knew she was not
being at all rational. Confusing thoughts muddled her
brain. Whenever she was around the man, she couldn't
put two pennies together for thinking they were a silver dollar.

But she could shoot. She prided herself on that. The
look of shocking respect stole over Tyler's face as he
had watched her take those shots. Some women had
wily ways with enticing men, and Lily...well, she had
a knack for learning new things easily.

And the more shots she took, the more confident
she became. She didn't like the thought of what a gun
meant in a person's life, but she found living way

outside of town on the Circle K practically required her to learn how to protect herself. And Bethann, if need be.

Tyler had assured her he wouldn't leave for roundup if he thought she and Bethann were in any immediate danger. Since he'd been shot six weeks ago, there'd been no further sign of trouble. She knew he'd pondered over it for weeks, night and day. He'd ventured to guess he might have spoiled a surprise attack of cattle rustlers. They'd had a fair share of rustlers stealing cattle through the years. Since Tyler never saw who shot him, he'd probably never know.

Lily reloaded the gun and spent another round. This time she aimed at a small log floating down the creek. The waters rushed by, but Lily had managed to hit the moving target many times. Tyler commented on how hard it was to hit a target moving at such rapid speed. He'd known many men who toted a gun for twenty years who hadn't been as good.

Lily holstered the gun. She planted her bottom down on the grass several feet away from Tyler and viewed the water. The sun felt good on her cheeks, warming them slightly. She sat in peaceful silence.

"Something else bothering you, Lily?" Tyler asked from beside her.

Lily gave him a halfhearted smile. "I was thinking of Bethann. What will happen to her when I find my uncle? I'll be leaving the ranch. Who'll watch her?"

Tyler leaned back on his elbows. Lily turned to him. He shrugged. "Don't know exactly. I suppose I'll have to try to find someone else suitable."

"I hope you do. For her sake," she added. "Of course, if you got married again…"

Tyler shook his head. "Don't think that's going to

happen. I can't see me taking on a wife again." Lily arched her brows at him. "I mean, in the real sense," he explained.

"Not even Letty Sue?"

Tyler chuckled. "Especially Letty Sue. She's okay and all, but that woman'd keep a man at loose ends. She's a handful of trouble."

"She's a beautiful woman," Lily said in earnest. She wasn't opposed to giving the woman her due. And in the looks category, Letty Sue had it all.

Tyler shook his head. "No denying. But a woman's got to have more than that to hold a man."

Lily didn't think so. She'd had a pure heart, but that hadn't brought any men knocking at her door. Lily sighed. "I remember my father used to say, 'A beautiful woman might turn a man's head, but inner beauty will turn a man's heart.'"

Tyler grinned. "Wise man, that Jonah."

"I never believed him. I thought he'd made that up just to make me feel better." Lily gasped silently. She couldn't believe what she'd just revealed about herself to Tyler. A gentleman would have to compliment her now, even if it weren't true. And Lily knew it wouldn't be true.

Tyler turned her so their eyes met. His fingers were gentle on her shoulders. "You know what I see when I look at you?"

Lily averted her gaze. She couldn't bear to see pity in Tyler's eyes.

"Lily, look at me," he demanded softly.

Obediently her eyes locked onto his. "Don't...you don't have to say a thing. I shouldn't have said—"

"I see lovely crystal blue eyes. Like shallow lake waters. And I see a head of incredible thick hair that's too often being pulled back or turned into a knot of some sort. I see a sweet, compassionate face.''

''Too skinny, too tall.''

''Slender, not skinny. And tall, like a delicate willow. Lily, you're too hard on yourself.''

''Lizabeth was beautiful. She used to come into the mercantile. Sometimes I'd find myself staring.'' With envy. She hadn't been proud of her feelings, but she had recognized them. Lily wouldn't reveal that to Tyler. She'd said far too much already.

''Yes, my wife was lovely.''

Lily looked toward the creek. She said softly, ''You must have loved her very much.''

Tyler was silent for a long time. Lily kept her gaze focused on the water coursing by. A breeze had picked up, rustling the leaves of the ironwoods. ''I did,'' he said finally. ''Her death was my fault.''

Lily turned to him. He sat as if in a trance. His gaze was focused to an unnamed point out on the horizon. Anguish obscured his handsome face. ''I heard it was an accident.''

He snorted, glancing briefly her way before finding that point on the horizon once again. ''The only accident was me meeting her and bringing her out to the ranch. Should never have done that. She'd be alive today.''

Lily was afraid to ask, afraid he'd get right on up from the patch of grass and walk away, but something told her Tyler needed to talk this out. That he'd probably never confided to anyone about Lizabeth's death. ''Tyler, what happened?''

Again, silence. Then, to her amazement, he began in a quiet, almost-reverent tone. ''My father and I drove the herd to Abilene that year. We'd had exceptional good luck with the drive. Only lost a few dozen head on the trip. Our pockets were bursting. I was heading to the nearest saloon for a good drink and damn good wh—''

When Lily turned and lifted her eyes in shock, he grinned, then apologized. After clearing his throat he continued. ''Anyway, I was headed for the saloon, when I nearly knocked down this beautiful young woman. She'd turned the corner in a fast hurry and didn't see me coming. She was about to fall and before I knew it, she was in my arms. That's all it took.''

''Was it...love at first sight?'' It was a romantic notion, she knew, but Lily believed in love at first sight. That it might be true for someone else made it seem all the more...possible.

''For me. I think so. I was discouraged to learn she was visiting family friends and she was heading back to St. Louis in a week's time. I stayed on in Abilene, determined to win her.''

''And you did,'' Lily said wistfully. The story seemed like one of the fairy tales she'd been reading to Bethann.

He nodded. ''Lizabeth was born in St. Louis. She was used to citified ways. I had no right dragging her out to the ranch.''

''But she agreed to marry you.''

Tyler frowned. ''I don't think she knew what she was getting into. Ranch living is a whole lot different than city living. We were both so young. We just wanted to be together. After my father died, the responsibility of the ranch landed on me. I had to make all the cattle drives. Lizabeth complained something fierce about me leaving her for so long. She convinced me that she and Bethann could come along. Bethann was just a tot.'' Tyler stopped to shake his head. ''I shouldn't have listened.''

''She died in a stampede,'' Lily stated softly.

''Yes, I was watching the herd late one night. It started raining unexpected like. The sky just opened up and poured down in big buckets. Lizabeth left the wagon to come looking for me. She was bringing me my rain slicker. I didn't know she was outside…till it was too late.''

Tyler stopped talking. He closed his eyes, but not before Lily saw moisture filling them. He shook it off and continued. ''Would've been all right if the storm hadn't turned ugly. Lightning and thunder always spook the cattle. She was caught right smack in the middle of it.''

Tyler bowed his head as if he was reliving the moment. His face filled with grief, his eyes half shuttered, and his body stiffened.

''I'm sorry, Tyler,'' Lily said with her whole heart. The pain and loss might have downed a lesser man. But although Tyler lived with his grief every day, he had managed to make a life for his daughter and himself.

Tyler stood and watched the small rapids travel around the bend in the creek. ''I've never told anyone this before.''

Lily stood, also, and looked into a face marked with pain. Her heart was splitting, watching him suffer so. If only she could ease a bit of his suffering. ''It wasn't your fault. You had no way of knowing there'd be a storm that night, or that she'd come looking for you.''

Tyler said nothing, but his eyes blinked. Lily reached out and touched his sleeve. ''I'm glad you told me.''

He nodded and before Lily had a real sense of what was happening, Tyler pulled her into an embrace. He held her loosely with his hands lightly touching her waist. She brought her arms up tentatively around his neck. Tyler kept his body away from hers but with his gentle coaxing her head came to rest on his shoulder. Long strands of Tyler's dark hair brushed the side of her face. A soft and warm flow of blood surged through Lily's body. She took in an unsteady breath.

"Thank you, Lily. I needed—"

"I know." She stood there locked in a delicate embrace, giving him all her comfort, all her compassion, and knowing deep in her heart she was in love with Tyler Kincaide.

They stood together long moments, the sound of rippling waters and an occasional bird chirping was all that interrupted the quiet. Lily wasn't sure when it happened exactly, but slowly, magnetically, their bodies moved closer to each other. Tyler breathed in the scent of her hair. "Lilacs. Lily, you always smell so good," he murmured.

She closed her eyes and relished being in Tyler's arms. Lily's breath caught in her throat. Unable to utter a word, she listened to the sound of Tyler's heart beating. His lips moved through her hair and she heard him groan. Gently moving his hands from her waist, he splayed his fingers just under her breasts. The tips of his fingers caressed the soft underside of her small globes. Lily trembled. She wanted his touch more than she wanted her next breath, but he hesitated.

Tyler, as if regaining his composure, bent his head and rested his forehead against hers. "I'm sorry, Lily. I shouldn't have."

"Tyler," she managed to hoarsely whisper.

"Forgive me. It's been so long since I've held a woman. I forgot you aren't...you haven't..." He stepped back and clasped her arms above her elbows. His eyes searched hers. "The right man will come along for you, Lily. I'm sure of it. I promised not to compromise you."

Lily swallowed hard. The ladylike thing to do would be to accept his apology and pretend the incident never happened. But she couldn't ignore the rapid thumping of her heart or the yearning Tyler had evoked.

Lily gave him a brave smile, then fastened her gaze to his. "I want to know, Tyler," she said in a hushed tone, but with such determination, Tyler blinked.

"No, Lily." He shook his head slowly as if trying to convince both himself and Lily. "It wouldn't be right."

Lily wanted to cry out. She'd spent a lifetime doing the right thing and where had it gotten her? Now, the one time she's willing to abandon her rigid morals for the man she loved, he'd turned her down.

Lily put her head down. She wasn't woman enough to hold on to a man like Tyler. She wasn't anything special, she knew. And Tyler, with all his good intentions, had just confirmed it.

Tyler stroked the line of her jaw with his index finger until it was under her chin. With gentle prodding, he lifted her face to view him. "I know what you're thinking, Lily. And you're wrong."

Lily knew Tyler had read her thoughts. "Am I?"

"I'm doing this for your sake, Lily. I made you a promise and I intend to keep my word. Tomorrow, you'll see that I'm right."

She doubted that. But she also knew tomorrow

she'd be too embarrassed to show her face. Good thing he would be leaving in the morning.

Tyler glanced out at the creek one last time. He cleared his throat. ''We'd best be heading back,'' he said, but then Lily thought she heard him mutter quietly to himself, ''before I change my mind.''

Small consolation. Lily had practically thrown herself at the man. And little did Tyler know, for Lily the right man had indeed come along.

Chapter Eleven

Tyler leaned back against his blankets and gazed up at the stars. The ground was hard and cold, but the air held a crisp freshness, a bite that told his senses he was alive. He shuffled down into the warmth of the wool and watched as a shooting star streaked along the night sky.

Smiling, he wondered if Lily had looked out her window and seen it, too. He'd tried in the past two weeks to put her out of his mind. And he'd been successful every day in doing just that. Busy with the grueling work of roundup, making sure his ranch hands were fed and well tended, he'd had little time during the day to think of much else.

At night he thought about Bethann, the little angel-faced child with devilish ways he'd brought into the world. He missed her. She was what made life worth living. He knew she'd be well taken care of. Then his thoughts would turn to Lily, the woman who had helped make his home a fit place for his young daughter. He couldn't place the title of housekeeper on Lily. She was so much more. There was genuine affection between she and Bethann. And that did his heart good.

But with a frown, Tyler realized that Bethann would be lost when Lily left. She was staying on at the ranch on a temporary basis. Even if she didn't find her uncle, Tyler didn't believe she'd stay on indefinitely.

And maybe it'd be best if she didn't.

At least for him.

Having a young female underfoot was trying to his willpower. And Tyler had loads of willpower. But he'd almost given in to temptation that day at the creek.

He'd spoken to Lily of things he'd not told another soul, Lizabeth's death and his guilt. The pain was still entrenched in his heart. He hadn't let anyone see it, until Lily. She'd lent him the comfort and support he needed. She had listened to him, tried to console him. And he'd almost taken unfair advantage of her.

I want to know, Tyler. The words had haunted him every night for the past two weeks. He conjured up a picture of holding Lily in his arms. She'd been soft and sweet-smelling. And it'd been too damn long since he'd held a decent woman. He shouldn't have brought her close, shouldn't have touched her. When she shivered, he'd realized he'd frightened her.

Tyler rolled onto his side, closing his eyes, blocking out the image of Lily's hope-filled face. She was an unsure, fragile flower. He'd not dare bruise her in any way. He admonished himself that he'd almost given in to temptation and shown her how it was between a man and a woman.

Only, he knew it was wrong. Tyler had no intention of committing to a woman again. He couldn't take Lily without offering her a true and honest commitment.

Tyler groaned when he again thought about her words. *I want to know, Tyler.*

He quelled the rising need below his waist. Damn. First chance he got, he was heading to the Golden Garter to look up the redhead who always greeted him with a welcoming smile and a guilt-free time. He fell asleep thinking of Renee Boudreau, the fiery Frenchwoman who would, if only for a short time, help him forget his past mistakes.

Morning dawned bright and cool. Tyler was greeted with a mug of piping hot coffee as he stoked the small campfire. "Thanks, Wes. Coffee smells good."

"It's good when we're out 'ere tryin' to keep warm, but it ain't comparin' to Lily's. She makes a mighty fine brew."

Tyler nodded and winced as his sip of the hot liquid burned his tongue. "Roundup ain't gonna be the same once all the fences go up in the territory. Ours are half up. Another couple of months and we'll be fenced in completely."

"Yup. Next year, about this time, we'll be keeping strictly to Kincaide land, 'cept for the strays that find a torn down fence or two. Won't take as long, neither."

"That's a good thing, I suppose. I hate leaving Bethann for too long. Girl's growing faster than one of Lily's cornstalks."

Wes laughed. "She is at that." He gave Tyler a sidelong glance. "Yore missing that li'l lady, too, are ya?"

Tyler spilled out the remainder of his coffee onto the fire. A small gust of smoke spiraled upward as the fire diminished to orange-red embers. "Damn it, Wes.

Every chance you get, you bring up Lily. What's got into you?''

Wes smirked and slowly straightened his wiry body. "Ain't nothin's got into me, boy. Nothin' at all."

"That's good." Tyler stood up and stamped down the fire. He kept his eyes on the broken branches, kicking dirt over the low-lying flames. "'Cause that's what'll happen between me and Lily. Nothing. She cares for Bethann and does the house chores. We have an understanding."

Tyler bent to roll his blankets and tie them off. Wes began walking to the mess wagon. The old man chuckled, then said over his shoulder, "Seems to me, ya two do a wagonload of talkin' about what's not gonna happen." Then he barked loudly over the whole awakening camp. "Breakfast's ready. Come and git it."

Tyler grabbed his plate filled with scrambled eggs and biscuits fried in bacon grease and leaned up against one of the wagons. He was halfway through his meal when Randy showed up. The lanky young cowpuncher took a spot next to him against the wagon. "Mornin', Randy."

"Mornin', boss."

Randy's lips were set in a thin line. Stiff-shouldered, he looked out toward the circle of cowboys having their first meal of the day. Tyler waited patiently. He knew Randy well enough to know something was eating at the boy.

"I, uh, got something to say and I want you to know this don't come easy for me, but I thought you had every right to know, since I've been workin' the Circle K for better than four years now."

Tyler recognized the tension in Randy's voice. Balancing his plate down on the wagon wheel, Tyler turned to face him. "Say it."

"Well, it's just this. I know you don't take kindly to trouble out on the range, but if I run into Jack McGee again, I'm going to have to take off his head. The boys held me off him yesterday. I had a mind to—"

"What's this all about? What happened yesterday I don't know?" Randy was a peaceable sort. As far as Tyler could remember he'd not had any trouble with him at the ranch or on the cattle drives.

"I told the boys I'd tell you first thing this mornin' and that's what I'm doin' now. You've always been fair with me and I thought to give you fair warnin'. We ain't had much trouble on the range since I came to work for you. But if that worm McGee makes one more indecent remark about Miss Lily—"

"Lily?" If a rattlesnake came up and bit him, Tyler wouldn't have been more surprised. "What's Lily got to do with anything?"

"Seems McGee and some others from the Double Diamond Ranch got a notion of Miss Lily that ain't right. McGee made the mistake of spouting off in front of me."

"You fought him?"

"I wanted to beat him senseless, but, like I said, the boys took me off him."

Anger boiled just under the surface. Lily was innocent of any wrongdoing, but she'd told him her reputation would be ruined if she took up his offer. And damn if she hadn't been right. But that hadn't stopped him from persuading her to stay on at the ranch. And now Randy had been the one to uphold Lily's honor. Tyler found himself envious of his young ranch hand.

If Tyler had been there, he'd have relished the chance to put Jack McGee in his place. He didn't know the ranch hand, but had heard tales of his manhandling the ladies in the Golden Garter. He'd been thrown out and told to never return. "What'd he say exactly?"

Randy cleared his throat. When he hesitated, Tyler nodded for him to respond, although Tyler knew he'd be better off not hearing what Randy was about to say. "He said Lily was nothing but a skinny little whore dressed all proper-like, pretending to be a lady. Said if he was you, he'd a not left her to her lonely bed. He's got a mind to get over to the ranch and have a turn at her himself. After that, my fist was in his mouth. He didn't have much else to say." Randy frowned and Tyler noticed for the first time, a large purple bruise on the young man's hand.

Tyler pushed himself away from the wagon. He paced back and forth. "Damn it all! If I get my hands on him, he'd better pray there'd be someone around to pull me off him. None of it's true. Not one damn bit."

Some of the tension eased from Randy's face. "I know, boss. I know Miss Lily. She's a decent woman."

Tyler stopped pacing to look Randy dead in the eye. "You did the right thing. I want to thank you. If I'd been there, I'd have done the same. The problem is, Lily is a young unmarried woman living under my roof. People are bound to get notions. Nobody'd say a blasted thing if she was round about the middle and graying at the sides of her head. Tom Harper's got a housekeeper. I haven't heard anyone speak unkindly about her."

"She's about twenty years older than Tom and at

least twenty pounds heavier.'' Randy grinned. ''If you don't mind me pointin' that out.''

''Exactly my point. You don't think the man would actually head over to the Circle K, do you?''

''Doubt it. He's a snake, but he's all talk. He ain't got an ounce of guts. He ain't goin' nowhere.''

Tyler put his hands on his hips. He took a breath slowly to calm his fury. A tiny shred of good sense was all that held him back from seeking out McGee and finishing the job Randy had started. ''All right, Randy. I'll take care of McGee from here on out. You best be staying clear of him.''

''Boss, what you plannin' on doin'?''

''Hoping to God Almighty I don't have a run-in with the man myself.''

''Ouch. Oh, damn it!'' Lily looked around the parlor guiltily then muttered, ''I mean, darn it!'' The sewing needle had pricked her finger, almost breaking the skin, but there wasn't anyone around to hear her outburst. Bethann had been asleep for hours. And Lily was too tired to really care. Her lips curved up slightly. She'd been spending too much time around Tyler Kincaide and his foul-mouthed ways. They were rubbing off on her. She'd have to be more careful. She'd never in her life taken to swearing. But then again, there were plenty of things she'd done since living on the Circle K she hadn't ever done before.

Lily spread the hem of her new dress out onto her lap. The deep blue satin shimmered under the glow of the lantern light. She'd stayed up late the past week working diligently on the dress, patiently making sure every line, every detail, was just right. And it was. She compared the dress time and again to the picture she had saved from years ago taken right off the pages of *Godey's Lady Book*. Her dress was an exact replica.

Lily sighed and wondered if she'd have the courage to wear such a fine dress to Henderson's barn dance next week. She wondered if Tyler would go, if he'd ask her dance.

Silly notion.

He'd already said he didn't much care for barn socials. Still, it'd be a dream come true if he'd ask her to dance. Just one time.

Lily got up and stretched. Stiff-necked, she tried to rub the weariness from her aching muscles. She'd been rising earlier than usual and going to bed later each night since Tyler had been on roundup. But for her efforts, she and Bethann had two new dresses each. The child had insisted Lily make them a set of matching dresses. Lily had obliged, sewing them each a colorful blue and yellow calico. Wouldn't Tyler be surprised when he viewed his daughter in a garment edged in lace and ruffles?

Lily had even splurged with her earnings, taking Bethann into town when Jose Morales had offered. She'd bought them both ready-made dresses from Wilbourne's Emporium. For Bethann, she purchased a lemon-yellow broadcloth with wide puffy sleeves. For herself, she bought a simple pale blue dress made of lightweight cotton with a bit of ruffle around the collar. The color matched the hue of her eyes and Lily had instantly loved it. And surprisingly enough, the dress needed only a slight tuck or two on the inseams. The drab colors of her tattered dresses were a thing of the past. In her new clothes, she felt more alive, more vibrant and much more feminine.

Morning dawned without ceremony. The sun overshadowed by dark gloomy clouds had scarcely made an appearance. Lily went about her chores, taking time out of the day to give Bethann her lessons. The young girl had an easy capacity for learning and had even begun reading three-word sentences. Lily was proud of Bethann's accomplishments over the past two months.

By afternoon Lily was bone-tired. "Bethann, I need to close my eyes for a few minutes. I'm giving you a list of chores to do."

Bethann groaned. "But I just fed Pint-Size and swept out her stall."

"I know, and I'm happy to see you've been taking such good care of your horse. But, you left your room a mess. The chores are easy and when you're through, come get me. We'll do something fun."

Wide green eyes lighted. "Like what? Can we play a game?"

"Well, sure. But I thought you'd rather learn something new."

Bethann's mouth turned down. Her small shoulders fell. "I don't want another lesson."

"It's not a lesson. Wait here." Lily went to her room. She found the jumping rope she'd had secretly hidden in her dresser. When she returned, she found Bethann staring out the window. "Bethann," she said softly, "this is for you." Lily handed the girl the shiny wood-handled rope. "I bought it the other day when we were in town. I thought I could teach you how to skip rope."

"Oh! Thank you, Miss Lily!" Bethann clutched the new rope to her chest. "Rhonda Mae has a rope for skipping, but it's dirty and worn 'round the edges and her rope don't have pretty handles."

"Doesn't have pretty handles," Lily corrected with a smile. "Then you know how?"

"Not 'xactly. I tried, but I couldn't. Rhonda Mae wasn't very good, neither. She kept gettin' her feet caught up all tangled like and she felled down a lot."

"Well, after I rest, and you do your chores, I'll be glad to teach you. It's really easy."

"Like riding a horse?"

Lily bit back a wry comment. Anything was easier than riding a horse for her. "For you, it'll be just as easy to learn, sweetie. Now, go make up your bed, dust your furniture and tidy up your room. When those chores are done, I want you to practice reciting the alphabet ten times. Out loud. Then come get me."

Bethann nodded. "Okay, Miss Lily. I can't wait to use my new jumping rope."

Lily needed to rest just a few minutes. And since her new dress was finished, she was determined to get to bed early tonight. Once inside her room, she lay down and closed her eyes.

Lily woke up and noticed the time. She'd been asleep for more than an hour. Bethann hadn't come to get her. Slowly, she rose, blinking her eyes and rubbing her face. She walked over to the pitcher of water and splashed her face several times. That helped.

She called out for Bethann. No answer. The house seemed too quiet. Lily made her way to Bethann's room, noticing her little charge had done her chores. Quickly she straightened her dress and tucked stray strands of hair back into her braid before going outside. She found Jose Morales by the barn. "Mr. Morales, have you seen Bethann?"

"No, Señorita Lily. She is not here. I have been working in the barn and corral. I have not seen her."

Lily called out again. "Bethann! Bethann!" Her eyes roamed over the ranch dwellings. Everything seemed to be in order. Lily sucked in a deep breath. "It's probably nothing, but could you help me look for her. She seems to be missing."

"*Sí.* I will look."

"Good, if you find her, bring her back to the house and wait for me. I'm going looking, too."

"Señorita Lily, I would not be too worried. The little *chica* is a bit of a...handful, *sí?* She is somewhere playing and we will find her."

"I hope you're right, Jose." Lily ran straight to her room. She lifted her mattress and pulled out her holstered gun. She flung the holster on the bed, loaded the gun and began her search. Since Tyler had been shot, Lily had no reservation about taking up arms. She was confident in her ability to shoot, if need be. And if Bethann was in danger, she wouldn't hesitate.

Lily headed straight for the creek, Bethann's favorite place to play. She'd been warned time and again not to go there without adult supervision. But Bethann was headstrong, like her dad. Lily prayed she'd find her there.

Lily's search lasted more than thirty minutes. She walked with a briskness in her step, calling out Bethann's name over and over. She tamped her panic down, her reasonable side taking hold, telling her Jose Morales had probably found the child and was waiting back out at the house for her. Lily raced the rest of the way home, hoping she'd been right.

But she stopped up short when the house came into view. The scene she witnessed stunned her so, she began walking very slowly toward the house. Bethann stood beside Jose Morales. Thank God, the child was safe, but Jose had his gun pointing at a tall, dapper-looking man with dark auburn hair. The man's hands were up in the air, by Jose's urging, Lily assumed.

Lily kept a hand on her gun as she approached. She sidled up to Jose and touched Bethann's shoulder but kept her gaze fixed on the stranger. "What's going on, Jose?"

"I found this man with our little *chica.* He says he knows her."

"Bethann, do you know this man?"

"No, ma'am, but he says he's my uncle."

Uncle? Tyler never mentioned Bethann having an uncle. Lily spoke up. "Who are you? What are you doing here?"

The stranger spoke with a deep husky drawl and a sureness that made Lily nervous. "Well, if you'd put that gun down, I'd feel a mite more like talking. I sure didn't expect this kind of a welcome."

Lily didn't budge, nor did Morales. They kept their guns pointed directly at the man. "Sir, please talk or get off Kincaide land."

"What the girl says is true. I'm Bethann's uncle. Lizabeth Muldoon was my sister." The man flashed a wide smile, showing white straight teeth.

Lily looked long and hard at the man claiming to be related to Bethann, and grudgingly realized his claims held truth. His auburn hair was the exact shade of Bethann's and they shared a similar smile, but the eyes were the telling. His eyes were dark green, like blades of winter grass, just like the precocious six-year-old's. "What's your name?"

"Brett Muldoon." He lowered his arms to point at

Bethann. "And that pretty young lady is my niece. I'm her uncle. Tyler around?"

Lily lowered her gun, but kept it aimed in Brett's general direction. "He's on roundup."

"Well, I came out here to visit my only niece. She's the image of her ma. A real beauty. Did you know my sister?" The man eyed her intently and Lily immediately knew where his thoughts were heading.

"No, sir, I didn't. I'm the housekeeper. I came to live here a few months ago."

"Ah, I see. Well, I'd be much obliged if you'd all put down those guns. Never know when one might go off...accidentally."

Lily holstered her gun and turned to Jose. "It's okay, Jose. I believe him. There's no danger here. You can put your gun down."

Jose gave her a cautious look. "Only, if you are sure. I do not trust a man who wears finer clothes than my very own mother."

Lily bit back a chuckle. It was true. Brett Muldoon was a fine specimen, handsome in his dark suit and embroidered vest. "I'll take full responsibility, Jose. He is who he says he is. You can put away the gun. And thank you for finding Bethann. Where was she, anyway?"

The stranger put his hands down and approached when Jose holstered his gun. Before Jose could answer, the man spoke up. "I was riding up when I spotted her by that crop of trees out yonder. She was jumping rope. We had a bit of a chat, then headed toward the house. Sorry, if we caused you both any worry."

"Apology accepted, Mr. Muldoon."

"Thank you, ma'am. I appreciate you taking me at my word. I am who I claim to be."

Lily smiled. "I wouldn't take a stranger at his word, but looking at the two of you," she said, glancing down at Bethann, "a person would have to be blind not to see the resemblance."

The man laughed heartily. "Very astute of you, Miss...?"

"Lillian. My name is Lillian Brody."

The man took her hand to shake it gently. "Very nice to meet you, Miss Lillian."

Lily glanced again at Bethann and thought about her lack of family. Now, suddenly, Bethann had an uncle. It would do them both good to get a chance to know each other. On impulse, Lily made Brett Muldoon an offer. "Would you care to stay for an early dinner? Bethann should get to know her uncle. You can head back to town before the sun sets."

The man smiled warmly. "I think I'd thoroughly enjoy eating in the company of two lovely ladies. Thank you very kindly."

"Bethann, your uncle Brett is going to stay awhile longer. Go on up to the house and wash, then come help me with dinner. We'll talk about you wandering off later."

Lily watched Bethann race up the steps of the house. Tyler would be happy to know that Lizabeth's brother was in town and wanted to spend time with his daughter.

Yes, she quelled any doubts she had about asking the man to dinner. Tyler would be pleased. Very pleased.

Tyler had pushed his horse hard. The last few miles to the house seemed to take an eternity. He'd left camp very early, before sunup, and asked Wes to handle the final day of roundup. He'd been satisfied with the smooth running of the operation. One man suffered bruised ribs after having been kicked by a stubborn calf and another man had burned his arm when he lost his hold on the branding iron. The injuries were minor and his men would recover. Considering the atrocities that often occur out on the range, Tyler was grateful this roundup had been successful.

He was anxious to get home to his girls. "Tarnation, Tyler Kincaide, what are you thinking?" he muttered, but only his horse Blaze could hear him. "Damn fool, is what you are."

He sorely missed Bethann. He had thought about her every day since he'd been gone. But had he missed Lily, too? Maybe he had. Tyler had to keep reminding himself Lily was leaving soon. She'd find her uncle one day and claim the family she'd always wanted. And besides, he'd already made up his mind to not have another woman in his life. Losing Lizabeth had cured him of all notions of falling deep and hard for a woman. He'd nearly lost his mind when she died. The pain and the loss were a constant companion.

But he was worried about Lily. Until he was sure that Jack McGee's threat was an idle one, he wouldn't rest easy. Lily was under his protection while she lived at the ranch. He'd not let that scum get within ten feet of Lily and he wanted to make sure nothing had happened while he was gone. That's what he told himself when he'd decided to head home a day early.

Blaze picked up his pace, loping at a steady gait when they neared the ranch house. The reliable cow pony always knew where his next meal was coming from, Tyler mused. The animal had earned his bucket-ful of oats. Tyler reined in his horse when he reached the barn.

Jose Morales came around the corner of the barn to greet him. "*Hola! Señor Kincaide.* Welcome home. The roundup went well?"

"Afternoon, Jose. Yep, one of the best I'd say." Tyler swept his gaze over the property. "Everything okay here?"

"*Sí,* it has been quiet here. I have watched over the women." Jose removed his straw hat to scratch his head. "Perhaps, Señorita Lily will tell you of her sur-prise."

"Surprise?" Tyler smiled. A surprise from Lily. With his curiosity sparked, he looked toward the house. "Are they inside?"

"No, they are out walking. The *señorita* said they would not go far."

Tyler nodded. "Appreciate you watching out for the womenfolk, Jose. Looks like you did a fine job here."

"*Gracias,* but the work was not too hard. And the *señorita* spoiled me with her delicious pies." He pat-ted his stomach. "Maria might not recognize her hus-band, eh?"

Tyler laughed. "After you bed down Blaze, why don't you go on home to your wife? I can handle things here. The rest of the crew will be back tomor-row."

Jose gave him a wide smile. "*Gracias, Señor Kin-caide.* I will do that very thing."

Tyler sought out Bethann and Lily. He heard the faint sound of a child's laughter and followed it. Walk-ing back behind the ranch house, he spied his daughter running through a field of buttercups. She was a picture of innocence wearing a new yellow dress. Coppery pigtails slapped haphazardly against her shoulders and her face lit with merriment.

Tyler folded his arms across his chest, leaned against a tall pecan tree and watched the happy scene. A giggling Bethann ran straight toward...Lily? Tyler blinked and refocused his eyes. Slowly he came away from the tree. He'd been gone close to a month, but certainly he wouldn't have mistaken Lily, the tall, slender, pale-eyed woman who had saved his life and befriended his daughter.

Only the Lily he viewed today had curves in places he'd have been sure to remember. Her bright-colored dress hugged her hips and even dared to flare out slightly. The soft lace-edged bodice clung to her upper torso, hinting at a ripeness, a fullness Tyler was sure hadn't been there before. He closed his eyes momentarily, wondering if this apparition might disappear. But when his eyes scanned over Lily once again from top to bottom, he knew that what he was seeing was real.

A vibrant smile graced Lily's face. Her cheeks, rosy from playful exhilaration only enhanced the sky-blue of her eyes. Light brown hair, shaken loose from its braid and kissed by the sun was the color of darkened honey. Silken tresses flowed down her back in long golden waves.

Lily was lovely.

When had this happened? And how?

Tyler was stunned. His memory flashed images of Lily eating heartily at every meal, of her tilling the soil under the warming sun's rays, of her enjoying the everyday aspects of ranch life.

He stood stock-still, captivated by the scene before

him. Bethann handed Lily a jumping rope and together they jumped up and down, bruising the golden flowers beneath them.

With eyes intent on Lily, he watched her feet leave the ground as her body lifted up. He heard the sweet sound of her laughter. And witnessed her feminine shape bouncing, heaving her chest up and down. Tyler swallowed hard. His heart thumped wildly and his whole body tightened.

He remembered Lily's slender legs the day he saw to her injury. Soft, shapely, graceful legs. He imagined how they'd feel wrapped around him in a fit of passion. He could actually picture it. Tyler swore silently, but couldn't take his eyes from Lily. It was bad enough he liked her. It was bad enough he admired her abilities. It was bad enough he'd come to care for her.

Now this.

He'd never expected her to…to blossom, just like those damned flowers she's always tending. The very proper, very rigid, Miss Lillian Brody had softened around the edges. And it was a remarkable change.

"Papa! Papa!" Bethann spotted him and came barreling forth. She ran into his arms and he lifted her high in the air. "You're back, Papa. We missed you!"

Tyler hugged his daughter, keeping her chubby body in his arms. "I missed you, too, sweetcakes. Papa missed you very much." He kissed the top of her head.

Lily approached with a broad smile. She was even lovelier close up. Tyler smiled back. "Hello, Lily."

"Welcome back, Tyler," she said breathlessly. Her blue eyes fixed on his. Tyler was helpless to tear his gaze away. In what seemed like a self-conscious move, she began redoing her braid. "I—I must look a mess."

"Your hair looks nice. And both my—you young ladies look beautiful." Tyler glanced at his daughter after witnessing Lily's blush. "New dresses?"

"Yep, Miss Lily made us a batch of new clothes and we even gots some from the store," Bethann offered eagerly.

"Well, now, they're real pretty dresses. Both of them." Tyler dared a glance at Lily. She was inspecting her shoes.

"You must be tired. I'll go in and fix chicken and dumplings," Lily said as she made her way past him.

"Mmm, my favorite. You're spoiling me, Lily," he teased as he set Bethann down.

Bethann grabbed his hand. "Papa, I learned how to skip rope. Lily surprised me with a new jumping rope with shiny carved handles."

"Did she now?" Tyler glanced at the sway of Lily's backside as she headed toward the house and wondered what other surprises she had in store for him.

Chapter Twelve

Lily dashed about the kitchen, stirring her meal, making lemonade and setting out the dishes. Minutes ago Tyler had seated himself down and stretched his long legs out at the thick oak table. Lily felt his eyes following her every movement. Self-conscious of his blatant scrutiny, she wiped her hands down her apron over and over again. They'd become clammy, as had her whole body when she'd seen him down by the pecan grove earlier.

It had been exactly twenty-four days since they'd spoken. Not that she'd counted the days, but, oh, who was she kidding? She'd made a small mark on her calendar in the privacy of her room every night he'd been gone. She thought she'd be too busy to think about him. She'd hoped. But since he'd touched her…that way, down by the creek, every free moment her thoughts drifted to him.

Now that Tyler was home, she wasn't sure which was worse, missing the very sight of him, or having him back, making her jittery and flustered again.

Why on earth was he staring at her?

He cleared his throat. "I like the color of your new dress, Lily. Does something to the blue in your eyes."

Lily continued to stir the dumplings and suppressed the thrilling shudder that wanted release from her disobedient body. "Thank you."

"Jose said you had a surprise. Chicken and dumplin's and a slice of pecan pie is a mighty fine welcome home. Thanks, Lily."

Lily twirled around to face him. Distracted by his return and all the crazy stirrings going on in her heart had made her forget his real surprise. "Oh, my goodness, Tyler," she gasped. "I can't believe I forgot to tell you."

Tyler noticed the flounce of her skirts when she turned, which made Lily even more self-conscious. She wasn't used to wearing such frilly clothes. He grinned when their eyes met. "Tell me what, Lily?"

Lily removed her apron and tossed it aside. She sat down to face him across the table. "Well, while you were gone, we had a visitor."

Tyler's eyebrows shot up. "Jose didn't mention—"

"I asked him not to. I wanted to tell you myself." A warm glow spread through her insides, thinking she could finally give Tyler something that would make him happy. She couldn't help but smile. "You see, this man showed up. And Bethann, well, I fell asleep and she sort of disappeared for a while, but it was okay, because she was jumping rope and I didn't need my gun after all and—"

"Lily, get to the point. And what's this about a man and a gun? I'd worry, but I know what a good shot you are," he teased. "Who came out to the ranch?"

Lily knew she'd babbled on, she was just so darn excited about the news. She rushed on. "The point is,

Bethann's uncle Brett came for a visit. Isn't that wonderful?''

Tyler's smile faded. In fact, his whole face dropped. His eyes narrowed and his jaw set rigidly. He stood up and glared down at her, resting both palms on the table. ''You don't mean *Brett Muldoon* was here at my ranch, do you?''

''Y-yes. He was here. Tyler?''

Blood rushed to Tyler's face. ''You say he saw Bethann?''

''Yes, the two of them got on nicely. She wasn't so sure about him, but once we sat down to supper, she—''

Tyler slammed his fist on the table. Lily jumped. ''You invited him inside. He ate here?''

Lily stood up on shaky legs. She didn't know what prompted Tyler's tirade, but he was clearly furious.

''Well, yes, I did. I thought you'd be happy. He is family, Tyler.'' Lily thought about her own uncle. Finding him had become a quest. How happy she'd be if she could locate him and finally keep the deathbed promise she'd made to her father. To Lily…family was everything.

''Lady, you are sorely mistaken. He's no family of mine.''

''But…he's Bethann's uncle.''

''Stay out of it!'' His faced flushed cherry-tomato red. He raised his voice and emphasized each word. ''This is none of your business, woman.'' Tyler grabbed his black felt hat, pushing it flat onto his head, then stormed out the back door. The string of his curses rang in her ear.

''Well,'' Lily said, jamming her fists onto her hips, ''of all the nerve!'' And here Lily actually thought she was helping. Her surprise had jumped up and bit her. The worst thing of all was Tyler's outrage at her.

In that moment she realized that Tyler held no warm feelings for her. She was, in his mind…just the house-keeper. She had no right interfering with family matters. She wasn't his "family," either.

Lily slumped into the chair. Her anger faded into something harder to handle, emptiness. She put her head in her hands and forced away tears ready to fall. Her mistake was innocent. Brett Muldoon led her to believe Tyler would welcome him into his home, but Tyler hadn't wanted explanations or excuses. He'd let her know without question her place in his house-hold—she was hired help.

Reality sunk in slowly, like a twig falling into a mud hole. She had come to love Bethann and…her impenetrable father. She had come to think of herself as a part of their family. She had cared for Tyler's home as if it were her own. She had cooked his meals with thoughts of pleasing him. She had laundered his clothes, schooled his daughter, befriended his ranch hands.

She had fooled herself into thinking she may just belong here. Earlier today, when Tyler arrived home and first glimpsed her, she had a fleeting feeling that he had missed her, too. His gaze never strayed far, and he seemed to welcome her with his smile, his tone of voice. Her heart had sped up and a flash of what it was like to be a true family, the three of them together, brought surging warmth through her body.

But the Kincaides were not her family. Tyler had made that abundantly clear just now. Jasper Brody was the only family she had. She had to find him and get away from here.

Before her silly notions and aching heart would do her in.

Randy stopped the wagon in front of the telegraph office and helped Lily down. "Thank you, Randy. I'll meet you in two hours at the supperhouse."

Randy removed his hat and scratched his head. "You sure, Miss Lily? I could stay and wait for you."

"No, that's not necessary. Go on. I know you have business in town. I want to do some shopping at the emporium. I'll be fine."

On a nod, Randy was back in the wagon, heading for the livery. Lily breathed a sigh of relief. She had to get away from the Circle K, if even for just a few hours. Tyler had been insufferable the past two days. He'd barely spoken to her, only responding to her questions with a curt nod or one-syllable answers.

Lily didn't understand his behavior. He was brooding and pensive, like a powder keg about to go off. She'd steered clear of him, but his eyes, when they lit on her, had been penetrating, suspicious. Lily vowed not to let one more day pass without trying to find out what had happened between Brett Muldoon and Tyler.

Wes Farley, usually a wealth of information, had kept quiet on the matter and told Lily it was best not to dredge up the past.

Lifting her skirts, she stepped into the telegraph office. "Morning, Charlie. Anything?"

Charlie swung around in his swivel chair. He gave her an apologetic smile. One Lily had become accustomed to. "Sorry, Miss Lillian."

Lily hoisted her shoulders, more determined to find Uncle Jasper than ever. Lifting a V-spot from her reticule, she handed the paper money to Charlie along with a list she'd been working on since Tyler's tirade two days ago. "I want you to send out this message to all these cities."

Charlie whistled as he perused the list she gave him. "All these, you say? Same message to all. Yes, ma'am."

"Yes, and if you hear anything in response, send a messenger to the ranch. Immediately."

"Guess you really need to find your uncle."

"Yes, Charlie, the sooner the better."

Lily didn't know how she'd handle the situation when she did find Uncle Jasper. She'd given her word to Tyler she'd stay on at the ranch until after the cattle drive. Lily wasn't sure if she could keep her promise—although in all her life, she'd not once reneged on her word. Tyler needed her services. They had a business deal.

It was clear now that Lily was Tyler's employee, nothing more. She'd been a fool to dare hope she meant anything to him. He'd told her time and again he didn't want love in his life ever again. Why didn't she listen?

A hollow ache in the pit of her stomach threatened to swallow her up. She bit down on her lip, refusing tears to fall, but one sole moist drop did escape. It traveled down her cheek to drip off her chin.

Heavens, Lily, don't let the whole town see what a lovestruck ninny you really are.

She took in a deep sobering breath. For all her flights of fancy, Lily was truly a realist at heart. She knew leaving the ranch would hurt her, but staying would hurt even more. Loving Tyler and not having that love returned would split her heart in two.

She had promised her father she'd make a new life

for herself with his brother. She intended to do just that. She didn't belong with the Kincaides. Just knowing she had a place to go home to, once Tyler returned from the cattle drive, would give her the peace of mind she needed.

But where was Uncle Jasper? Why was he so hard to find?

Lily headed down the sidewalk hopeful one of the wires she sent today would bring her some news. She came to a stop when she found herself in front of Wilbourne's Emporium. Colorful fabrics and hair accessories were on display on a narrow table in one corner in the front of the store. The table was covered in a fine lace tablecloth.

She viewed the lovely items from the window and thought what a brilliant scheme—to put the finest womanly items on view so they may be seen through the window, tempting all the female passersby.

Lily found herself measuring the coins left in her reticule to the price of a lovely hair comb inlaid with tiny white pearls. The comb would be a perfect complement to her new blue dress she planned on wearing tomorrow night at the barn dance.

Lily still needed to be frugal. She'd just spent a good deal of money at the telegraph office. Her savings would have to see her through when she left the ranch, if she hadn't found Uncle Jasper by then.

She entered the store and wandered down the aisles, grateful for this reprieve from Tyler's oppressive scrutiny. She couldn't afford the comb, but she found herself standing over the table lifting it up to finger the delicate pearls.

"That's a right fine comb, Miss Lillian."

"Oh!" She whirled around to come face-to-face with Brett Muldoon.

He cast her a charming smile. "Good morning. You're out early today."

"Y-yes. I had a bit of shopping to do."

She couldn't very well tell him he was the reason she'd had to get away from the Circle K this morning. Whatever went on between Brett Muldoon and Tyler in the past had brought a great deal of tension to the Kincaide household.

"You planning on buying it?" Brett focused his deep green eyes on the comb she held in her hand.

Abruptly she placed the comb back down. "Oh, no. Just admiring it."

"I wanted to thank you again for your hospitality the other day. It did my heart good to see my niece. She's a beauty, just like her ma."

The man had such an honest face, open, filled with obvious love for Bethann. She wondered if Tyler was justified in his hatred for his brother-in-law. "Yes, she's a special child."

"I can see you mean a great deal to her, too. The little time I spent with her, she spoke on and on about her Miss Lily."

Lily smiled. "We have a special bond, Bethann and I. But I've never tried to replace her mother."

"No, no." He rubbed his jaw. "I'm glad she has a friend in you. Tyler back yet?"

Lily tensed. How much should she divulge to Brett? She didn't want to interfere and have Tyler's wrath brought down upon her once again. But the man came out to the ranch, obviously unaware Tyler harbored any hostility. Should she warn him? "Yes, he's back. But, Mr. Muldoon—"

"Call me Brett, please."

"Brett, I think you should know, Tyler doesn't...well, he was not pleased you came out to the ranch the other day. I don't think it's a good idea for you to plan on coming out again."

Brett took in a breath. "I was afraid of that." Two customers strolled down the aisle toward them. Brett glanced their way, then focused his attention back to Lily. "Listen, do you have a few minutes? This is a private matter, but I would like the chance to explain. We could take a walk, it's a beautiful day, or I'd be honored to buy you a meal at the supperhouse."

Lily shuddered to think what might happen if Emma Mayfield got within earshot of that explanation. Tyler's private affairs would be up for public scrutiny within the hour. "A walk sounds lovely."

"Fine, then. I'll finish making my purchases and meet you outside in a few minutes."

Lily took a deep breath once she stepped outside. She was curious, perhaps overly so, about what had transpired between Tyler and his brother-in-law. Tyler had warned her to stay out of his affairs, but she deemed it only fair to let the unsuspecting Brett Muldoon know he was not welcome at the Circle K.

Brett joined her minutes later, and took her elbow. They began a slow leisurely walk east, toward the church. "Miss Lillian, I must thank you for agreeing to hear me out. You see, when my sister died, I was distraught. We were close, not just in age, but in every way a brother and sister could be. She was all I had in the way of family."

"I've never had siblings, but I can understand the closeness you must have shared."

He nodded as they made their way past an ancient

oak that bordered the edge of town. "It's no secret I wasn't happy when my sister decided to stay on out west and marry a rancher. I resented Tyler Kincaide. He kinda barreled into Lizabeth's life, then nothing was ever the same."

"I understand they loved each other very much."

"Ah, but my sister wasn't happy. In the beginning yes, she was besotted, but the reality of what she'd done finally hit her. Her letters sounded more and more desperate. When little Bethann came along, I think my sister finally knew some joy. She'd resigned herself to living west. And then, the accident."

Brett's handsome face contorted, twisting his mouth into an ugly snarl. "When I heard the news about Lizabeth, the gruesome details of her death, I blamed Tyler. I hated him."

Alarmed at the venom in his tone, she asked, "Do you hate him now?"

Brett became thoughtful, giving Lily a long look. "No. I treated him unkindly. We had a misunderstanding. Both of us were aching from losing Lizabeth. He told me never to come back. But, you see, I love Bethann. She is a part of my sister. I came back to make amends."

They stopped when they reached the whitewashed picket fence surrounding the church. The sun shone brightly overhead and the sweet smell of jasmine lingered in the air. "Will you be here long?"

"I have business in Sweet Springs—a venture I'm thinking of investing in. I shall be around for some time. I'm hoping to see Bethann again. I'd like her to come to know her uncle Brett." He smiled crookedly.

"Bethann would like that, but Tyler…"

"I just wanted you to hear my side of the story,

Miss Lillian. Now, I think I best get you back. The sun's scorching those pretty cheeks of yours.''

Lily's eyes grew wide and her cheeks flamed. She put her head down as they changed direction. Once they reached the middle of town, Brett took her by the hand. ''Thank you again, for listening.'' He reached into his vest pocket and placed the pearl comb she'd admired at the emporium into her hand. ''This is for you.''

Lily stared at the comb in complete surprise, then lifted her eyes to him. ''No—I couldn't.''

''Please take it. A token for treating me kindly the other day. After all, you could've shot me.'' He chuckled. ''And letting me spend time with Bethann, well, that was real good of you.''

''But I—we aren't…is this proper?'' she asked on a breath.

Brett cocked his head to the side. ''It's proper. You're the first friend I've made in Sweet Springs. I hope, one day, you'll think on me as a friend, also.''

Lily wound her hand around the comb. ''Thank you. It's a thoughtful gift.''

''Lily!'' The sharp warning from behind made Lily's breath catch. She froze, recognizing the familiar jingling of spurs. Tyler's approaching footsteps sounded more menacing the louder they became.

The pearl comb fell from her grasp. Brett bent to retrieve it. He handed the comb back to Lily, covering his fingers over hers just as Tyler reached them. Brett Muldoon's eyes were steady as they reassured her.

''Get away from her, Muldoon.'' Tyler practically spit out the words, yet he stood with a deceptive calm.

Brett smiled sardonically at Tyler. Lily, still frozen on the spot, felt Brett's fingers travel over hers before releasing his grip. "Just helping out the lady, Kin-caide."

"The *lady* doesn't need your help."

"Tyler!" Lily came to her senses when she realized the men were speaking about her as if she were transparent. "Mr. Muldoon and I were having a conversation."

The grim set of his jaw told Lily what he thought about that. His chest heaved; he seemed to be struggling for patience. At the moment Lily didn't care about his disposition. He'd been unbearable these past few days.

Tyler glanced at the comb she held in one hand and gave her an accusing stare. "Fine, finish your conversation." He folded his arms around his middle and rooted his boots to the sidewalk.

Brett stepped back, smiling at Lily. "I think Miss Lillian and I have finished our talk." He tipped his hat. "Thank you for the stroll and I'm glad you like the comb. Wear it well." He turned and left Lily alone with Tyler.

Tyler grabbed her under the elbow and began pulling her in the opposite direction. Lily tried to remove herself from his grasp, but his fingers dug in and wouldn't let go. "Tyler, let me be."

"No, Lily. Not until I have my say."

She struggled to keep up with his long strides. "Where are we going?"

"Quiet, Lily, just quiet." There was anger in his tone, but oddly, Lily thought it seemed directed at himself.

He continued to drag her along. Lily was too irritated at his abrupt behavior to give much mind to the stares she was receiving from curious onlookers. Men smirked, woman gazed with knowing smiles. Emma Mayfield came out of the supperhouse with dishtowel in hand, wide-eyed, registering each step she and Tyler took. Tyler's tirade would soon be headlining the *Sweet Springs Chronicle,* no doubt.

But Lily balked when she realized Tyler's intent. With a slight shove, he nudged her into the Springtime Hotel.

"Tyler, please." Lily's eyes darted around the lobby. No one but the desk clerk was present. Thankfully.

"I need a room," Tyler barked.

"Yes, sir," the clerk said, noticing the dangerous look Tyler was casting him. The clerk made a hasty turn, lifted a key from its hook and handed it to Tyler.

Tyler didn't bother signing the register. He shoved some bills at the clerk and turned back to Lily.

"No, Tyler, please," Lily hissed under her breath. Her humiliation equaled her anger. And confusion was attempting to wedge itself in to make a trio of emotions clamoring in her brain. Why was he doing this? She'd never seen Tyler so…out of control. He ignored her attempts to remove herself from his grasp, tightening his hold even more.

"Lily, we have to talk." His tone brooked no argument. Tyler was the most stubborn man she'd ever known.

"But not here, please." Her plea went unanswered. She supposed the damage was already done. Scores of people had seen her enter the hotel with Tyler whisking her along.

Tyler put the key in the door of Room 217. "We need privacy."

He opened the door, and allowed her entrance in a

gentleman-like manner. Lily wanted to cry from the irony. If her reputation wasn't ruined from living at the ranch, it surely was now. Tyler wanted to…talk. But who would believe that's all they would do up here?

Lily shrugged and resigned herself to this talk. She stepped into the room. Tyler closed the door from behind. Lily had never been in a hotel room before. The room overlooked the east side of town. Dark crimson curtains, tied back, welcomed the bright afternoon sun and dust swirls appeared in the streaming ray of light pouring in. The mahogany furniture was sparse, but the double-wide bed seemed to loom like a Brahman bull in a horse stall. Lily swallowed hard.

She heard the distinct click of the latch from behind. Tyler had locked them in. Lily pushed fallen tendrils of hair from her face and glanced at the man who stood with hands braced on the windowsill, looking out.

"You had no right to bring me here like this, Tyler."

Tyler Kincaide swore silently upon hearing Lily's softly spoken but firm reprimand. He continued to stare out the window, calling himself a coward. He didn't want to witness Lily's condemning gaze, but he sensed her boring a hole smack through his back.

She was right. He *had* no right to bring her here. It was the dumbest blame stunt he'd ever pulled. He asked himself why he'd done it and the answer muddled up his brains. He feared he knew the reason. Seeing that man put his hands on Lily made Tyler crazy.

Brett Muldoon, with his high-priced suitcoats and charming ways, could turn just about any young innocent's head. Muldoon wouldn't care that Lily was inexperienced. He wouldn't give a damn that Lily was naive in the ways of the world. The man would take advantage of her. Tyler couldn't let that happen. Lily was under his protection.

Protection? Tyler scoffed at the notion. His gut clenched. He shouldn't have brought her to the hotel in view of half the townfolk. But as Tyler brought his reasons to the surface, the only one that held fast was he *wanted* to lay claim to Lily for the whole town to see. He'd compromised her, yes. He'd vowed to her he wouldn't, but seeing her with Muldoon had changed all the rules.

Was he right in assuming Muldoon had gifted Lily with that pearl comb? Hell and damnation. Tyler'd never thought to give her a gift, especially one she held in obvious affection. Didn't the naive woman know accepting such a fine gift constituted certain liberties for the man to take?

Another knifing pain stabbed at his gut. Had Lily wanted Muldoon to take those liberties with her?

I want to know, Tyler.

Her plea that day by the creek when he'd touched her echoed in his ears. And a nagging thought crept in, one he spent nights awake pondering. He was the one who wanted to show Lily the ways between a man and a woman. He wanted to teach her how passions ignite when a man takes a woman to his bed.

Hell, when she'd first come to the ranch she'd been a shy, plain, tall woman who kept a proper house. He admired her talents, liked the manner in which she carried herself, was grateful for the way she'd taken to Bethann.

She hadn't aroused him in the least.

Coming home from roundup had changed all that. And it wasn't just how she seemed to have bloomed into a lovely, rosy-cheeked, golden-haired woman with soft curves that sent his mind wandering—no, it was more than that. She had simply taken to ranch life without a qualm. Her quiet confidence, her ability to get things done, her devotion to Bethann, had all contributed to the way he was beginning to feel about her, the way he wanted her.

He hadn't even realized it until he'd nearly lost all semblance of self-control when he saw Brett Muldoon making cow eyes at her.

And hadn't he gone about the very way to secure his desire? He hadn't given Lily a choice in the matter. By dragging her up here, he had laid his claim. Now there would be no doubts. No man who respected Tyler would ever disturb Lily in any way.

The damage was already done.

"Look, Lily—maybe I shouldn't have brought you up here, but there's things you must know about Muldoon." Tyler finally turned to her, fearful that his expression would betray what he'd been thinking.

"Brett has told me something of himself." Her chin up, Tyler knew so were her defenses. "He came back here to make amends. He loves Bethann."

It rankled that she had become somewhat familiar with the man. "He'll not step foot on Kincaide land ever again, Lily. I don't want that man near my daughter."

"But, Tyler, he's…family. Brett wants to get to know his niece."

Tyler shook his head. He reined in his anger. Blasting Lily would get him nowhere. It was clear she'd been taken in by the man. "I said no. He's not the man you think he is."

"I barely know him, Tyler. But I see the love he has for Bethann. He said you two had a misunderstanding when...your wife died."

"Humph." Tyler didn't know how much longer he could keep hold of his temper. "Hardly a misunderstanding, Lily. Tell me, are you smitten with him?" He held his breath, caring overly much about her answer.

Lily jerked back, as if she'd been slapped. "I, uh, no. Of course not."

"You served him dinner at my ranch."

Lily stared at him, her blue eyes wide with confusion. "He was a relation. I thought it the hospitable thing to do."

"You spent time alone with him this afternoon."

"It was an accidental meeting."

"Was it?" Tyler narrowed his eyes and stepped closer. The fresh scent of Lily's soft hair teased his nostrils.

"He gifted you with that pearl comb, didn't he?"

He saw her swallow, then nod her head. His suspicions had been correct. Tyler's heart hammered, the fast sharp pounding throbbed in his head. Lily had accepted a gift from Muldoon.

"Suppose Muldoon expects more than hospitality from you, Lily. You giving it to him?"

Lily flinched. Blue eyes sparked angrily and the meaning of his words sunk in. She gasped, then slapped his face. Hard.

Tyler grabbed her wrist. His body shook. "You damn fool woman. Don't mess with the likes of Brett Muldoon. He'll bring you nothing but heartache."

"Let go of me, you...big...stupid...fool." Lily struggled to get loose from his grasp. Tyler decided to release her, but stepped back to protect himself against another sharp smack to his cheek.

He rubbed the spot where she'd slapped him. She packed a powerful punch. His face still stung. "Ah, Lily. Don't you know what accepting an expensive gift from a man means?"

Lily planted her fists on her hips. He was grateful she'd found another spot to put them besides his cheekbone.

"And what do you suppose it means to the fine community of Sweet Springs when a man drags a woman halfway across town to a hotel room?"

Tyler tugged on his ear, hesitating. "I had to warn you. Men like Muldoon take advantage of kindhearted women. I don't want him near you again, either."

"Ha! You don't have any right to tell me who I claim as a friend, Tyler."

"I'm telling you right now, do not see that man again."

Lily pursed her lips. Her blue eyes shot sparks of anger. "What will you do, *fire* me?"

Tyler pounded his hat against his thigh several times. "Damn it, Lily. I'm telling you this for your own good."

"And I'm telling you this, Tyler Kincaide. I won't be spoken to that way. I won't allow you to tell me who I may have as a friend, and I certainly won't stand here in your company one second longer. I'm leaving!"

Lily lifted her skirts and turned to the door. She yanked on the knob, then realized Tyler had locked them in. Her face flushed with irritation, she gave him a look so cold it would rival a winter snowfall.

Tyler planted his hat on his head and sauntered to the door. "I'll escort you home."

Lily waited until the key was in the lock. She scurried out the door, calling over her shoulder. "No, thank you. Randy will be bringing the buckboard around."

Tyler stood at the top of the staircase, letting go of a barrage of curses as a few stunned hotel guests stared up at him from the lobby.

Bethann sat on the bed and ran the comb through Lily's hair. "You got such waves in your hair, Miss Lily. Sure is pretty."

Lily met Bethann's reflection in the mirror, watching the child admire her hair. "Thank you, sweetie. Your hair's just as pretty. We've just got to keep the dirt and dust from getting yours so darn matted down."

Wide-eyed and wrinkle-nosed, Bethann asked, "How'm I supposed to do that?"

Lily turned on the bed to put a finger under Bethann's chin. "There's time for that. You can be a little girl as long as you want. But when you're ready, sweetie, then I'll curl your hair real pretty."

Bethann smiled and lifted her braid to the top of her head. She studied herself in the cheval mirror. "You can do up a fancy bun, with curls and all?"

"Sure can, if that's what you want."

"But you're leaving your hair down. How come?"

Lily's mouth twisted. Tyler liked her hair down. And ever since he'd told her that, she'd made a point of wearing it in one long plait running down her back.

She always thought to please him, even in the simplest ways. But she wouldn't admit that to Bethann. The little one might just find the need to inform her father. Lily had already made enough mistakes where Tyler Kincaide was concerned. She wasn't planning to add to the list, especially tonight.

Tonight was a special occasion—Henderson's barn dance. And Lily wanted to look her best, even if Tyler wasn't going.

She was still angry and hadn't spoken one word to him since yesterday afternoon when he dragged her into that hotel room and ordered her not to befriend Brett Muldoon.

"Sometimes a lady needs a change. Your uncle bought me a fine comb as a thank-you for the hospitality shown him when he was out at the ranch. I thought I'd leave my hair loose and stay the waves with the comb." Lily walked to her dresser and handed Bethann the comb. Even though it had been a sore subject with Tyler, Lily wanted his daughter to know her uncle Brett had a kind and giving heart.

"It's so fancy." Bethann's chubby fingers followed the path of the delicate pearls, touching each one as if they were the most precious of gems.

Lily wanted to offer the comb to her, but knew Tyler wouldn't allow it. Tyler wanted his daughter to have nothing to do with her uncle. A notion Lily still couldn't reconcile. Bethann had no other family. And once Lily left…she could only imagine the hurt Bethann would feel, for Lily, too, would be in anguish when the time came to leave. She loved Bethann with all of her heart. And Tyler, her heart still belonged to him, too—pigheaded as he was.

If only things were different, she thought wistfully.

An image of Tyler, handsome in his Sunday finest, escorting her to the dance and gazing at her with admiring eyes, flashed in her mind. He'd take her into his arms and whisk her around the dance area, neither one noticing another soul at the festivities but each other.

"Miss Lily?"

Bethann's curious voice interrupted her thoughts.

Lily, stop your daydreaming!

"Uh, yes, Bethann, it's a lovely comb. Someday you'll own a pretty comb just like it."

"Really?"

Lily leaned over to take Bethann's chubby face in her hand. "Why sure, you'll have loads of beautiful things when you grow up. Just remember," Lily said, placing her fist to her heart, "nothing is more beautiful than a kind and loving heart. That's where real beauty lies."

Bethann nodded and bounded from the bed. "This here the dress you fixin' to wear?"

The sapphire blue silk had been carefully laid over the chair. "Yes, it is. Now, you'd better get your chores done and let me finish dressing. I promise I'll come get you when I'm all ready, so you can see the dress on me."

"Yes, ma'am," Bethann said adamantly.

Lily chuckled. "Okay, then, off you go. I'll see you a little later."

When the door closed behind Bethann, Lily took off her everyday dress, added three layers of petticoats over her chemise and donned the silk garment she'd worked on for almost a month. With a twist of her lips, she glanced at the low cut of the bodice and wondered what had possessed her to sew the garment so snugly that it pressed and lifted up her small breasts, making them seem full to overflowing. She struggled with the fabric trying to lift it higher on her chest to no avail.

Lily closed her eyes and took a deep breath. "Don't be silly, Lily. This dress is the prettiest thing you own and you're going to enjoy yourself tonight."

Smiling at her reflection in the tall mirror, she lifted the smooth flowing fabric and twirled around. Yes, tonight she would have fun. She fiddled with the comb, adjusting it until soft waves streamed down her shoulders. Satisfied, she lifted her shawl and was off to find Bethann.

With any luck, she wouldn't run into Tyler Kincaide.

Chapter Thirteen

Tyler deliberately stayed away from the ranch house all day, spending a tedious day riding the line, checking fences. He hadn't wanted to witness Lily's departure to the barn dance, but had to return in time enough to watch over his daughter. All the ranch hands aside from Wes were planning on kicking up their heels this evening. He'd eat a quiet dinner with Bethann, then retire early.

That had been the plan.

Until he heard a rustle of skirts and caught a glimpse of Lily, rosy-cheeked and eager, bounding down the steps of the house. He stayed behind the barn door and watched.

Randy helped her up onto the buckboard amid a cacophony of compliments given by the other ranch hands that were seated in the back of the wagon. Her eyes sparkled with delight as she turned and made a ceremonious little bow. "Thank you, boys. You're all too kind," she said with a gracious smile.

Tyler swallowed hard.

Her honey-brown hair flowed past her shoulders in waves caressing her creamy skin. The blue silk fancy dress hugged her soft curves and brought out a flush of color in her face. He'd never seen Lily in such a dress. His heart reacted, hammering erratically in his chest. Good Lord, Lily looked beautiful.

And he knew he wouldn't be the only man to think so. His ranch hands, who respected and befriended her, were testimony to that. Tyler slapped the dust from his clothes, watching the buckboard head out the Circle K gates.

"Damn fool, you are."

Wes's voice, low and hoarse, resounded in his ears. Tyler didn't acknowledge the man who had just stepped up.

"That's a mighty fine woman yore lettin' go."

He took in a deep breath. "I'm not *letting* her go. She's going on her own accord."

"That ain't what I meant. Yore gonna let every mangy cowpoke in the county put his hands on her tonight? Some young smitten wrangler might be a claimin' her as his afore the night's through."

Tyler had had similar thoughts all afternoon. He'd worked himself hard today trying to block out images of Lily dancing, throwing her head back in laughter, smiling up at her dance partner. But the thoughts had filtered through, muddling his brain. And a tenuous knot in his stomach expanded like a fist in the gut hearing Wes speak of it.

"Lily can take care of herself." Tyler did turn to Wes now, and met his wrinkled eyes directly. "Besides, she's leaving us all soon."

"Humph. You ain't asked her to stay."

Before Lily came to the ranch, Tyler had resigned himself to raising his daughter and herding his cattle. He had no room in his heart for another woman. No, sir. Couldn't afford that. He'd been devastated and besieged with guilt when Lizabeth died. He wouldn't put himself in that position again. He wouldn't fall for Lily. She was leaving. It was best they all remembered that.

"She's determined to find her uncle, keep the promise she made to her father. Besides, I don't want her to stay."

Wes laid a hand on Tyler's shoulder. "Then yore a bigger fool than I originally thought, son."

Bethann raced out of the house and ran into his arms. He welcomed her, anxious to end the conversation with Wes. "How's my sweetcakes?" he asked twirling his daughter in his arms.

"Oh, Papa, did you see her? Miss Lily looked like a princess."

"Someday you'll dress up fine like that and then Papa's going to be a sorry man."

Bethann ignored Tyler's attempt to change the subject. "Papa, you ain't goin' to the dance?"

"No, sweetcakes, Papa's fixing on spending the night with you. You'll like that, won't you?"

His daughter put her head down. Her pink lips came together in a pout. "But you won't git to dance with Miss Lily." There was pleading in her voice.

"Seems the daughter's more intelligent than the father," Wes chimed in.

Attacked from both fronts, Tyler put Bethann down and placed his hands on his hips. "You really want me to go?"

Bethann nodded eagerly.

"I'll watch the little 'un tonight. You go on, fix yoreself up, put on fancy duds and give Miss Lily a twirl about fer me."

Wes's offer and his daughter's smile were more than one man could take. On a deep sigh, Tyler relented. "I guess you two settled it. I've got to take a quick bath."

Tyler tuned out his daughter's ramblings about Miss Lily's fancy dress and her pretty hair as they walked into the house. A thought nagged at him. He realized he'd forgotten one very important thing. Lily wasn't speaking to him. So how was he going to get her to dance with him?

More than an hour later Tyler strode purposely into the Henderson's huge barn filled with fellow ranchers and neighbors. Streamers hung from the loft, fiddlers stomped their boots and played a polka, long tables laden with every manner of foodstuffs were set against the far wall.

Tyler removed his felt hat, straightened his suitcoat and looked around for Lily. He spotted her dancing with Byron O'Grady, ranch foreman for the Hendersons. The man kept a decent distance away, holding Lily almost at arm's length. That suited Tyler just fine. As soon as the music ended, Tyler would approach her.

"Tyler Kincaide, my word, you made it, after all." Letty Sue batted her eyelashes and sauntered over to him. He groaned silently. He wasn't in the mood to entertain the little vixen tonight.

"Evenin'. You're looking mighty pretty tonight."

The woman giggled and curtsied, treating him to a view of her ample bosom.

"Thank you. You're looking handsome, too. And goodness," she said breathlessly, "you're just in time to save me from all these toe-tappers. I swear, they don't give a woman a chance to rest."

"That's why they're here—to dance." He tried to hide his irritation. "Isn't that why you're here?"

"Why, yes, of course. But right now I believe I need some refreshment. Would you be kind enough, Tyler?"

Letty Sue tucked her arm through his. He had no choice in the matter, but as he walked her to the food table, his eyes followed Lily, who was presently dancing with Randy.

Tyler ladled the punch into a glass and handed it to Letty Sue. She smiled up at him with adoring eyes. Tyler winced. Letty Sue, the young woman with a body that could turn most men's heads, did nothing for him. He preferred Lily's slight curves to Letty Sue's obviously feminine figure. He found Lily's soft sky-blue eyes more appealing than Letty Sue's deep azure ones. He enjoyed Lily's quick wit and intelligence over Letty Sue's flirtatious demeanor.

Minutes later, peering over the festive party-goers, he spotted Lily, once again dancing. This time, Sheriff Singleton was spinning her around. Her face flushed, her chest heaving, her soft eyes twinkling, Tyler wanted nothing more than to take Lily into his arms and keep her there, where no other man could claim her for another dance.

"Tyler," Letty Sue said, pouting as she finished her punch, "I'm disappointed you haven't asked me to dance."

He was too much of a gentleman to hurt Joellen's daughter. He respected the woman and had put up with Letty Sue's antics through the years for the sake of friendship.

Stiffly, he offered, "Would you care to dance?"

"Yes, I most certainly would." Letty Sue attached herself to his arm and they moved onto the dance floor.

Lily had held her breath when she caught sight of Tyler entering into the festivities. She'd stumbled, missing a beat in the music, completely thrown by surprise upon seeing him. He'd said all along he wasn't coming tonight. What made him change his mind? Then she'd seen Letty Sue, eyes fluttering and all aglow as she sauntered over to him. Lily's heart sank to the floor.

He'd come for Letty Sue. Tyler, handsome in his dark brown suit and brocade vest, and Letty Sue in her cherry-red chiffon frills, made the perfect couple. Lily tried to ignore the sting of jealousy burning within.

She was still angry with Tyler, she reminded herself. Even if he did ask her to dance, she...wouldn't accept. At least, she didn't believe she would. Hoped she wouldn't.

Probably would.

Heavens, how could she deny herself one dance with Tyler? It had been a dream of hers for years—to be the envy of all the other women, having the handsome rancher take her in his arms, give her his full attention and swirl her around the dance floor. Just once.

But she wouldn't let him know how seeing him glide the saucy woman around the perimeter of the barn, hurt her. Lily was a fool to think he cared.

A tall stranger introduced himself and asked her to dance. Winded, Lily didn't want to injure the man's feelings, so she had accepted but after their dance, she excused herself. She needed to get a breath of fresh air.

"Be my honor, ma'am, to escort you," he said. "I'll get us some refreshment. The barn's a mite stuffy for me, too."

Lily waited outside for the man to join her. Handing her the glass, he sipped his in one long gulp. They walked around to the back of the barn. Lily leaned against a post and gazed at the stars. "Sure is a nice night."

"Hmm, nice," the big man answered. He stood close to her.

"Let's see," Lily pondered, "you work for which ranch?"

"Double Diamond, ma'am. Been there a while now. And you work for Kincaide, right?"

"Y-yes, th-that's right." Lily didn't like the way the man moved closer to her. His breath touched the skin on her shoulders. He hadn't taken his eyes off her chest. She placed her hand just above the lace of her bodice and he gave her a crooked smile. Nervous, Lily thought she'd best get back inside. He'd seemed so polite earlier—now he frightened her. Lily hadn't had much experience with men, but something told her this was potential for danger.

When she stepped away from the post, the man caught her wrist. "You do more for him than watch his brat, don't you, honey?" The man's lips twisted and Lily's stomach clenched. His eyes, black as soot, again slithered down to her bosom, blatantly watching the heaving of her chest.

"I d-don't know what you mean." She struggled to get out of his grasp. "Let go of me!"

"Not till I get a little of what Kincaide's been getting.'' He grabbed her other hand and locked both hands behind her back.

She struggled wildly to get free. His foul breath smelled of too much whiskey. He wouldn't release her and she couldn't break free on her own. Her heart thudded heavily in her chest. She fought down a wave of panic. Then cold hard lips crushed hers, brutalizing her with a kiss so vile, Lily wanted to vomit. She kicked him in the shin and nearly broke free when he leaped up startled. He grabbed at her, tearing the short sleeve on her dress. Her scream was cut off by a sharp slap to her cheek.

Tears streamed down her face from the sting of his palm. He pulled her into him and fondled her breasts, trying to kiss her again. She wrestled with him, flailing arms and legs, kicking, shoving, screaming. His next slap knocked her to the ground. ''Quiet, you little wh—''

''Shut your damn mouth, McGee.'' Tyler's fist shut it for him. Lily shuddered when the man's body landed next to her. She rolled away from him.

Tyler, his face reddened with fury, grabbed the man up from the ground and began to pummel him. The man fought back, landing a fist to Tyler's cheekbone. Lily stood up, bracing herself against a post. Trembling, her knees nearly buckled as she witnessed Tyler fight the man.

''Kincaide, you think you're so high and mighty,'' McGee said, rubbing his jaw as he barreled toward Tyler again. His right jab missed, leaving Tyler open to come at him with both fists over and over again. Lily had never seen Tyler so enraged. His dark eyes, black and dangerous, never left their mark as each blow struck home.

The man fell in a heap and this time didn't get up. He covered his bloodied face in his hands. Tyler stood over him, shaking. With a face contorted in disgust, he pointed a finger at the beaten man. "You go near the lady again, you even dream of touching her, you whisper her name in your sleep, and I'll kill you. You got that?"

The man uttered some unintelligible words. Tyler walked away from him, picked up his hat and jacket then strode to the post that held Lily upright. Tears coursed down her cheeks when she saw Tyler's bruised face.

His eyes, sympathetic and warm, roamed over her. He touched a finger to her cheek where she'd been struck. "I'm sorry, Lily."

Lily shed a flood of tears, hearing his quiet apology. None of this was his fault. She'd been foolish, coming out here with a stranger. "Oh, Tyler."

He wrapped an arm around her shoulder and led her away from the scene. Stopping behind a tree, both inhaled deeply. Lily controlled her sobs until finally only whimpers came out in short spurts. Tyler took her into a tender embrace. The soothing feel of his hands stroking her back quelled her trembling.

"What happened, honey?" he asked in a soothing, almost apologetic voice.

"He, um…" Lily began, biting her lip. "He seemed so nice at the dance. I wanted to get a breath of air. He said…he'd escort me. Then, once we were behind the barn…" Lily couldn't bring herself to say the words. She put her head down.

"He *touched* you, didn't he?"

Lily couldn't deny it. The marks of his hands were on her skin. Her dress was ripped. She nodded slowly.

Tyler's body stiffened. He tightened his hold on her. "I'm sorry you were hurt," he said soothingly.

Lily sank into his comfort, letting it seep into her skin. She lifted her head to look into his eyes. "He said awful things."

"Tell me," Tyler demanded softly.

"He said...he wanted a little of what...of what... you w-were g-getting."

There was a quick flicker in Tyler's dark eyes. Emotion flashed like a torrid rain over his face. "Bastard. I should've killed him."

"No, Tyler, no. I made a mistake. I shouldn't have been so trusting." She kept her voice low. "I didn't know. I, no man...has ever...wanted me."

"Ah, Lily," he murmured, kissing her forehead, "you really don't know how lovely you are."

His lips felt wonderful brushing over her eyebrows. "I...am?"

Tyler swallowed, then lifted the torn sleeve on her cerulean dress. His fingers caressed her shoulder, bringing an onslaught of heat to her insides.

"Yes, and if things were different tonight, I'd show you just how appealing you are."

Lily stared at his lips. "Show me, Tyler, please."

She watched as emotions, raw and deep, flowed over his face. He hesitated—she could almost hear the debate going on inside his head.

"Tyler," she pleaded, "I want to know. Just once," she whispered.

"Lily," he said in a tortured voice. He cupped the back of her head with tender care and slowly brought her closer. His coal-black eyes pierced her with their intensity, sending warm shivers of delight down to her toes. She wrapped her arms around his waist. When his lips touched hers, Lily's heart soared.

This is what she'd dreamed about, what she'd always wanted. Tyler's mouth caressing hers, his body close, keeping her warm, safe, protected. When she murmured his name, he slipped his tongue into her mouth.

A hot sensation flowed down below her navel. Her woman's center ached sweetly as his tongue delved deeper, stroking her gently at first then more boldly. Stroking him back, she leaned into him until no space separated them. They stood chest to chest, hip to hip, thigh to thigh. She heard a rich deep sound coming from his chest and she knew she had pleased him.

Abruptly he broke off the kiss.

Taking her shoulders, he squeezed with gentle pressure. He almost looked angry. "I'd better get you home, Lily. I'll talk to the sheriff about McGee. Wait for me at the wagon." He took his suit jacket and laid it over her shoulders.

Puzzled by his odd behavior, Lily did as she was told. Tyler had answered her innermost dreams with a kiss so potent and passionate, her head swam with vivid images. No fantasy she could ever conjure up would have equal measure to the reality. Tyler Kincaide has kissed her, but good. But he'd stopped too soon, seeming to berate himself as if he'd committed a terrible sin. She saw the look of regret in his eyes, then condemnation.

Why hadn't he enjoyed the passion they shared as much as she had? Was he just being kind?

Lily leaned against the buckboard and stared up at the night sky. A warm breeze drifted lazily by, calming her nerves. Her dress was in ruins, her hair smattered with dirt, her body bruised, but Lily had never felt more alive.

And Tyler was taking her home.

"Hold still, Tyler," Lily said, dabbing at the blood caked onto his face. "You don't want to wake Bethann with all your grumbling."

Tyler sat on the kitchen chair in the dimly lit room, breathing in Lily's lilac scent. "I'm not grumbling, Lily," he defended. Having her bend over him while she administered to his bruises was causing havoc to his insides. Her breasts, plumped up from the tight fit of her dress, were directly at eye level. He couldn't resist taking a sneak peek. But the peek did him more harm than good. Soft and creamy smooth, he itched to touch her there. He fisted his hands.

Hell, he itched to do more than touch.

"Does it ache?" she asked innocently.

Oh, yeah. It ached. "No, not much."

"Good," she said softly. Her breath caressed his cheek. She brought her face close, pouting with a twist of her lips. Surveying him, she shook her head. "I'm afraid there'll be a bump." She fingered his cheekbone. He didn't flinch, he wanted her hands on him. Anywhere.

Tyler closed his eyes and tried to quell this need he had for her. She was an innocent. She was under his protection. She would leave soon.

It didn't matter. None of it. Tyler wanted Lily in his bed. He couldn't have her, he knew, but he wanted her all the same.

Having her touch him was torture. Not having her touch him was…torture. When she slid her fingers in his hair, he looked up, surprised. "Lily?"

She was busy, caressing his scalp. "I'm looking for more bumps, Tyler."

He groaned inwardly. She stood beside him, the soft curve of her breast brushed against his arm.

"Nothing seems to be coming up," she said resolutely.

She was dead wrong. Thankfully the lower half of his body was hidden under the wooden table or she'd see what was coming up. "Th-that's good," he mumbled.

Lily sat down on the chair at an angle to his. She rested her elbow on the table and smiled at him. "I never thanked you for coming to my rescue."

"No thanks necessary."

She straightened. He loved it when indignation lit her soft eyes, darkening them to a deep sky-blue. "Oh, but it is. I don't know what would have happened if you hadn't come along when you did."

Tyler knew, and the thought didn't bode well. He still wondered whether he should have sent McGee to his maker. An image of that man's hands on her made Tyler's blood boil. He couldn't fathom anything else happening to her. Not to Lily.

"I did and that's all that matters." He took hold of her hand. "Try to put it out of your mind, honey."

"But why did you come outside?"

"When I learned you went outside with McGee, I went searching for you. I knew the man was trouble. Randy was your escort. Where in blazes was he all night?"

"Oh, he spent time with me. We danced, then I, uh, well, I don't want to get him in trouble."

"I'm not ignorant to how my men celebrate, Lily.

When I found him, he was booze-blind and emptying his gut.''

Lily flinched.

''Oh, sorry.''

She chuckled. ''I'm not that delicate, Tyler. Your description of Randy surprised me, is all.''

Tyler squeezed the hand he still held. ''It's good to see you laugh tonight.''

''I *was* having fun at the dance.''

''Humph, dancing with every cowpoke west of Louisiana.'' He shot her a narrowed look.

''How would you know? You spent every second in the company of Miss Letty Sue Withers.'' She hoisted her chin.

''Only 'cause I couldn't get near the woman I wanted to dance with.''

Lily gave him a genuine, heartfelt smile and Tyler's heartbeat sped up. ''And who would that be?''

''You.'' He met her eyes directly, the pull of them holding him to the spot. A man could get lost in those eyes, he thought, and not even know it until it was too late.

''Why did you come to the dance, Tyler?''

He pulled his hand off of hers. Admitting the reason, the real reason, would not be wise. He hoped Lily wasn't expecting things of him he couldn't give. He didn't want to hurt Lily, but Tyler had closed off his heart long ago. Nothing much was going to change that. He hesitated answering, rubbing his jaw. ''Wes convinced me I was too young to be put out to pasture.''

''Oh,'' she said, disappointed. ''So it was Wes's idea.''

''Not exactly.''

"You came for Letty Sue, then," she stated quietly in a shaky voice.

The hurt look on her face injured Tyler more than the fist fight he'd just had defending her honor. He closed his eyes briefly, knowing encouraging Lily now would do her more harm than good. "Not exactly. Ah, hell, Lily. What do you want me to say?"

Lily put her hand to her chest. Her blue eyes rounded. "Why I—"

Tyler glanced at her overflowing bosom. His groin throbbed with need of her. He sunk his head in his hands. "It's late Lily, go on to bed."

"But—"

"Please, Lily. For once, no arguments. Just go."

"Well, it is late." She cleaned up the rags and water bowl she'd used administering to him and was halfway out the door when she stopped. Turning, she ran to him quickly and kissed his good cheek. "Thanks again for saving me."

"'Night." This time she made it all the way out of the kitchen and Tyler could breathe again.

Damn. That little peck on the cheek reminded him of the kiss they had shared earlier in the evening, the one he hadn't been able to shove from his mind. Lily's lips, soft, warm, inviting, had felt like heaven. Her mouth was sweet. He doubted she'd been kissed by too many men. He relished her innocence and knew her response to him had been spontaneous and pure. It made him want her all the more.

Heaven help him. He was in deep trouble.

Chapter Fourteen

Lily fingered the delicate blossoms with care. Three beautiful lavender-blue flowers were beginning to bloom. Their vivid color lifted gently toward the sun. With a sigh of contentment, Lily wandered to the side of the house where she'd planted sunflowers and corn. The stalks of both were two feet high, developing evenly in size and color. The sunflowers, blooming now with wide yellow-orange bursts swayed in the slight breeze.

Lily smiled amid her endeavors. Her garden was only one source of her joy. The other, Tyler, had been especially quiet lately. Since the kiss. Lily closed her eyes to the warming rays of sunlight and remembered the texture and taste of his mouth covering hers just two days ago. Each time she recalled the kiss, she tingled inside. Shivers of excitement flowed through her veins. She wanted Tyler to kiss her again.

But he'd been evasive since the night of the dance and overly polite when their paths did cross. She'd catch him at times, in the parlor, puffing on a cheroot, sipping brandy with a look of deep concentration, or out by the corral, arms flung over the fence, staring out.

"Afternoon, Lily."

The rich deep tone of Tyler's voice startled her out of her musings. She turned to find him watching her. "Tyler," she said on a gasp. The sight of him made her head swim with delightful thoughts.

He cast her a brief half smile, flashing only a portion of white teeth. His eyes bore a solemn look, partly narrowed and penetrating. "We need to talk, Lily. Tonight, after Bethann is asleep."

Lily was shocked at his serious tone. Was he angry with her? She bit her lower lip. Tyler's eyes caught the movement, glancing down at her mouth, then back up to gaze steadily into her eyes. He took in a deep breath, waiting for her response.

"All right." She bit down on her lip again, which drew his focus to her mouth a second time. Lily restrained herself from asking what was so darned important. She smiled at him instead.

He took one last glance at her lips, said, "Tonight then," turned on his heel and walked into the barn.

Lily retreated to her bedroom. She poured water from a pitcher and washed her hands and face, throwing a bit of lilac oil into the water. The fragrance helped refresh her and calm her jittery nerves.

Darn the man.

He could still make her heart hammer hard in her chest.

He seemed so intent and serious earlier when he had summoned her. What did he want? She admonished herself for simply not asking why he wanted to speak with her. Now she'd have to go the rest of the afternoon and evening before finding out what was in that man's head.

Lily changed her clothes, putting on a cornflower-blue dress with a lovely lace collar. She glanced in the mirror, perusing her appearance. She wanted to look pretty tonight. For Tyler. And the new blue dress she'd sewn had made her feel that way. The dress was more feminine, hugging her slight curves more tightly, than any other she owned. Not that it was indecent. The dress held to the modest tastes of ranch-town society. And the lace made her feel a bit more...confident. For some unknown reason, Lily felt she'd need all her wits about her tonight.

Three hours later, seated at the kitchen table, Lily took her eyes off of Bethann sinking her teeth down on a biscuit, to look at Tyler. He sipped lemonade and stared at the wall straight ahead. He hadn't even noticed her new dress. Or if he had, he hadn't said a word.

Lily leaned in, trying to snap him out of his silent brooding mood. "How was the meal? I was afraid the chicken roasted a bit too long."

Tyler set down his cup and glanced at her. "It was delicious, Lily. Thank you."

"The potatoes—"

"Were perfect," he offered without a smile.

"And the biscuits seemed too—"

"Light and fluffy, as always, Lily."

Lily slumped back in her chair. The man wanted no part of her conversation tonight.

"Papa, can I ride Pint-Size after supper?" Bethann chimed in after devouring two biscuits.

"Not tonight, darlin'. After you help Lily with the chores, you're off to bed."

"But, Papa, you promised I could ride her."

"Tomorrow is soon enough. You need to get into bed early tonight." Tyler's gaze flickered Lily's way, before glancing back at his daughter.

Bethann's mouth twisted into a disappointed pout. Lily's heart went out to her. Any other evening Tyler would have allowed his daughter the ride.

"How about I read you another chapter of *Little Women*. Would you like that, sweetie?"

Lily knew her offer held little consolation. She lifted her brows slightly to coax her. Bethann had enjoyed listening to the first chapter the other night, but this evening her heart had been set on riding her new pony.

"I guess," she said, looking at her impenetrable father.

It was clear to Lily that Tyler was preoccupied. And Lily had the sinking feeling it had something to do with her.

"Well, then, let's get the dishes cleared." She stood and began gathering the plates. Tyler moved with efficiency, helping her load the dishes into the tub of water by the sink. Bethann wiped down the table.

When the kitchen was cleaned, and all things put back in order, Lily turned to Bethann. "Time for you to wash up and get ready for bed, sweetie. I'll meet you in your bedroom in ten minutes."

"Yes, ma'am," Bethann replied, her face still a picture of disappointment. With a little loving shove, Lily moved her toward her bedroom.

"Go on now, you'll ride Pint-Size tomorrow."

When Lily turned, Tyler's eyes were on her. "She doesn't have to get her way every time, Lily."

Shocked, Lily lifted her eyes to his. "I don't believe

she does. She's just a little girl, Tyler. She needs lots
and lots of love and security. Every girl does.''

Tyler raked his fingers through his hair. He let out
a pent-up sigh. ''I know. And you're doing a fine job
with her. She minds both of us better since you've
been here. It's just hard to always be the one to discipline her.''

''I do my fair share of that, too,'' she stated evenly.

''True enough, you do.''

''But she was disappointed tonight. No harm in
making her feel a little better, is there?''

He shook his head. ''I guess that's what mothers
do. Make their children feel better when they're hurting.''

Lily blinked. ''I do love Bethann, but I'm…I'm not
trying to replace her mother.''

Tyler looked away. His mouth tightened into a fine
thin line. ''I know,'' he said quietly.

Lily ventured further, ''Is that what you wanted to
speak with me about?''

''Uh, no,'' he said, looking at her again. ''Go on
and read her a story. I'll wait for you in my office.''

''You'll come in to kiss her good-night?''

Tyler smiled. ''Sure. I like to listen to her prayers.''

Tyler leaned on the window jamb, the cool spring
breeze blew in and lifted the curtains, causing them to
flap and sway against the window frame. He stared
skyward, noting the smattering of stars out tonight.

Minutes later he heard the door close softly from
behind. He turned to find Lily watching him. She
looked lovely in her cornflower-blue dress, clinging
enticingly to her small bosom, dipping in at the waist
and flaring slightly at the curve of her hips. Blue-eyed

and rosy-cheeked, she looked somewhat hesitant as she stood against the door with hands behind her back.

Hesitant and beautiful, he noted.

"Hi," she said with a shaky smile.

"Lily, please sit down." He gestured to the wing chair facing his desk and watched her approach.

Once seated, he began pacing with arms behind his back. "I know I owe you a deep apology for the other day. I, uh, well, I'm not good with words, but dragging you into the hotel, just wasn't right." He shook his head.

Lily said nothing, but her eyes stayed on him.

"I owe you more than an apology. I owe you an explanation. You see, when I saw Muldoon with you, I...went a little...crazy."

"Why, Tyler?"

"He's not a decent man."

"He said you and he had bad feelings, but he wants to rectify that."

Tyler snorted. "Hardly, Lily. The man would like to see me dead."

"What!" Lily said, coming to the edge of her seat.

Tyler stopped pacing long enough to look her straight in the eyes. "He blamed me for Lizabeth's death, you know that. At the time, I was blaming myself pretty badly, too. Felt I deserved every awful thing that happened to me. Except, for Bethann, I had nothing."

"You had the ranch."

"In my heart, I had nothing. I would get spitting drunk every night. It was the only way I could forget. One night, I was coming out of the saloon when I was jumped and pulled into an alley. Two men beat me near to death."

Lily stood and gasped. Her hand flew to her mouth. "No!"

"I know it was Muldoon who put them up to it. I wasn't so drunk that I couldn't make out what they were saying. They were robbing me, beating on me and laughing. The voices were distorted, but I could swear I heard one say Muldoon would have loved to see the pulverizing I was taking. The other man said the boss paid them to see me beg for mercy."

"Dear heavens. Tyler, what happened?"

"They did nearly kill me. One held me, the other, well…the alcohol I'd consumed nearly cost me my life. I couldn't fight back much. If I'd had my wits about me, they'd have never got the jump on me. I guess luck was on my side, because a group of local cowhands came out of the saloon, saw what was happening and chased the men off. I was laid up for a month after that. I swore I'd get revenge, but Bethann needed her papa and I realized I couldn't go chasing after Muldoon."

"Oh, Tyler," Lily said, coming forward. She placed her hand on his arm. "I'm sorry. I didn't know."

Tyler took Lily's hand into his. "You see, Muldoon is a dangerous man. And I don't want him on my property ever again. I have no way of proving that he was behind what happened to me that night, but I know it was him."

"Yes." Her lovely blue eyes filled with compassion. "I won't let him near Bethann ever again."

"Or you, Lily?" he asked with a warning in his voice. "I don't trust the man at all."

Lily's eyes flashed with fear. "No, I won't let him near me, either."

"Good," he said, releasing her hand.

Lily sat back down. She folded her arms under her chest and shuddered. "I wish you would have told me this earlier."

"It's hard reliving bad memories." With a slight shrug, he added, "And I wanted to spare you this unpleasantness. I thought my asking you to steer clear of Muldoon was enough."

Lily frowned. "It should have been. I should have listened to you. After all, this is your ranch. I have no right imposing my beliefs on you."

"Lily, I'm not putting blame anywhere but with Muldoon. Since he's come to town, I've spoken with the sheriff and there's more. Seems Muldoon was incarcerated for quite some time. He was just recently released."

"He was in prison? Why?"

Tyler took a deep breath. Lily's sweet innocent face was stark now and pensive. He hated that he'd put that look there. No decent woman should have to hear of such things. But this was for her own good—to make her see the kind of man Brett Muldoon really is. "He abused a woman. Beat her so her own mother wouldn't recognize her."

Lily gasped. "Oh, my, Tyler. That's just so awful."

"I'm sorry, Lily. But you had to know."

"I understand everything more clearly now." Lily stood and made her way to the door. "I'm glad you trusted me with this information. I'll be on my guard from now on."

"Lily, don't go. There's more I need to say to you."

A puzzled expression crossed her features. "More?"

"Yes." He rested his hands on the window jamb. With his back to her, he was able to conjure up the words he needed to say. "I, uh, the truth of the matter is, what happened to you the other night at Henderson's barn dance—"

He heard Lily suck in a breath. She probably hated discussing the incident, and Tyler hated putting her through the anguish again, but he had spent long hours thinking on this and had come to a conclusion.

"What about it?" she asked quietly.

He turned to look into her sorrowful eyes. Bracing himself against the window, he conceded, "It damn well shouldn't have happened, Lily."

"I know. It was my fault." Her voice was low in self-condemnation.

"No! It wasn't. But the fact remains, as long as people get notions in their heads, there's bound to be talk. I'm afraid your reputation is at stake. It's partly my fault and I aim to correct the situation."

Lily took a step forward. Her eyes, big as silver dollars, honed in on him. "How?"

He scratched his head, looked down at his boots, glanced at the hem of Lily's dress then mustered the courage to look her straight in the eye. "Well, uh, I think...I really think we...we should get married."

"M-married?" Lily's face flushed. Why did her voice squeak so?

"Yep, Lily. Married." There, he'd said it.

Lily stared at him in disbelief. Hell, he had a hard time believing he was offering marriage to her again. True, he wasn't proposing for the reasons most men do. He didn't want a wife, and Lily deserved more than what he could give, but what better way to keep her safe?

"You'd have my protection, my name. No man would ever get the wrong idea about you again, Lily."

Lily paused, as if deep in thought. Lord, if he only knew what she was thinking. With a tilt of her head, she said slowly, "But you don't want to get married."

The woman could be exasperating at times. "I asked you, didn't I?"

"No, you suggested, commanded. Whatever it was, it certainly wasn't a proposal in the proper way. Do you want to get married?"

Tyler closed his eyes momentarily. "Lily."

"I'd like an answer, Tyler. Then I'll give you mine."

She came within inches of him. He could smell her fresh lilac scent wafting up from her skin. Her hair flowed down around her shoulders. But her face was void of all emotion. She stared blankly, waiting.

"Not actually, no. But I'm willing."

"For my reputation," she said, folding her arms and tapping her foot like a stern schoolmarm.

He nodded slowly. This wasn't going well. Hell, he couldn't figure women out. Weren't most ladies eager to jump into matrimony? He was a decent sort, owned a nice parcel of property and had a daughter Lily loved. What did Lily want, anyhow? He'd already told her he couldn't marry again, least ways not in the real sense. His heart wouldn't allow it. But marrying him would solve all of Lily's financial problems. She'd have a home, and all that went with it, including upholding her reputation.

"And how do you feel about me?" she asked with sugary sweetness. She eyed him speculatively. Her change of mood put him on alert. It was a trap, Tyler was sure. And the room suddenly seemed stifling. Tyler's pores began to leak moisture. He loosened his shirt, undoing a button. "Feel? Uh...I l-like you.

You're good with Bethann. You know how to cook, shoot—''

''I see.''

Her eyes condemned him at that moment. She had a way of making him feel guilty. True, he wanted her in his bed, but he wasn't offering that, unless she chose to come to him. Lord, he wanted her to come to him. But what he was truly offering was a way to keep her reputation intact.

And keep other men away from her.

Ah, hell, he thought, he couldn't afford to have feelings for her. Not real, genuine, you're-the-light-in-my-life sort of feelings. No, he'd had that kind of love once. And the hurt was deep to unbearable, losing it.

''You like me enough to make the sacrifice and marry me?'' Lily's face flamed, her words sharp, cutting.

''No, I—damn it, Lily, you're turning this all around.''

''Don't curse, Tyler.'' She planted her hands on her hips. ''And no, I won't marry you! Not for those reasons. Are you forgetting I'm leaving as soon as I find my uncle?''

Anger seemed to give way to tears. They streamed down her face now. She wiped at them and continued. ''In fact, I—I got a wire j-just the other day, that he'd passed through Fort Worth. S-so you s-see,'' she said on a muffled sob, ''I'll probably find him soon and you won't have to worry about my reputation. I'll be gone before you know it!'' She hoisted her chin and strode to the door.

''Tarnation! Lily!'' he shouted, but was too late. The door slammed right smack in his face. ''I don't want you to go,'' he murmured quietly to the closed door, stunned that he'd voiced what had been pounding in his head for days now. The thought of her leaving etched a hollow ache in his gut but the thought of her staying made him shudder in fear.

Tyler slumped into his desk chair, undoing the rest of his shirt buttons. It did nothing to quell his heat or his frustration. The woman made him burn with…hell, he knew why he was so frustrated. He needed a woman. One that wouldn't make him feel guilty or angry or anything at all. He stood and strode to the door with new determination. It had been too long since he'd visited the Golden Garter Saloon.

Lily caught her breath the minute she closed her bedroom door. She stopped crying immediately and berated herself for letting that man cause her such heartache. Imagine his nerve! *Now* he wanted to protect her reputation, when it was all but ruined, anyway. His was the poorest excuse for a marriage proposal she'd ever heard. Did he believe giving her his name would justify denying her his heart? Because, Lily wanted his heart. She wanted to love and be loved. Was that so wrong? She wished the fool man would open his eyes and see the love she had for him shining in her eyes.

Darn him, anyway.

For a brief moment when he'd offered, Lily had contemplated being his wife. Many women marry for sake of convenience. She needed a home, wanted a family, loved both father and daughter—but she couldn't do it. She had always been prideful. Even when she was penniless, Lily always kept her head held high and expected no less of herself than she expected of others.

Marrying Tyler Kincaide for all the wrong reasons wouldn't be fair to either of them. Besides, Lily deserved love. If the man couldn't open his heart, she'd have to move on. Besides, she couldn't ignore her father's last dying wish to find Uncle Jasper and make a home with him. It was a promise Lily meant to keep.

With that thought in mind, Lily wrapped a shawl around her shoulders and walked outside for a breath of air. The cool breeze lifted her spirits somewhat and she began strolling down a path. The moonlight and hundreds of bright stars lit her way. Ambling along, breathing in the crisp spring air, gave her renewed strength. She'd find her uncle. And once she was settled in her new home, she would write to Bethann each week and when she was old enough, the young girl could come visit Lily. The thought soothed her. She felt a sense of calm, a feeling of peace.

One hour later, Lily was frantic.

"Bethann!" Clutching Miss Daisy, the little girl's doll, Lily scoured the rooms in the house. Bethann wasn't in her bed, or in any other part of the house. She always slept with her doll and the fact that Lily had found it outside the doorway of Tyler's office, didn't bode well. If Bethann overheard the heated conversation Lily'd had with Tyler, no doubt she'd be upset. Maybe upset enough to run away.

Tears pooled in Lily's eyes. She couldn't afford to cry right now. The most important thing was to find Bethann. And Tyler was nowhere to be found, either.

She raced outside, calling Bethann's name. The first place she looked was the barn, where Pint-Size was stabled. It was dark, but she was able to make out images of the animals and no sight of the little girl.

Then she ran to the corral all the while calling out

for Bethann. Lily's heart thundered in her chest. Her mind spun with terrifying thoughts. Bethann by the creek, Bethann injured, hurt and alone.

Pounding on the bunkhouse door, Lily shrieked for Wes to open up. When the door opened slowly, she grabbed at the old man's arms. "Have you seen Bethann?"

Wes scratched his head. "No, missy, I ain't. I been sleepin'."

"Wake up the boys and start searching for her. She's missing. She could be anywhere. Oh, Wes!" Lily held back tears, blocking out the frightening thoughts threatening to filter in. "Please hurry, Wes. I can't find her!"

Then a thought struck that gave her cause for hope. "Tyler's gone. Maybe he took her with him. Where is he? Do you know?"

"Yes, ma'am, I do. But it ain't likely she's with her pa. Tyler rode out a while ago. He went into town."

"Town?" This late? Why would Tyler go all the way into town at this hour? When Wes didn't offer more, Lily pressed the issue. "I need to know where he is, Wes. He's got to know Bethann's missing."

"I'll go git him," Wes offered automatically.

"No! You stay here and organize the search. We need every able-bodied man to look for her. Wake up the boys. Tell them to search by the creek. Send someone to Rhonda Mae's, others should spread out over the land. We've got to find her, Wes. I'll get Tyler. Now tell me where he is."

Wes hesitated about a second under Lily's scrutiny, then finally relented. She noted a flicker in his wrinkled eyes. "He's at the saloon."

"The Golden Garter? Fine, I'll take the buckboard."

"You ain't goin' to town by yoreself. Tyler'd have my hide. And it ain't fittin' a lady steppin' in a saloon."

"Let me worry about that. Bethann's the important one here. Now, please have someone hitch up the buckboard. We're wasting time."

With a nod, Wes woke up his crew and began barking orders. The old man could move fast in a crisis. Years of experience, Lily thought. As she headed for the barn, she said a silent prayer for Bethann's safety.

Nothing else mattered.

Chapter Fifteen

The taste of whiskey soured in his throat. Tyler held the glass up, peering through the amber liquid and recalling a time when liquor had controlled his life. He'd lost himself in its mind-numbing depths after Lizabeth died. Now, seeking its comfort once again, left an empty void inside. He slowly lowered the glass.

"What's the matter, sugar? Don't you like what we're serving up tonight?"

In the dimly lit room, Tyler glanced at the redhead with the pouty crimson smile. Her face, just a little too bright with color, the shine in her flickering moss-green eyes a little too stoic to be considered genuine. He caught the glitter of gold from the garter she wore around her thigh as she sat next to him on the bed.

"Guess not, Renee."

"Aw, I bet I can fix that," she cooed, scooting closer. Her hands worked at the buttons of his shirt. When the imprint of her hand scorched his chest, Tyler glanced up. "Why don't you stretch out on the bed," she said in a low sultry voice.

Tyler covered his hands over hers, stopping her

from going further. With a shake of his head, he took her hands off him. "Sorry, darlin'."

She seemed momentarily disappointed. "You're sure?"

He hung his head. "Sure as anything. Sorry, again."

She moved away from him and chuckled. "Don't be. This happens from time to time." Lifting his glass to her lips, she took a quick sip of whiskey.

"What does?" He raised his eyes to hers.

"One of two things." She glanced down at the area between his outstretched thighs. "I don't believe you've got a physical problem."

Tyler widened his eyes, feeling lines form on his forehead. "No," he choked. He didn't have that kind of a problem at all.

"Then it's a woman," the redhead said with certainty.

Tyler braced an elbow on his knee and rubbed his jaw. "A woman, you say?"

Renee gave him a smug smile. "Am I wrong, Tyler?"

Tyler pursed his lips, ready to deny her claim. He huffed. "No, guess not."

He couldn't lay a hand on Renee without thinking about Lily. Damn, the woman was driving him crazy. He wanted her, but knew he couldn't have her. Maybe if she had agreed to his marriage proposal, she would have come to him. But knowing the futility of the situation didn't squelch the strong desire he had for her.

Renee sat down on the bed and crossed her legs, swinging them out. "You're in love, Tyler Kincaide."

Tyler opened his mouth to definitely deny this

claim, but a boisterous commotion coming up from the first floor of the saloon interrupted his thoughts.

Hoots, hollers and loud laughter filled the small room.

"You can't go up there, lady!"

"Aw, let her go. We need some excitement 'round here."

"I'll be damned if I let my woman up there!"

Curiosity sparked, Tyler stood and opened the door. Then his mouth fell open. Lily stood on the opposite side of the doorway, ready to knock. She took in his appearance, then glanced past him to Renee, sitting casually on the bed. Her eyes rounded, taking on the appearance of giant-size sapphires. Tyler blocked her view with his body and tucked in his shirt. He gulped. "Lily! What in tarnation are you doing here?"

"I wouldn't have interrupted, if it wasn't urgent." She stared at his exposed chest. Realizing how this must look to her, he began buttoning his shirt. Renee's laughter from behind didn't help matters.

"You're not interrupting."

Lily ignored him. She had a determined look on her face. And a fearful one. "Bethann's missing. I can't find her anywhere. I thought you should know. I've got all the men out looking for her."

"What do you mean, missing? Lily, we put her to bed early tonight."

"I know, I think she overheard us...arguing about..." She glanced past him once again, into the room then she lowered her voice. "About getting married. I found her doll on the floor out by your office."

On a heavy sigh he said, "That little one's got to learn not to eavesdrop." He turned to retrieve his hat. Renee came up from behind and handed it to him. She flashed her moss-green eyes, then winked. Tyler cringed inwardly. He was sandwiched between two women. One was grinning like a miner who'd just struck gold, the other was frowning, casting him a look of disgust.

Slowly, Tyler slid his hand into his pocket.

"No charge tonight, Tyler." Renee winked again. "Go on, and find your little girl."

Tyler nodded, feeling heat rise up his neck to singe his face. Glancing from Renee to Lily as both women watched him, he jammed his hat onto his head and took Lily by the arm. Tight-lipped, he said, "Come on. Let's get out of here."

Tyler worked the reins of the buckboard expertly, bringing the wagon to a stop right in front of the barn. He hopped out and reached for Lily's hand. She was too quick for him. She jumped down by herself, nearly tripping on the hem of her new blue dress. Both raced over to Wes, who was leisurely smoking a cheroot by the corral gate.

They reached him at the same time. "Well, did you find her?" Lily asked, nearly out of breath, more from fright than from the run.

"Randy found 'er halfways to Rhonda Mae's, sound asleep in a patch a grass."

Lily slumped with relief. "Thank God!" She leaned her body against the corral railing. "Where is she?"

"In bed, where she ought to be."

Lily made a move to leave. Tyler took her arm. She didn't want his hands on her. She just wanted to forget the whole evening. It had gone from bad to worse real fast. The shock of seeing him with that woman was just settling in. In one instant, he was asking to marry her. In the next, he was in the arms of a prostitute. And her humiliation equaled her mortification when she'd dragged him out of that room to search for his daughter.

Lily was glad she'd listened to her pride and refused his offer of marriage.

"We'll check on her together," he said resolutely. Lily couldn't deny him the chance to see his daughter safely tucked into her bed. And she had to see the little girl herself, before she'd get one wink of sleep.

Wes sighed. "Seems the little 'un, caught a whiff of a marriage proposal."

They both turned to Wes. "Is that why she ran away?" Lily asked, almost certain it was. A sense of dread engulfed her already-fragile heart.

Wes puffed on his cheroot. "Appears so. She was hurtin' real bad. Seems to me, the two of you ought to make up yore minds, before that little 'un gets all confused."

Tyler put his head down. "That conversation wasn't meant for her ears, Wes."

"I know it, but she loves Lily, wants her to stay on."

Lily gasped. Her heart tightened with sorrow for Bethann. She'd never meant to bring sadness to that dear child's life. If only Tyler had feelings for her, Lily would come back after she found her uncle. She'd not abandon Bethann. But Tyler didn't love her. How could she marry a man just because it suited their practical needs? No, Lily couldn't do it. She couldn't deny her heart Tyler's love. The pain of staying on would be far worse than the pain of leaving.

Lily wrestled free of Tyler's grasp. "I've got to go see her." She ran up the steps and into the house.

Tyler's footfalls fell into step with hers. She quieted once in the hallway. Tiptoeing into her room, Lily viewed Bethann, swollen-eyed, clutching her pillow, sound asleep. Her breaths came in irregular puffs, the result of so much crying. Lily bit her lip to catch her own sorrowful tears from escaping.

Tyler sidled up next to her. He was too close for comfort as his breath caressed her neck. It was dark in the room, and having him stand so close as they both watched Bethann sleep, seemed so intimate, so right. But it wasn't meant to be. Lily scooted away and focused all of her attention on the sleeping child.

"Poor little angel. She's had such a tough time, losing her mother, trying to adjust." Her innermost thoughts came out in a whisper. Lily saw Tyler stiffen his shoulders.

"I'm doing the best I can," he said quietly.

Turning to see the pain on Tyler's weary face, for an instant Lily thought she could just marry him. And give Bethann the security and love she needed. And Tyler, too, stubborn as he was, needed love. Her love. But he wouldn't see it. Her thoughts softening to him, she wondered if she could stay. Maybe in time, he'd grow to love her.

Then a vision of the near-naked redhead on the bed in an upstairs room of the Golden Garter Saloon flashed like lightning into her head. And Tyler, looking guiltier than sin itself when she'd found him there, made Lily bristle with anger. And regret.

She bent and gently brushed a soft kiss on Bethann's forehead, then turned to leave the room. Tyler followed her.

"Lily, wait. Please," he asked in a soft plea.

She couldn't look at him. She stopped at her bedroom door and glanced down at her hand as she grasped the knob. "You're doing a fine job with Bethann. I—I'm tired, Tyler. Good night."

"But, Lily," he said, stepping closer.

Feeling the heat of his gaze on her back, she quickly entered her room.

She slumped against the door and once hearing Tyler's hesitant footsteps retreat, Lily sobbed silently.

"You know what you did last night put a fright in both your pa and me, Bethann." Lily kept her voice calm, soothing. In a crouched position, she worked her fingers around the base of the flowers that were beginning to bud. Lifting and tossing any wayward weeds in the garden, she spied Bethann doing the same in a patch next to her.

"Sorry, Miss Lily," she said, not looking up. Her little fingers worked the soil, the way Lily had taught her.

"You were upset. It's understandable, but, sweetie, that conversation wasn't meant for little ears." With a small shovel, Lily upended the soil, giving it a good turn, then took her watering bucket and doused the roots.

"But don't you want to stay with us?" Bethann's round eyes beseeched her.

Lily took her gloves off, giving them a swat against the porch steps to loosen the mud. She reached for Bethann. "Come here."

Bethann scooted into Lily's arms. The two sat on the ground. Lily rocked her. "I don't want to leave you, Bethann, you must remember that."

"But you won't marry my papa."

"I—I can't. I don't expect you to understand right

now. But we'll always be friends, you and I. You'll never really lose me. I promise.''

''Papa says you havta find your uncle.''

''That's right, you know that. We've talked about it. It was my father's last dying wish that I find Uncle Jasper and make a home with him and his family. My papa worried over me, the way your papa worries over you. I promised him, Bethann. It's something I have to do.''

''Will you come back when you find him?''

''If I say I will, no matter how far away I am or how long it takes, it's my promise to you. I'll come back one day for a visit. And when you get older, maybe your papa will let you come to stay with me a while, too.''

''But,'' she whimpered, ''I don't want you to go a'tall.''

''Oh, Bethann! I wish I could stay.'' Lily closed her eyes and hugged her tight, rocking in a swaying motion. ''I'm sorry, little one. I truly am.''

Bethann nuzzled deeper, pressing her head into Lily's chest. ''I love you, Miss Lily.''

''I love you, too. And when people love each other, they stay right here,'' she said, planting a fist on her chest, ''right in our hearts. So you see, they are always with you. *I'll* always be with you. And you'll always be with me.''

Bethann poked her fist at her chest. ''Right here?''

Lily covered her tiny fist with her hand and applied slight pressure. ''That's it. That's what love is all about.''

She stroked Bethann's long unruly hair. She couldn't fathom not seeing her every day. Lily had once told Tyler she wasn't trying to replace Bethann's mother, but deep in her heart, Lily knew she had done just that.

Unintentionally she had become more than Bethann's nanny, she had come to love her as a mother loves a daughter. The child meant everything to her.

"What about my papa?" She moved her fist from her chest to Lily's. "Is he here, too?"

Lily sucked in a breath. "Oh, yes, Bethann, he's here, too." She loved Tyler more each day—there seemed no hope for it. But it was futile to love a man who refused her at every turn. Lily realized the truth in that now. Tyler would never be hers. "Let's not think about all this right now. It's far too depressing for such a beautiful sunny day. I need you to promise never, ever, to run away again."

Bethann nodded. "I promise."

Lily kissed her on the cheek. "Good girl." She stood and reached for Bethann's hand. "Let's go check the sunflowers. I bet there's a tall one ready to pick."

Bethann jumped up. "Okay," she said, placing her hand in Lily's.

They were partway there when the rumbling sound of an approaching horse made them both turn toward the entrance gate off in the distance.

"Uncle Brett!" Bethann exclaimed with a shrill of excitement.

Dapper as always, the tall, thin man, wearing a dark suitcoat, tie and vest, rode proudly in the saddle. Lily glanced around. The ranch hands all seemed to be gone at the moment. She knew for certain, Tyler was tending to a sick steer in the east pasture.

With a shiver, she realized she'd have to handle this

situation by herself. "Go on inside, Bethann. Wash up and stay put until I call for you."

"But," the little girl said, pointing to the approaching man on horseback, "Uncle Brett's here."

Lily made her voice as stern as she ever had in the past. "Do as I say, Bethann. Now. Don't come outside unless I call for you." She swatted the little girl's behind gently for emphasis. "Go on."

Thankfully, Bethann obeyed. With one battle won, Lily readied herself for the next. It would probably be her most challenging. She stood tall, straightening her spine, and waited for Brett Muldoon.

He reached her moments later, wearing a charming smile. Tipping his hat, he greeted her, "'Morning, Lillian. You sure do look pretty today."

Lily brushed dust from her skirt, then looked at him directly. "What are you doing here, Mr. Muldoon?"

His charming smile faded. "Why, that's not a very hospitable welcome. Have I done something to offend you?"

She wanted to tell him just what he could do with his engaging ways. If what Tyler told her was true, and she believed him wholeheartedly, then this man shouldn't spend another moment with Bethann. He most certainly shouldn't be on Kincaide land. Or expect friendship from her. "Tyler doesn't want you here. You'd better leave right now, before he returns."

He leaned over in the saddle. "I have a right to see my niece. Lillian, you've helped me in the past. I thought we were friends."

"You're right," Lily said, realizing her blunder, "stay here. I'll be right back."

Glancing his way, she noted his smug expression. In a minute she hoped to wipe it clean away.

When she returned, Brett had tethered his horse and was standing by the front steps.

"Where's Bethann?" He cocked his head in question.

"I've asked her to stay inside, Mr. Muldoon. I have to give this back to you." She handed him the pearl comb he'd gifted her with days ago. "I no longer have need for it."

Muldoon looked at the comb, then twisted his lips. "I see. You don't need the comb or my friendship, is that it?"

Lily swallowed. "Yes. It's better this way. Tyler wants you off his land and nowhere near his daughter."

"And do you think that's best, to deprive Bethann of her only other relation?"

Lily balked. Hadn't she been looking for that very thing herself? To seek out and find her only living relation. But Tyler's words rang true. She was beginning to see the dangerous side to Brett Muldoon. She needed to get him off Kincaide property before Tyler returned, or there would surely be trouble. "You've seen her. Spent time with her. That's all Tyler will allow. When she's old enough, Bethann can make her own choices, but until then, I must insist on carrying out Tyler's wishes."

"And that means I can no longer visit her?"

"Yes, I'm afraid that's exactly what it means."

His eyes flickered, then narrowed. Lily took a step back. The movement did not go unnoticed by Muldoon. "He's poisoned your mind against me. At one time you believed me worthy of your friendship. What's changed?"

Lily thought it unwise to engage in further conversation with him, especially since she knew what this man was capable of doing. "I told you, I'm upholding Tyler's decision. He is a man I respect and admire. I'm being paid to see to Bethann's welfare while I'm on the ranch. And right now, it's in everyone's best interest if you leave immediately, Mr. Muldoon."

Fury heated his gaze. The charming mask he wore disappeared, replaced by an icy glare. "Tyler is a bastard. He killed my sister. You'd be wise to take my advice and leave here before he destroys you, too."

"That would never happen." Lily hoisted her chin in defiance. Tyler may not love her, but he'd never let any harm come to her. She knew that as sure as the sun shining up in the sky. She softened her voice, hoping to convince the man of Tyler's innocence. "Everyone knows what happened to your sister was an accident. Tyler was no more to blame than you or I. It was unfortunate."

She watched Brett Muldoon throw his foot in the stirrup, then lift himself up onto his horse. With a snarl on his lips he said, "The only unfortunate accident was the two of them ever meeting."

It was no use. Lily couldn't get through to the man. His mind was made up. "I think you'd better go."

"Oh, I'll go. Remember my warning, Lillian. Get away from Kincaide before harm comes to you, too."

Lily stared into eyes burning with hatred. She wondered if his warning was just that, or had it been a threat? Standing on the porch steps, Lily watched him ride off until his image was no more than a speck on the horizon.

That evening, Lily and Bethann ate a quiet meal together. Tyler had left word with Wes earlier in the day that he wouldn't be joining them for dinner. Lily wondered if he'd gone back into town to finish what he'd started with the buxom redhead from the night before. Not able to touch her own food, Lily watched Bethann eat heartily, happy to see the events of the past day hadn't hurt the little one's appetite in the least.

But Lily worried about Tyler's whereabouts. Her stomach knotted at the thought of him returning to the Golden Garter. Jealousy ran deep. She didn't want Tyler with any other woman. It didn't matter that he'd pay for her services or not. She was a woman and Tyler would be… Oh, she didn't want to dwell on such notions.

And her stomach twisted even more, pondering Tyler's reaction hearing about Muldoon's visit today. She had to tell him.

After hours of reading in her room and weary from today's incident with Muldoon, Lily undressed and got into bed. She must have dozed off, because a soft knocking at her door startled her. She rose abruptly and rubbed her eyes.

"Lily, you awake in there?" Tyler whispered.

"Yes, uh, just a minute." Lily ran a hand through her hair, leaving it to flow down her back, then grabbed for her white cotton robe. Quickly jamming her arms into the sleeves, she wrapped the tie around her middle as she reached to open the door.

"Evenin'," he said with a crooked grin. His eyes danced, taking in her appearance.

"Tyler, I tried waiting up for you. We have to talk," she said in a hushed tone. She stood in the open doorway, wearing nothing more than a thin chemise and robe, staring into twinkling dark eyes. He was the most handsome man she'd ever known. And right now, the intent look he was giving her made her heart flutter.

Living under his roof and seeing him every day, still didn't temper the strong emotions Lily had every time she laid eyes on him. If anything, the close proximity heightened her feelings.

"I know, that's why I'm here. May I come in?"

Come in? When she hesitated, he added, "We're going to wake up Bethann if we talk with me half out and you half in your room."

It was highly improper, she should suggest the parlor, but she hadn't been the picture of propriety lately, anyway. She opened the door wider and allowed him entrance, then closed the door behind him.

"I don't know how you've heard," she began on a whisper, "but I suppose it's good that you know."

The lines on his forehead wrinkled and his eyes narrowed. "Know what, Lily?"

"Why, that Brett Muldoon showed up here today."

Tyler's calm expression faltered. He took a step closer and glared at her. "Did anything happen? Did he hurt you? Bethann?"

"No, no. Nothing like that. I told him to leave. I thought you knew."

Tyler shook his head and lowered himself down on the bed. Bracing his elbows on his knees, he raked his fingers through his hair. "Damn, maybe you better tell me everything."

Five minutes later, after undue questioning by Tyler, she had related the entire conversation, nearly word for word, that she'd had with Muldoon.

Tyler stood and stepped closer to her. His eyes pinned her down with a look so...intense Lily wanted to back up against the wall. But she didn't, she remained where she was, rooted to the spot.

"What you did..." He began softly, but didn't finish the sentence. It was as if he wanted to say more but couldn't.

"I didn't want that man near Bethann. Not after what he'd done to you."

Tyler took another step closer. There was less than a foot separating them. Lily held her breath. His gaze pierced hers, capturing her with a slow burn. He reached out with his hand and skimmed a finger down her arm. She trembled from his touch. His eyes shone with what Lily regarded as admiration. "You stood up to that man, defended me. Chased him off my land."

Lily swallowed, then nodded. "He, uh, you were...right. He still blames you. I was afraid..." Lily couldn't think beyond the sensations Tyler was creating along the path of her arm. She tingled with awareness.

"Did he frighten you?" he asked, taking his eyes off her arm long enough to look at her.

She gulped, seeing his dark lashes lift to her. "No, not in that way. I was afraid you'd come back and he'd...you and he would..."

"You were worried about me?"

She nodded. "I—I didn't w-want any trouble."

He slid both hands up and down her arms. Lily thought to turn away. Or to send him out of her room. For half a second. Then she banished the thought. Tyler was staring at her lips. She wanted him to kiss her. She hoped he would.

"If he's your enemy, Tyler, then he's mi—"

Tyler's mouth covered hers. Lily relished the warmth and firm texture of his lips pressing her into a deep kiss. He cupped his hand behind her head and her loose hair flowed over his arm. His other hand wrapped around her waist, bringing her closer yet.

His rigid, well-honed, muscular body enveloped her. Lily felt wrapped in a cocoon of safety. Desire flared in her woman's center, bringing on a hot, moist heat. He continued the kiss, slanting his lips over hers, moving her body in tune with his rhythm. A deep groan escaped as he brought his lips to her throat and pressed his hips into hers.

Lily braced a hand to his chest and pulled away slightly. She gasped for a breath, then rasped, "T-Tyler, is this w-what you did with that w-woman last night?"

Chapter Sixteen

"Tarnation, Lily! You sure do know how to break a mood." A bucket of ice water splashing Tyler right smack in the face wouldn't have startled him more. He stepped away and stared at her. Rounded sky-blue eyes sparked with curiosity questioned him.

Lily's face flamed. She touched a finger to her swollen lips. "I can't get it out of my head, Tyler." She turned away from him and hugged her middle. "I know I shouldn't have gone up there last night. The barkeeper warned me. And now I'm paying the price, because the vision keeps tormenting me."

Tyler scraped his boots across the wood floor noisily, moving to the window. He needed a distraction, something to restore his wits. Lily's blunt question nearly undid him. And her response to his kiss was potent enough to destroy any man.

Gazing up, the sky was filled with hundreds of stars shining brightly. But he couldn't enjoy the view. Lily's lilac scent permeated the room, reminding him of the woman he'd held in his arms just seconds ago. He opened the window to let the cool evening breeze dilute her feminine scent. "What vision exactly, Lily?"

"Of you and that...that woman," she said breath-lessly.

Tyler winced. How had life become so compli-cated? If only he could make Lily understand why he went there. But to do so would mean revealing things he wasn't sure he wanted to face. "It was a mistake, my going there."

"Men go there for one reason. You can be honest with me, I won't break in two hearing the truth. I know what you wanted," she said quietly.

Tyler closed his eyes and knocked his head against the glass of the window. He could envision the blush creeping up her lovely neck. This conversation was costing her a measure of her pride. But she was dead wrong. He should let her go on believing what she was thinking. It would be better all the way around. And he should get out of her room right quick. But he couldn't do it.

"No, it's not what I wanted."

"I...see."

By the doubting tone of her voice, Tyler knew she hadn't a clue as to what he really wanted. "No, I don't think you do, honey." He turned to look at her. The length of the room separated them.

"Then," she said, darting her tongue out to lick at her swollen lips, "what is it that you want?"

Tyler held back his retort for one brief second. He walked over to stand in front of her. She stood boldly, looking beautiful in the moonlight slanting its way across the room. "The only woman I want is...you, Lily."

Lily swallowed and stared up at him.

He brought his hand to her soft rosy cheek. "I couldn't touch another woman. Lord help me, but you're the only one I want."

He moved away from her and put his hands into his back pockets. "You won't agree to marry me, and I won't compromise you, so—"

"Tyler," she said on a breath, "I want you, too."

To his surprise, Lily came forward and lifted her mouth to his, kissing him soundly. Her sweet taste, her immediate passion, nearly knocked him to the ground. She was bold and beautiful and so terribly innocent. He enfolded her in his arms to keep her close. "Ah, Lily, this isn't proper."

She kissed him again. "I know."

"You know and you're still willing?" A smile was beginning to emerge from beneath all of Tyler's rising qualms. How he wanted this woman.

There was a light in her eyes, shining like the clearest river waters on a bright sunny day. And the smile that graced her face beamed with delight. "I'm twenty-five years old, Tyler. It's time for me."

"But—"

"You *do* want me?"

"You know I do, but—"

"Damn it, Tyler, kiss me again. I won't change my mind."

"Cursing again, *Miss Lily?*" He grinned and swept her up in his arms. "Now that's highly improper."

"You see? I'm a fast learner," she teased.

"That much I know." He looked down at her clinging to his neck, the tie on her thin cotton robe falling away to reveal creamy skin and a tempting view of treasures that lay hidden beneath her chemise.

"And maybe it's time I did some improper things, Tyler," she offered with a sweet sigh.

Tyler groaned his pleasure and kissed her lips. "I doubt you could do anything really improper, Lily, but I'll try my best to teach you."

Lily snuggled closer in his arms. With his heart thudding in his chest and his body tight with desire, he carried her to his room.

Tyler closed his bedroom door with a soft kick. He lowered Lily down onto the bed. Nervous, and biting her lip, she remained there in eager anticipation. More than anything, she wanted to be in Tyler's arms. He looked down at her. The hunger in his dark eyes smoldered and a shiver ran up Lily's spine.

"You're so beautiful, Lily," he said softly.

"My heart's pounding so fast, Tyler."

"Mine, too."

He lay down next to her and took her into his arms. His lips brushed over hers lightly then skimmed her eyelids, nose, cheeks and chin. Lily caught his lips once again and he stroked his tongue over the contours of her mouth. Instinctively, Lily allowed him entrance by parting her lips. His touch let off an explosion of reactions all over her body. Like dynamite, the tiny blasts took her by surprise and she wiggled and squirmed, then a soft whimper erupted from her throat.

Sensations swirled. Lily was enveloped in a hazy glow of passion. Tyler slipped the robe from her shoulders, unlacing the tie. Then slowly, keeping his eyes steady on her, he raised her chemise over her head. Lily thought to be embarrassed, to hide from his scrutiny, but Tyler's eyes never wavered from her, and the appreciation she witnessed there assured her more than any words he could utter at the moment. As he let his gaze roam slowly over the slight curves of her naked body, his swift intake of breath made Lily feel, for the very first time in her life, truly beautiful.

No man had ever made her feel that way. She doubted any other man could. Lily gave her heart freely, loving Tyler, wanting so much for him to love her back. She held on to that notion, a flourishing flutter to her insides, like a butterfly spreading the wings of hope.

She put her hand to his cheek, bringing her lips to his. The kiss was filled with emotion, pent-up from years of wanting, a desire too strong and potent to be denied any longer. She whispered into his mouth, "Touch me, Tyler."

A slight slant to his beautiful mouth told her she had amused him. "I'm trying to go slow, Lily. For you."

"Don't," she said in a quiet plea. "I'm not afraid." And the honesty in her words struck her with powerful force. She wasn't afraid to trust in this man. Tyler would never hurt her. She cared little for propriety now, the rules of society had no import on what she was feeling. Her reputation mattered not. Being here with Tyler, loving him with every fiber of her being…was right. She knew it deep in her heart, the truth bursting forth like a glorious new dawn. She loved this man wholly and completely and that was all that truly mattered.

Tyler stroked her cheek. "You are a special woman."

He stood and shed his clothes quickly. Except for the time she administered to him when he was near death, she had never seen a man fully unclothed. And she certainly had never seen a man...aroused.

Lily gulped, but the sight to behold was too magnificent to turn away. She kept her gaze focused on him as he stood in front of her. The rapid beats of her heart thudded in her chest and she wondered if the town of Sweet Springs could hear her and know what sizzling sensations whirled inside her trembling body.

"Are you afraid now?" he asked gently.

She lifted her eyes to his and shook her head slowly.

Another smile from him and Lily's heart rate accelerated even more. He was the most breathtaking man she had ever known. And when he lay back down beside her and took her into his arms again, Lily's love poured out in a passion so deep, so natural, so stirring, she may have even shocked Tyler from her responses. Although his soft agonized groans and the way he caressed her body told her she had done nothing but please him.

His lips left her mouth and traveled a path down her throat. A rich aching exploded below her waist when he cupped her breast and slid his tongue over her awaiting peak. She arched up, hips riding high and Tyler moved his other hand to the center between her thighs. When his fingers touched her there, she felt a jolt of heat and a moan of ecstasy escaped her parted lips. She bit down on them, containing the sound and endured the torturous pleasure he was evoking.

Her body wanted to dance, to move, to undulate under his bold stroking. She held back, wondering at the pressure building. "Tyler?"

He kissed her. "It's natural, Lily. Let go, honey."

Trusting him, she did just that. Her hips dipped and rose with a rhythm that both were creating. His mouth moved over the length of her, touching her, kissing her, caressing her everywhere. She felt treasured. Cherished. And a deep and potent sensation coursed through her, heightening her awareness as she reached out for more.

Tyler gave her a deep satisfying kiss, then lifted himself over her. He closed his eyes as he entered her carefully. "Lily," he said on a low breath.

There was a small bursting pain. Lily gasped, then the ache subsided. Tyler waited, she thought, patiently. "Sorry, honey. Happens like this the first time."

She nodded. Tears of joy threatened. Lily couldn't believe she was joined with this beautiful man. Tyler had once been her dream, a fantasy that lay hidden in the deep recesses of her mind. Only in her most private times would she allow herself to peek inside to wonder what it would be like to join with this man. Oh, how she had wondered. But the dream was real now and better than any of Lily's vivid imaginings. His body slowly began moving over her; she marveled at the rightness of his touch. He was her reality and no matter what happened between them afterward, she would always have this one wonderful night.

"How do you feel, honey?" he asked minutes later with concern in his voice. He slid down next to her and enfolded her into his arms.

She laid her head on his chest and smiled when his hand toyed with tendrils of her hair. "Like I've just gotten down from Pearl after a long ride."

Tyler's chest lifted and rumbled when he broke out in a deep chuckle. "Ah, Lily." He kissed the top of her head.

"It was wonderful." That was an understatement. Lily's heart burst in wonder and delight. She was in the arms of the man she adored and he had just made love to her. She never wanted this night to end. She wanted an eternity of nights like this to block out the harsh reality of day.

But if all she had was this one night with Tyler, then Lily knew she would summon up the recollection with a clarity and truth that would belie the sad and lonesome years to come.

Sitting up, Tyler adjusted a pillow behind his head, then did the same for Lily. She made sure she covered herself, almost up to her chin, with the sheet.

Tyler bent over and lit his bedside lamp. The room took on a soft yellow glow. Reaching down from his side of the four-poster, he brought out a large rectangular package. "I rode into town today to pick this up. I was going to give it to you tomorrow, but now seems more fitting."

"For me?" Lily glanced at the large box, both surprised and excited. Discounting Muldoon, she couldn't remember the last time she'd received a gift from anyone. But this wasn't a gift from just anyone—it was from Tyler.

"Go ahead, open it."

Lily glanced at him. He gave her a reassuring nod. Slowly, she raised the top of the box and moved aside the wrapping paper. "Oh, it's beautiful." She lifted up a tan doeskin split riding skirt. The fabric had a firm texture, but was soft to the touch.

Tyler pointed down to the box. "There's a vest to match."

Lily stroked the vest that lay at the bottom of the box. The rich brown stitching along the lapel formed an intricate swirling pattern, both delicate and bold.

"Oh, Tyler. This is so lovely…and thoughtful. It's the most beautiful gift I've ever received. Th-thank y-you."

"You deserve it, Lily. And so much more," he said softly. "I had Emma Mayfield's sister make it up. She's quite handy, owns her own shop in Abilene. It was fortunate for me she's visiting Emma for a spell."

Lily came out of her daze hearing Emma's name. She breathed, "You mean, Emma knows about this?"

Tyler nodded. "Uh-huh."

"Now the whole town of Sweet Springs will know."

Tyler frowned. "I thought about that. Your reputation again, Lily. You know how Emma gossips. But I wanted you to have the finest and that meant asking Emma's sister."

Tears pooled in her eyes. The gift was truly a sweet gesture from Tyler. He wanted her to have the finest. Didn't the man know, all she wanted, all she had ever wanted since she'd known him, was his love? Oh, to have Tyler whisper the words she so desperately wanted to hear. The gift of his love would make her heart soar.

And that would truly be the finest gift of all.

"Don't cry, Lily. It hurts to see you cry." He brushed the tears from her cheeks. His touch, ever so gentle, reminded her of the way he had made love to her just moments ago. Tenderly. He had given a part of himself to her tonight, and the sharing of their bodies had been glorious.

Lily wasn't a greedy woman, but was it so wrong to want his heart, too? She knew now, she'd been right to refuse his proposal of marriage. Her heart would splinter in two if she'd married him without his love.

She'd settle for nothing else now. Nothing else would do.

Bravely and taking in a deep breath, she gave him her brightest smile and halted any more tears from flowing.

"That's better, honey. No more tears from now on."

From now on? Dare she hope of a life filled with love and laughter with Tyler by her side and Bethann in tow? "I love my present, Tyler."

"I hoped you would. I wanted to show you how much...never mind." He frowned, then looked out the window.

"I gave the pearl comb back to Brett Muldoon. I didn't want it or anything else that man offered."

"Ah, Lily."

"I guess I was a fool to believe him."

"Shh," he said with a finger to her lips. "Let's not speak of it again." Tyler removed the parcel from her lap and scooted her back down on the bed.

"Tyler?"

His lips met hers briefly in the softest kiss. He spoke into her mouth. "There's more to learn, sweetheart."

Lily caressed his muscled chest, letting her fingers lace into the spiraling hairs there. Bringing her lips to his throat, she drizzled kisses up to his chin and gazed into his eyes. "Teach me *everything,* Tyler."

Pleasantly shocked, Tyler's mouth dropped opened. He guided her hand under the sheet to feel the silkiness of his thick manhood. Lily looked at Tyler in wonder, stroking him gently.

"Ah, Lily, you do learn fast, don't you?"

Tyler dragged her under the covers and gave her a passionate lesson she'd not soon forget.

* * *

Lily's coughing woke him. Lying behind her, he huddled her closer in his arms and breathed into her satiny thick hair. But instead of the familiar scent of lilacs, he smelled...smoke.

Tyler jolted upright and lifted his nose in the air, but that proved unnecessary because once fully coherent, he witnessed the smoke streaming in from under his doorway. "Lily, honey, wake up. Quick, get dressed."

He bounded from the bed, putting on his clothes in a fast hurry. "I've got to check on Bethann!"

Lily donned her nightdress and robe then opened the bedroom window. Tyler watched the smoke escape, then carefully creaked open his door. He turned his head away as a blast of smoke from the hallway bombarded the room. The orange-blue blaze of fire seemed to be coming from the kitchen area. Thankfully, Bethann's bedroom at the other end of the hallway was not already engulfed in flames.

He raced to her room, throwing open the door. "Bethann," he shouted, looking at her empty bed. Lily was just behind him. She covered her nose with a cloth and gave him one, too. "Dear God! Where is she?"

Lily screamed Bethann's name while Tyler looked under her bed. He couldn't think of anywhere else she'd be.

"I'll check my room." Lily hurried out and came back seconds later shaking her head. "She's not there, either. Oh, Tyler!"

"I'll check the other rooms. Lily, get outside. We've got to alert the others." Smoke billowed around them. The house would soon be destroyed if they didn't act fast, but Tyler didn't care. He needed to find his daughter. He fought down an overwhelming attack of panic. Moving quickly, ready to search the rest of the house, he stopped suddenly when he caught sight of Lily's pearl comb lying on top of Bethann's armoire. Remembering what she'd told him about returning the comb to Muldoon, he called for Lily.

She peered in horrified shock at the comb he held. "Oh, no! I gave that back to him. He's been here, Tyler!"

Tyler rummaged through Bethann's armoire. "Her clothes are missing." At that moment Tyler realized the extent of Brett Muldoon's hatred. He'd bet his ranch Muldoon was behind his being shot all those weeks ago. And now this. Saying the words out loud scorched his throat. "Muldoon's got her."

Lily raised a hand to her mouth in horror. Tyler's mind had moved behind the initial shock and was bent on getting his daughter back, then seeing Muldoon pay for his crimes.

He grabbed Lily's hand and raced back to his bedroom. Yanking his gun holster from the peg on the wall, he fastened the belt, tying the thin strip of rawhide around his thigh. "Get Wes to wake up the men. They'll have to try to control the fire. Tell Randy to notify the sheriff. I'm riding out. I've got to find her."

Lily nodded, taking the hand he offered as they ran outside. "I'm coming, too."

"No," he said, stopping to give her a stern look.

"Tyler, I—"

He took a firm grip of her shoulders. "No, Lily. I can't risk it. He's a dangerous man. You stay here."

Lily's voice rose to an uneven pitch. "But you don't even know where to look."

"I have an idea. He's heading north, then he'll probably catch a train back east. He's not worried about being caught. He set the fire, leaving us for dead.'' Tyler raked a hand through his hair. "I've got to go now, Lily. Don't worry, I'll find her.'' He bent to kiss her hastily.

"Be careful,'' she said in a shaky voice.

"Go on and get Wes. He'll know what to do. And stay away from the fire.'' Tyler doubted Lily would heed his advice. She was a headstrong woman. He only hoped she wouldn't see fit to getting injured or worse dousing the blaze that threatened to obliterate Tyler's home.

By the time Tyler gathered the necessities he needed and rode out, the ranch was a mass of commotion. Men formed lines, passing bucket upon bucket of water onto the fiery blaze. And Lily was in the thick of it, working as hard as the men, just as Tyler suspected she would.

He shuffled down his concern, trusting that Lily was a woman who could take care of herself. But his fears for Bethann's safety in the clutches of that wild man made Tyler's gut knot with apprehension.

Tyler rode his horse hard. He figured Muldoon had at least an hour's head start. He was banking on the notion that Muldoon wouldn't expect to be followed so soon. He'd left them all for dead. It would be daylight before the fire at the house was put out and his men would discover that Bethann's body wasn't among the ashes.

But Muldoon was no fool. Tyler knew to tread carefully. He prayed his instincts were right about where the man was heading with his daughter. Brett Muldoon was a city dweller. He hated the west, hated how living out here had killed his sister. He wouldn't subject Bethann to a life in Texas. No, Tyler was certain, he would head east. Maybe not back to St. Louis where he'd be expected to go, but some other large city where he and Bethann would blend into society and no one would be the wiser.

The nearest railroad was in Amarillo. Muldoon would have to ride across the plains to the rim of the Palo Duro Canyon. Having Bethann along would slow him. Come daylight, Tyler hoped to pick up their trail.

Blaze, lathered and gleaming with sweat, wouldn't last throughout the night at the pace Tyler set. He slowed the horse to a halt. His only consolation was that Muldoon also had to rest his horse from time to time. Throwing his wool blanket near some tall brush, Tyler figured he had two hours to rest before dawn. After seeing to his horse, he lay down, his Colt .45 nestled under his arm. He forced his eyes shut. He needed some rest, although the events of the past few days ran in patterns through his head.

And Lily's image, like a sweet dream, came floating in. Thinking of her gave him the only sense of peace he had all night. A smile curved his lips as he remembered the passion in which she responded to him tonight. Had that been only hours ago?

Lily made his house a home, Bethann adored her, and she'd proven herself to be capable at the ranch. Tyler let out a deep sorrowful sigh wondering if it was enough.

He didn't know if he could open his heart completely, to love wholly and unconditionally again. He'd lived all these months, hardening himself to ever care for a woman again. The pain of the loss almost too much to bear. He'd been content with his life, accepting his fate to live a life without love. And then came Lily.

Now he didn't know what was better for her, to stay or to find her uncle and fulfill the deathbed promise she'd made to her father.

And he didn't know if he could give Lily the life that she deserved.

Rustling sounds jarred his light sleep. Keeping his eyes closed, Tyler inched his fingers around the handle of his gun. He sensed a glimmer of predawn light emerging. Blaze nickered softly. More sounds, closer this time. The brush was thick in the area he'd chosen to bed down. He slit his eyes open, catching movement in the thicket in the opposite direction of his horse.

All at once, he jumped up, with gun ready to shoot, and pounced down on the tall unsuspecting figure from behind. Fully alert now, he overwhelmed his opponent, bringing him down to the ground. With gun positioned at his head, Tyler straddled the slim man, trapping him under.

But from beneath his legs, the thighs he imprisoned were soft and delicate, the body too familiar.

Tyler yanked off the man's overly large hat.

He stared straight into a beautiful, blue-eyed bewildered face. "Lily!"

Chapter Seventeen

Lily rubbed her sore bottom. The split skirt she wore, gifted to her by Tyler just hours ago, and rummaged out of the burning house, did little to cushion the blow to her backside when Tyler had thrown his full body weight on her. "I won't slow you down," she insisted.

"No!" he shouted, pacing back and forth in front of her. "You're going back."

She looked up at the angry man. "I'm coming with you."

Tyler closed his eyes momentarily. "I don't want you getting hurt, Lily. It's bad enough I've got to worry over Bethann. I won't take unnecessary risks having you along."

Lily stood up to meet his heated glare. He'd been furious with her once the shock of seeing her had worn off. "You're forgetting what a good shot I am. I can help."

"No." He folded his arms in typical Tyler Kincaide stubborn style and planted his boots firmly. "It's too dangerous. Hell, woman, I nearly shot your head off just a minute ago. Don't you realize you might get hurt."

"Tyler," Lily began, softening her voice. Oh, how her backside ached, but she wouldn't let him see her flinch with pain. "I made it all the way here, found you, and if you'd given me an instant to speak, you'd have realized I didn't sneak up on you. I saw you sleeping, kept my distance for a time, so you'd get the rest you needed. I only came over when I thought you'd be waking." Then on an added note in her defense, she said proudly, "And I didn't fall off Pearl once. I think she likes this split skirt. Gives us both confidence when I ride her."

Tyler looked at her in utter disbelief. "That's the damnedest fool thing you've ever said, Lily." He looked away from her and shook his head.

She heard his stomach grumble. "I brought biscuits and cheese," she said, retrieving the foodstuffs from her pack on Pearl. "I bet you didn't pack any food."

"The kitchen was on fire," he stated blankly.

"I took these from the bunkhouse. Wes made sure I had what I needed."

Tyler cursed, taking a biscuit from her hand. He gave her a scathing look, but she noticed a flicker of admiration. "I suppose you think this makes it all right." He bit down on the biscuit.

"I've got more food and water packed and my gun."

The mention of her gun made Tyler wince. He took a deep breath. "I'm riding out now. I've had some rest. You haven't."

"I'll keep up with you. I'm strong and I love Bethann just as much as you do. I couldn't wait back at the ranch, not knowing what was happening. Tyler, I promise I won't slow you down." She hoped to cut into his stubborn streak.

He swallowed hard and stared at her, then pointed his finger at her nose. "You listen to me at every turn. I mean it, Lily. Follow my orders, no matter if you agree or not. You got that?"

Relieved, Lily nodded her head. "Yes!" She threw her arms around his neck and kissed his cheek. "You won't be sorry."

Tyler removed her arms and shook his head. She knew he wasn't pleased with his decision. "I'm already sorry, honey. Let's go. We've got a hard ride ahead of us."

Lily shoved her hair under her hat and shook trail dust off her new riding clothes. She wouldn't ask Tyler for a boost up onto Pearl. Instead she walked the horse over to a large boulder, then mounted. Tyler eyed her silently. Lily lifted her chin, determined to help the man she loved find his daughter.

Riding over the plains was a boring, hot, dusty endeavor. Lily's bottom was sore. She shifted countless times in her saddle trying to find a comfortable position. After three hours she gave up trying for comfort, resigning herself that her derriere would never be the same again.

Tyler said little. He was still angry. He'd get over it, she mused. And she'd rather have her fingernails plucked out than to admit how tired she was. She wouldn't ask to slow down. But, an hour later, Tyler reined in his horse. Lily glanced at him when he approached.

"We'll rest a bit, have a bite to eat."

He reached for her and helped her down from Pearl. When her boots hit solid ground, Tyler didn't release her. Instead he wound his arms around her waist and brought her into an embrace. She felt his lips brush her forehead. "I'll never forgive myself if you get hurt, honey."

"I...won't," she said breathlessly. But all she could think of was the way he held her and the dark shining gleam in his eyes. How his slightest touch caused such dire yearnings deep in her heart. This was as it should be, she thought, the two of them together, searching for Bethann.

He took her hand and they lay down on a blanket he'd spread out. "Try to get some sleep."

She laid her head on his chest, listening to his heart-beats, and within minutes Lily was breathing heavy.

They were on their way in less than an hour. Tyler insisted she eat something to keep up her strength, but in truth, the events of the last day, with all that had occurred, had damaged her otherwise healthy appetite. Still and all, she grabbed a handful of pecans and ate them to appease Tyler's watchful eye.

The sun beat hot. Lily was glad Randy had insisted she take his felt hat. The wide brim helped to shade her face. When she'd left the ranch, he'd given her a sober look of admonishment, but hadn't tried to stop her from chasing down Tyler. He'd saddled up Pearl for her, then rode off to alert the sheriff about Beth-ann's kidnapping.

Lily had a difficult time holding back tears when-ever she thought of Bethann being whisked away from everything she knew, everyone she loved. How fright-ened she must be. That little imp had stolen Lily's heart. She had better be safe. Something deep inside told her Brett Muldoon wouldn't let any harm come to his niece. She held on to that thought, but she also blamed herself for encouraging Muldoon to get to know Bethann. When she thought about how she'd gone directly against Tyler's wishes to befriend the man, Lily gritted her teeth. She'd made a terrible mistake and now Bethann was paying the price. Tyler, too. She knew he would hunt Muldoon to the ends of the earth to find his child. Lily had to be a part of her rescue, perhaps to ease her own conscience. They had to find her.

Dusk settled onto the horizon in a blast of color. Lily relished the sunset for it meant rest. She had nearly fallen asleep astride her horse three times, each time, Pearl's snort or a sound from the whispering plains would give her the start she needed to right herself on the mare and take control of the reins.

Tyler slowed his horse and sidled up next to her. "We'll camp for half the night, then we'll move out slowly." He gave her a sympathetic look. "You did real good today, Lily."

Lily was too tired to nod. Her half smile made Tyler grab for her reins. Pearl followed Blaze to a clearing packed with dense deep grass. After dismounting, he reached up to take Lily by the waist and carried her off her horse. He set her down gently.

Tyler laid out their blankets then made a small fire with kindling he'd gathered. Rummaging through her bags, he found a tin of Arbuckle's coffee and a small coffeepot. He smiled and looked over at her. "I was hoping for some coffee. You're a smart lady, Miss Brody."

"Wes was angry with me for leaving the ranch, but he helped pack the provisions in a hurry. He's a good man. You can thank him when you see him."

"I'll not thank him for allowing you to come after me."

Lily sighed deeply. She wasn't up to another argu-

ment with him. Besides, she'd gotten her way. He
hadn't sent her back so she could stand to hear Tyler
grumble a bit if it made him feel better.

Tyler made the coffee, sharing with her the one mug
Wes had packed. They took turns sipping, then
munched on biscuits and cheese. Lily's strength was
returning. The food and the rest helped to restore some
of her usual vigor, but her bones did complain something terrible.

She peered at the two blankets Tyler had laid out.
His next to hers. Things had changed rapidly in their
relationship. It warmed Lily's heart to see the man
who had been so closed off when they'd first met finally share something of himself with her. She needed
more from him, but for now this would have to be
enough.

"You're tired, honey," he said, adjusting stray
strands of her hair behind her ear. "Get some sleep.
I'll let the fire die out since it's not such a cold night.
The blankets will keep you warm enough."

Lily made quick work of braiding her hair. Tyler
watched her quietly, then when she laid down on her
bedroll, he covered her with another blanket.

To her surprise, he lay down beside her and took
her into his arms. Facing her, he stroked her cheek
with a finger, then cupped her chin with his hand.
"Good night, Lily."

His mouth covered hers with a deep desperate passion, a mating of lips, tender yet rough in need. A
need that would go denied tonight. Their thoughts
were on Bethann, on finding her and bringing Muldoon to justice. Tyler held Lily so snugly she prayed
he'd never want to let her go. She couldn't fathom
letting him go.

She responded to him the only way she knew how, giving him all her love, her comfort. It was all she had to give him tonight as they snuggled deep into the blankets.

She hoped it was enough.

"We will find her, Tyler."

"Planning to, Lily. If it takes my entire lifetime."

She held him tight until the troubled man she loved finally fell asleep.

They were getting close. By midmorning Tyler found Muldoon's camp. The embers from the night's campfire were still warm. Not an hour ago Lily had spotted Bethann's yellow ribbon lying off the side of the road. They were nearing rugged rocky canyons. The going would be much tougher from now on.

As they rode on in silence, Tyler looked behind him, noting Lily casting furtive glances in every direction, the Colt .45 she practiced with at the Circle K resting against her hip. As soon as they had dismounted, finding the site where Bethann had obviously spent the night, Lily had gone straight to her pack and holstered her gun. Tyler hadn't said anything about it then. He was too relieved to have finally found evidence they were on the right track.

But now as he studied her, he felt a pang of regret for allowing Lily to stay on. The soft sweet woman he'd made love to looked incongruous astride the saddle in her dirtied riding clothes, packing iron. Tyler winced. Yes, Lily was a good shot—when she was aiming at bottles set up on a rock ledge, but how would she react in a true crisis? Would she freeze up, or worse, make a bad shot and hurt Bethann? He couldn't risk it. Somehow he'd have to convince her to give over her gun.

He wasn't looking forward to it.

Lily sped up her horse to reach his side. "We're going to find her soon." Her voice held an excited edge. "I can just feel it."

"I'm hoping to find her before nightfall," Tyler said, keeping his voice level. Blaze lifted his head and nickered as if in agreement.

"I can't wait to get Bethann home," Lily said wistfully.

He subdued the rush of excitement he felt hearing Lily's softly spoken words. An image of the three of them sitting around the parlor with Lily reading to Bethann by the fireplace entered his mind. But those could be dangerous thoughts. He needed to stay alert, keep his wits about him. He couldn't afford to get sentimental. Keeping wary, staying apprehensive, was a means to survival. Tyler knew retrieving his daughter wouldn't be easy and now that they were closing in, he wished he'd turned Lily away and sent her back to the ranch.

She would be safe there and he'd not have to worry about both his girls.

"Lily, Muldoon's not just going to hand her over to us. You know what that man's capable of doing. We have to tread carefully." He gave her a stern look. "I want your gun."

Lily's startled look turned into sheer stubbornness in the beat of a second. "No." Her hand automatically covered the handle of her gun.

"You promised to obey me, no matter what, Lily. I'm asking nicely, give me your gun." He extended his hand.

"Tyler," she said briskly, tightening the hold she had on the Colt .45. "I...can't." Then in a pleading voice, she offered, "You might need my help."

Her concern and the soft look in her eyes offering to protect him touched Tyler. But Lily had not seen any real conflict in her life. He'd been a party to skirmishes with his men on cattle drives, broken up fights at the saloon and had to defend himself against rowdy cowhands a time or two. Although he didn't relish using it, his gun had been known to keep the peace and save his hide on more than one occasion.

"Hand it over, Lily. I can't be worrying about what you might be doing with that gun when we finally catch up with Muldoon. It'll distract me. Might even get us both killed."

Lily twisted her mouth and seemed to regard what he was saying. When she lifted the gun from the holster and handed it to him, Tyler hid his surprise. "I think this is a mistake, but since you don't trust me—"

"Damn it, Lily. I'm trying to keep you safe."

"And I'm trying to keep you safe," she said adamantly.

The woman was one hundred percent sheer determination. Tyler loved that about her under normal circumstances, but not at the moment. "I appreciate the thought, honey."

She lifted her chin and rode ahead of him. He thought it best to let her stew a bit on her own. There wasn't anything he could say to make her feel better right now.

They rode just east of the newly furrowed cotton fields of Llano Estacado. The high plateau, treeless plains would not lend them the cover they needed, so they kept to the lowlands. Tyler followed the banks of

the White River, looking for a shallow place where
they might cross.

"Lily, slow down!" he called to the woman who
had managed to ignore him for the last hour and a
half. She turned to him in haughty resignation. What
had happened to the shy, unassuming woman he'd
hired all those weeks ago? "We're crossing the river
here."

Lily nodded and with a soft kick to Pearl began
making her trek across the quiet river. Tyler moved
closer, keeping a watchful eye. He wanted to take the
reins from her and guide Pearl across behind him, but
Lily probably would shoot him daggers with her blaz-
ing blue eyes and never forgive him.

With a sigh, he kept a slight distance away, clamp-
ing his mouth from calling out any orders. Lily, as far
as he could see, was doing fine on the back of a horse
upon which, just two weeks ago, she couldn't manage
to stay on the northern end.

When Pearl sidestepped then made a half turn, probably after stepping on a large rock, Lily righted the
horse with soft words and a pull up on the reins. Water
splashed up onto Lily's riding skirt, but she didn't
flinch. She turned to Tyler, who'd had his mouth open,
about to bark a command. "I'm fine, Tyler," she
called before he could say one word.

"Well, who was asking?" he said, then cast her a
big grin.

Lily cast him a generous smile. She didn't know
how much her sweet smiles affected him.

Once reaching the opposite side of the river, Tyler
reined in Blaze. "Do you want to rest up a bit?"

Lily kept her horse at an even gait. "Not unless you
do."

"Then I guess we'll keep going."

Hours later, as the sun began its descent, Tyler slowed his horse. He whispered to Lily, "We've caught up to them."

He directed Lily's gaze to the large boulders off in the distance where smoke billowed up from the darkening sky. "Unless I miss my guess, they've settled down there for the night."

Tyler dismounted then helped Lily down. They both took deep breaths of air, then set their gaze to the spot where Muldoon had Bethann.

"What'll we do now?" Lily asked, biting her lip.

Tyler found an area of several tall, scattered shrubs where they could tie up the horses. Under the cover of darkness they wouldn't be spotted. "You're going to stay here and watch the horses. Keep them quiet. I'm going to get a closer look. If I can catch Muldoon off guard, I'll make my move."

"But—"

Lily's slight protest fell on deaf ears. Tyler wasn't going to debate the issue. "Do as I say. Keep the horses quiet and out of the way."

Lily nodded.

"Okay, then." He kissed her quickly, turning to leave. Then he stopped to look at her one last time. "I've got to know something."

When Lily's beautiful soft-eyed gaze fell on him, he asked, "I'd like to know if anything happens to me, well, since Bethann doesn't have any other kin, would you—"

"Oh, yes. I'll take her, Tyler. I love that little girl. But, Tyler…please, please, don't let anything happen to you."

"Don't plan to, sweetheart."

He took her in a sweeping, long kiss. Her lips warmed him to the very core and gave him the strength he needed to return to her. "I'll be back soon."

Lily paced, wringing out her hands, trying to keep hold of her sanity. Tyler had been gone almost an hour. *Patience, Lily, have patience.* She must have glanced in the direction of the campfire smoke one hundred times, hoping to hear or see something. But she couldn't make out any figures in the darkness. The sky tonight was ominous and darker than usual. No big bright moon cast its light to illuminate the earth, instead a tiny pearl-like sliver shrouded with a grayish haze was barely discernible. There was a chill in the air. Lily donned the heavy slicker Wes saw fit to pack her, thanking him for his insight as the long canvas coat warmed her. Guiltily, she wondered if little Bethann was warm enough tonight.

Lily took two carrots out of her pack and fed the horses a treat. They'd been pushed hard today. She stroked Pearl's long snout, earning a sweet-sounding whinny. She closed her eyes and said a silent prayer for Tyler and Bethann's safe return.

Prairie dogs scrambled nearby, making a slight rustling sound as they burrowed into the ground, then the hoot of an owl made her jump. "Enough of this, Lily," she said quietly. Her nerves were raw with worry. She couldn't wait any longer. Tyler might very well need her help at this very moment.

Without a moment's hesitation or remorse, Lily wrestled with Tyler's pack and withdrew her gun. She welcomed the feel of cool metal against her hand as she holstered the Colt .45. The long slicker she wore would hide the gun from Tyler's immediate view. She'd deal with his wrath later, once all three of them were safely on their way back home.

Chapter Eighteen

Tyler watched his daughter sleep. Coiled like a snake and tucked safely into her bedroll near the fire, exhaustion marred her usually animated face. Tyler said a prayer of thanks at finding her. Bethann looked frazzled, but healthy.

Muldoon sat by the fire sipping at his coffee mug. Tyler wanted to pounce right now, but Bethann was too close by. Instead he waited and watched. Then, finally, Muldoon stood, stretched out his arms and glanced at the slumbering child. He left the camp, heading toward a rocky slope. Tyler followed him from a distance.

It was easier than he thought it'd be. Coming up from behind, Tyler jabbed his gun into Muldoon's back. "Hands up and turn around." He kept his fingers tight on the trigger.

Muldoon made a slow turn, raising his arms in the air. "How many lives do you have, Kincaide?"

"Just one, no thanks to you."

Muldoon's wry laugh resounded against the wall of the rocks. "You should've died out on the range that day."

"Your aim wasn't that good."

"You're one lucky son of a—"

"Shut up and move." Tyler poked the gun into Muldoon's chest and pushed him toward camp, restraining his trigger finger from ending the man's life right here and now. "Two attempted murders and a kidnapping ought to put you away for a long time, if you're lucky. Otherwise, you might see the end of a rope. Good thing for you my daughter appears to be fine."

"I'd never hurt that little one," Muldoon growled adamantly, his mouth twisting. With eyes wild and dazed, the man had a deranged look about him.

Tyler gritted his teeth and spoke with tightly controlled anger. "Setting the ranch house on fire, trying to kill the people who love her, wouldn't *hurt* her? That's sick, Muldoon, real sick."

"You killed her mother," Muldoon ranted. "Lizabeth would've been alive today if it weren't for you. As soon as Bethann understood that, she would have forgiven me for taking her."

"You're crazy. And I'm through taking the blame for Lizabeth's death. She chose to marry me. What happened to her, I'll never forget and I deeply regret, but I can finally see that her death was an unfortunate accident."

Just steps away from the billowing smoke of the campfire, Tyler stopped up short. He blinked back his stunned surprise and his heart hammered with dread.

"Lookee what I found, boss." A sardonic smile curled the corners of Jack McGee's mouth as Lily struggled in his arms. He had one hand around her waist, the other pointing a gun to her head. His beady eyes gleamed with pure hatred when he directed his attention to Tyler. "Seems I found myself a woman."

Lily's gaze skittered until it rested on Tyler's. Her expression was one of deep apology.

"Drop the gun, Kincaide."

When Tyler hesitated, stalling for time enough to think of a plan, McGee jammed the barrel of his gun to Lily's temple. Tyler opened his fist and the gun fell to the ground. He couldn't chance it.

McGee laughed. Muldoon grabbed the gun from the ground. "Good work, Jack. It's about time you showed up. Funny thing," he said to Tyler, "how my friend here, has such a dislike for you. Right, Jack?"

"Right, boss. I been following behind just like you asked, when I came upon this pretty little thing." His wide arms squeezed Lily's waist tight, bringing her up closer. She put up a valiant struggle, kicking and squirming, but McGee was too powerful to let it faze him.

"Let her go, McGee," Tyler said with warning in his voice. With great restraint he held himself back. An impulsive move would get them all killed, but he hated like hell seeing that man put his hands on Lily.

"Not even close, Kincaide." He skimmed the tip of his gun along Lily's throat. Tyler winced inwardly. Then amid Lily's movements, he caught sight of a flash of metal from underneath her slicker. A gun. Tyler's gaze held Lily's for the slightest second in time. She blinked in understanding.

A quick glance at Bethann's sleeping form twenty feet away told him the commotion thus far hadn't woken her. She'd always slept heavily. Tyler didn't want Muldoon to have any more leverage when he made his move.

Muldoon looked over at Lily with scorn. "Sorry, but you had your chance. Now you're going to pay for knowing Kincaide here." He gave McGee a nod. "Take them both out by the rocks. That canyon is mighty steep. Nobody will ever find them. You know what to do."

Muldoon shoved Tyler forward. He made another quick glance at Bethann who was thankfully still sleeping. He'd make his move once his daughter was out of sight. But he couldn't wait too much longer.

"Kincaide goes first. I have me some big plans for the lady here," McGee said with disgusting glee. Tyler cautioned Lily with his eyes. She stopped squirming and settled down. McGee reflectively loosened his grip on her.

Muldoon stayed in the circle of the campfire but motioned Tyler to walk straight ahead until he was standing next to Lily. He turned to face her. "I'm sorry, Lily," he said, reaching out his hand to stroke her face. McGee attempted to pull her away, but Tyler's quick reflexes had his other hand drawing Lily's gun out of her holster. Surprise was on his side. Lily jerked herself out of McGee's arms. With one shot, McGee went down.

But Muldoon had witnessed the whole scene and before Tyler could shift positions to take aim, Muldoon fired his gun.

"No!" Lily screamed. She threw herself in front of Tyler. Before he could shove her to safety, the bullet met its mark and Lily slumped to the ground. Horrified, Tyler stared at Lily's limp body, then without another wasted breath he shot Muldoon in the hand. Metal flew as his gun flipped into the air and landed with a heavy thud next to Bethann.

Muldoon immediately clasped his bleeding hand and let out a loud bellow of pain. He dropped to his knees, clutching his hand, cursing. Tyler itched to pull the trigger again. His brain warred with his heart. He wanted to see that man dead for what he'd done to Bethann and to Lily. He aimed the gun at the man's head.

"Papa!" Bethann's startled cry rang out. She ran into Tyler's arms and sobbed. He kept his gun trained on Muldoon, brought back to his senses by his young daughter. The man would live to go to trial. A jury would decide his fate. He hugged Bethann tight. "Papa...M-Miss Lily's...hurt."

"I know darlin'," he said to his grieving daughter. He made short work of tying up Muldoon, then ran over to Lily. He bent by her side. "Lily." He tapped her face. With a quick perusal of her injury, he determined the bullet went clear through her upper arm. She was bleeding from both sides. And she'd lost a lot of blood already.

"Lily, dear God, wake up. Bethann, quick, get me some water from a canteen."

"Is she gonna die, Papa?"

"Not if I can help it," he said, reassuring his child. He sucked in a deep breath and tried to not let guilt seep in. He needed to concentrate. There'd be time enough later to blame himself for almost losing Lily. Tyler ripped off part of his shirt and managed to swab at the blood. Then he tightly tied a long strip of cloth to her wound.

Bethann handed him the canteen. He let a few drops of water drizzle onto her parted lips. Tyler crouched down and put her head in his lap. Then he gestured for Bethann. "Come here, sweetheart."

Bethann kneeled by Lily's side. Her teary face tore at his heart. "Are you okay?"

His courageous daughter nodded. "Papa, Miss Lily—"

"I think she's going to be fine. We'll rest with her here until she wakes up." Tyler prayed Lily would recover. Right now, she was pale and lifeless.

"I'm proud of you, darlin'. You've been very brave."

"I didn't want to go with…Uncle Brett. He s-said you w-wanted me to see where he l-lived," she said between soft sobs. "I didn't believe him, Papa. But he took me away anyhows."

Tyler hugged his daughter to his side and kissed the top of her head. She was precious to him. In one horrible night, he'd almost lost the two people in the world that meant the most to him. The thought of losing either one of them made him shudder.

"He was wrong, Bethann, and he'll pay for taking you. Nobody will ever take you away again. You belong on the ranch with me."

Bethann smiled and glanced down at Lily. "That's right, Papa. You, me and Miss Lily."

Tyler stroked his daughter's hair. Dear heaven, Bethann wanted Lily to stay on at the ranch. Tyler, too, wanted Lily. As soon as he saw that bullet hit its mark, he realized how much he cared for her, how much she meant to him. Tyler couldn't take another loss. He was a strong man, having overcome a great deal of hardship in his life, but he couldn't survive losing Lily.

Damn it, she'd been hurt because of him. Just like Lizabeth. How could he selfishly ask Lily to stay on?

He'd been right all along not to open his heart to her. He'd been right not to allow love in.

But you do love her.

With a sorrowful sigh, Tyler retreated emotionally. Yes, he may love her, but she'll never know. He'd not tell her. She deserved more than the hard life he could offer her on the ranch. Gazing down at Lily's lovely face, unconscious to the world, soaked in blood, Tyler's gut twisted. He was dying a slow agonizing death seeing her suffer so. She'd be better off without him. When she found her uncle, they would have to say goodbye. It would cost he and Bethann their happiness.

But that was the way it had to be.

Smoke filled her nostrils and Lily immediately woke in a panic. She thrashed her head, opening her eyes, recalling the last time she'd woken up to that smell. Thoughts of last night registered slowly. Images she'd like to put away forever flashed before her eyes. But dawning knowledge filtered in and Lily breathed a sigh of relief. The nightmare was over, the real danger passed. Bethann was safe. Soon they would all be home.

Home.

Lily smiled. She was weak, exhausted really, from losing a great deal of blood, and her arm ached terribly, but she'd never been happier in her life. She loved Tyler, had loved him a very long time and now they had a real chance at happiness.

The rising sun overhead was a glorious sight. She lay in her blanket and glanced at Tyler making breakfast by the fire. She tried lifting up but the pain in her arm stabbed like a knife. She sunk back down into her blankets.

"You all right?" she heard Tyler call. He was by her side instantly, his face deep with concern.

She lifted her good hand to his cheek and stroked his solid jaw with her fingertips. "I'm fine."

He shook his head. "You've got to rest, honey."

"I'm resting. You won't let me do anything *but* rest."

Tyler winced when he looked at her arm. The bandage he'd applied last night had soaked through again. "I've got to change the bandage."

Lily noticed deep lines around his eyes. "Tyler, you look tired. I bet you didn't get a wink of sleep last night." Each time Lily woke from the pain last night, Tyler had been by her side, lending comfort, soothing her with soft words. He'd checked the bandage several times during the night, changing it when the blood had soaked through.

Lily would have had a fitful night, if it hadn't been for Tyler. Just knowing he was there and that he cared had made all the difference. Finally, late into the night, Lily had fallen asleep sandwiched between Bethann and Tyler.

"Don't go worrying about me, Lily. I'm not the one injured this time."

"But you don't have to dote on me. You've got to get some sleep. I promise to be good today. It's not like I can dance a polka or anything."

He heaved a big sigh. His face masked an emotion Lily didn't want to acknowledge. Guilt. Tyler felt guilty for her becoming injured. It wasn't his fault, she wanted to scream. But she knew the feeling ate at him, like a boll weevil attacking cotton.

"Sorry if it hurts, but I've got to keep the wound clean." He unwound the strip of cloth he'd used as a bandage, taking his time, glancing up at her as if making sure she could deal with the pain. She bit her lip and didn't make a fuss. She'd not let him see how much her arm really did hurt. Lily was tough. She'd take any amount of pain if it eased his suffering.

And she knew he was suffering. His smiles were brief, his eyes filled with regret. How could she tell him she didn't blame him for any of this? It had been her choice to come trailing after him. She'd made the decision. How could she not? Both the people she loved dearly in this world had been in danger.

Tyler poured water over her wound from the canteen. Lily sucked in her breath. She managed to ward off a burning ache to smile up at him. "When will we head home?"

"Soon as you're strong enough to ride." With diligence, Tyler began to wind another clean piece of cloth around her arm, making sure to not secure it too tightly.

"I told you I'm fine."

He scoffed, giving her a disgruntled look. "You're weaker than a baby bird with clipped wings."

"I can ride."

"No. Not today." He finished the bandage off with a knot, then picked up the used bandage, wrapping it into a ball. He glanced at her arm again, shaking his head. "Maybe I should have sent you off with the sheriff and his deputies. They'd have gotten you to a doctor by now."

"I didn't want to go with them." Lily could be stubborn, too, if the need arose. Last night, after the shooting, Sheriff Singleton had ridden up with two of his men. They'd been tracking Muldoon and come upon the scene shortly after Lily had been shot. McGee's body had been carted away and Muldoon was promised a long stretch of prison time. Lily didn't want to be in his company any longer than necessary. Besides, her place was with Tyler and Bethann now.

"We're staying here, at least for one more day. Tomorrow, if I think you're ready, we'll head on out."

There was no arguing with Tyler when he took that tone. But as long as they were together, Lily wouldn't complain.

"So what smells so good? My stomach's doing flips, Tyler. It's got to be better than stale biscuits."

"The sheriff left us some supplies. Bacon and coffee. It's not elegant dining, honey."

"But it sure smells wonderful. Seems you can cook, after all," she teased.

"Only out of necessity." He adjusted the blankets behind her head. "Lay back and rest. I'll bring it over when it's done cooking. Bethann, come sit with Lily."

Bethann had been chasing a wild rabbit in the clearing. She ran over to Lily. "How you feelin', Miss Lily?"

"Much better. Thank you."

"Papa says we have to wait for you to heal up some, but I don't mind."

"I'm glad. Looks like we'll be spending the night here. How are you, sweetheart? Were you scared when you were taken?"

She nodded, putting her head down. "Uh-huh. I didn't want to go. But Uncle Brett told me lies. That's what Papa said."

"Yes, your uncle's not right in the head. He meant

to do us all harm. I'm just glad you're all right. Come close so I can give you a big hug with my good arm.''

Bethann sat down beside her and leaned in. Lily brought the child close and wrapped her arm around Bethann's shoulder. ''Oh, I'm so glad we found you in time. Your papa and I were sick with worry.'' She gave her one last gentle squeeze before letting go. Her eyes misted with tears. If Bethann were her own child, Lily couldn't love her any more.

Bethann looked at Lily, her heart reflected in her eyes. ''Now we can go home and be a family.''

Lily wanted that more than anything. But the decision wasn't hers to make. Tyler hadn't asked her to stay. The kidnapping had taken all priority. Perhaps once they returned to the ranch and things got back to normal, Lily's future would be determined. If Tyler would only let her into his heart, Lily knew she could make him happy. She loved him now more than ever, if that were possible. When she'd seen Muldoon point that gun his way, Lily knew her own life would surely end if Tyler died. She had done the only thing she could do—she saved his life, because her life blended with his. There was no beginning, no end. Why couldn't Tyler see that they belonged together? The three of them—a real family.

She had no choice but to be patient.

Tyler Kincaide was a man worth waiting for.

''Tyler, I can ride Pearl just fine,'' Lily said softly. Her voice was still weak, but slowly over the last three days, her strength was returning. Her biggest obstacle was the man who insisted she ride with him. He'd coddled her, as if she were the child instead of a capable adult. The trip back to the Circle K had been at a snail's pace.

"Quiet, Lily, we're almost home. You've been nagging me for the last twenty miles." There was a teasing hint in his voice.

"Me, nagging? Why, Mr. Kincaide, you're the one always hollering for me to be careful so I don't re-injure my arm. And who's always looking over my shoulder making sure I eat my meals so I can recuperate. I believe you're worse at doctoring than being the patient. That's saying something."

Bethann giggled when Lily made a face at Tyler. He pretended not to notice, but a crooked smile made its way to his handsome face. Lily, too, smiled, hoping she was just imagining the look of regret in his expression when she'd caught him watching her lately. He'd tried to make her smile, cajoling her with silliness at times, but the merriment never quite reached his dark soulful eyes.

Tyler had taken to heart the job of tending her, not allowing her to lift a finger in any manner, other than to feed and dress herself. She had the feeling he would have done that, also, if she would have allowed him.

But other than his concern over her welfare, Tyler had been extremely quiet on the trip home. He seemed deep in thought, withdrawing into himself. Only when Bethann asked a question or Lily needed something, did he come out of his long stretches of silence. So much had happened over these past weeks to fill Tyler's mind. She sympathized with his worry, but her heart rejoiced just the same. Sitting astride Blaze, with Tyler's arms around her, how could Lily feel anything but elation?

Bethann was safe and heading back to the ranch

strapped into the saddle on Pearl's back. The little one had held up wonderfully, caring for Lily, giving her sips of water, brushing out her hair at night. Lily had been taken by Bethann's voluntary gestures of love.

And best of all…they were almost home.

It was early in the afternoon when they made the round in the bend that led them to the Circle K Ranch. The bright sun glistened on the branches of familiar pecan trees, casting gleaming twinkles of light as the wind caught the leaves. Maybe it was just coming home that felt so good. The horses plodded down the path, trampling on wayward buttercups that had grown alongside the road, and Lily had never felt more alive, more exhilarated.

But the sight that welcomed them as they caught their first glimpse of the house Tyler's father had built nearly a half century ago made Lily's stomach contort with anguish.

Destruction, plain and simple.

The house, if one could still call it that, looked more like the skeletal remains of some ancient dwelling. The fireplace stood proud and tall where the parlor had once been. The kitchen was gone, as were the other rooms, except for Tyler's bedroom at the far end of the house. That space, the last the fire must have reached, still resembled a room with charred vulnerable-looking walls poised at ninety-degree angles and the once formidable-looking doorway leading to nothingness now.

Lily held back a gasp, glancing at Tyler's face, resigned in his expression of pain. He had dismounted, leaving Lily on Blaze, to walk over to his daughter and unstrap her from the saddle. Bethann came down into his arms and he hugged her to his chest as quiet tears fell from her little cheeks.

"Papa?" she asked in question. Tyler had thought it best not to tell her of the fire. She'd been through enough of an ordeal. Tyler had contended they didn't know the level of the damage so why disturb her young thoughts with worry.

Now they knew. Everything, just about, had been lost.

"There was a fire, darlin'. Looks like you get to sleep in the bunkhouse for a spell. How'd you like that?"

No degree of cheerfulness could coax a smile from Bethann's pitiful face. She began to cry anew. "Miss Daisy."

Lily wanted to shout to the high heavens she'd make her another doll but it wouldn't be the same and she had sense enough not to say anything.

Like wooden soldiers, they ambled toward the house. The devastation was even worse closer up. And Lily thought she made out the figures of two men standing on the charred remains of the porch steps. One she believed was Wes, she never could abide by his dilapidated worn-out old straw hat. The other man looked familiar. She pushed Blaze to a trot until she could focus solely on the man standing rather forlornly in front of Tyler's home.

Then she realized who he was. "Uncle Jasper."

Chapter Nineteen

The decision Tyler had been struggling with since Lily had leaped into his path to take a bullet intended for him was all but made now. Her uncle had arrived. She'd be leaving soon, and he wouldn't have to be the one pushing her out of his life. A deep ache lodged itself in his chest. It would be his constant companion, he knew, for years to come.

Tyler would let her go. Guilt over almost losing her had eaten at him all through the trip back home, and now as he watched Lily rush into her uncle's inviting arms, he knew it was the answer.

He'd lost one woman he loved already. Death is too final to be ignored. Lily had saved his life, almost at the price of her own. Her devotion wrapped around his heart like a barbed wire, securely, but with piercing sharp edges that meant to wound. If he had lost Lily, the woman who owned his very soul, it would have been too horrible to bear.

He had to let her go.

For both their sakes.

"Uncle Jasper," Lily said with a proud smile, "I'd like you to meet Tyler Kincaide."

Tyler took the man's hand. His grip was firm, like that of a man determined. And judging from the cut of his clothes and the way he held himself in dignified fashion, Tyler knew this man was wealthy.

"Proud to meet you."

Tyler nodded the same and introduced Bethann. How much more could his daughter take? When she realized that this man would soon take Lily away, Bethann wouldn't be offering any more tentative smiles.

Lily went on to explain the events leading up to the fire while Bethann raced to the barn to check on her pony.

The gray-haired man nodded, taking all of it in. Tyler stood back slightly. He should be checking out his property, talking to Wes who had disappeared from sight when they'd made their way to the house, but instead he stood by, listening. His fate would also be determined by what Jasper Brody had to say.

"I've booked a room at the hotel for you. I'm sure you could use a few days' rest. I was worried sick when Sheriff Singleton told me what had happened to you. Lily, you're my only family. I lost your aunt Helen and my own daughter in a terrible fire in '71."

"Oh, Uncle, I didn't know. I'm so sorry. I read about the fire in Chicago."

"It nearly crippled the city. After losing my family, I threw myself into my work. My lumber mill was at the edge of town, well away from all the turmoil. After the fire, my small company was the only one within miles, so you can imagine the business I did. Everyone wanted to rebuild quickly. I made a small fortune, but had no one to share it with." His eyes filled with regret as he spoke of the past.

A look of sympathy spread over Lily's face. "Father asked me to look you up. He'd died months ago, but I couldn't locate you."

Jasper sighed deeply. "It's been a lonely existence. One year ago I sold off the business. I've been moving around, making my way west. I'd always planned on visiting my brother. Stubborn as he was, I still loved him. About three weeks ago, one of your wires caught up with me. That's when I knew I'd been too late."

"My father died of consumption. He held no ill feelings for you when he passed. He told me he hoped you'd feel the same."

"He was a good man. What can I say? The war does things to men. I have nothing but fondness in my heart for him. Except that he left you pretty much penniless from what I understand."

"It hasn't been so bad. Tyler," she said, casting him a heart-melting smile, "he offered me a job. I've been working here while trying to contact you."

Jasper Brody gave Tyler an assessing look. "I thank you kindly for helping Lily out."

"She's been more help to me than otherwise."

Lily's uncle glanced at the makeshift bandage around her arm. He knew the details of the shooting. Probably knew Lily had risked her life to save his. He raised an eyebrow at Tyler, but didn't respond.

"You must all be exhausted. Lily, I hired a buggy to take us back to the hotel in Sweet Springs. You have a room there now," he said with an uncertain smile. "Will you take me up on the offer of going back to town to get to know your uncle again?"

Lily glanced at Tyler. This was it. He was losing her. But he had to let her go. She'd searched all these months for her uncle. He had to give her the chance to find the family she'd always yearned for. He mustered a bit of enthusiasm, though it cost him. His gut clenched. "Go on. This is what you've wanted from the start."

Lily didn't smile or appear happy. Instead he saw disappointment and hurt in her eyes. Did she want him to deny her time with her uncle? Hell, Tyler didn't know what she wanted or expected. He only knew he had to let her go.

And the tightening in his gut intensified.

"But—" Lily responded softly, glancing around one more time at the devastation. Tyler knew she felt like a traitor leaving him to deal with all this alone. He knew it, just as he knew his heart was shredding.

"We'll manage here. We always have, Lily. You go on."

Lily stared at him for a long drawn-out minute. She searched his eyes for the truth. Tyler steadied his gaze, keeping firm resolve in his expression. He couldn't allow her to see him weakening. He was doing this for her.

Finally she glanced away, and Tyler nearly slumped with relief. She nodded to her uncle. She'd leave with him.

Tyler had given her no choice.

"I want to say goodbye to Bethann."

"It's best that you don't," he said as softly as he could. Tears brimmed Lily's eyes, but she didn't argue the point. Tyler felt worthless for hurting her.

"Tell her...tell her, I'll be back soon."

"To what, Lily? It'll take weeks, maybe months, to rebuild the house. There's nothing here for you. I'll explain to Bethann."

Lily chewed her bottom lip, keeping her tears at

bay. Thank goodness for her stubborn pride. She'd not let him see how much he'd hurt her. Good for Lily, Tyler thought. Good for them both.

"Ya gonna eat that meal or just stare it to death?" Wes asked, eyeing Tyler as they sat in silence at a long wooden table outside the bunkhouse. Bethann had only eaten a smidgen herself.

"You call this a meal?" Tyler shoved the breakfast plate away and grimaced. Hell and tarnation, Wes had been a pain in the backside lately.

"Ya been starin' down my food for better'n two weeks now. Skin and bones, is what ya'll be gettin'."

"I'm not hungry."

Wes didn't even try to hide his smirk. "Wonder why that is?" He casually scratched his whiskered face. "'Course that house is going up faster'n a spirited kitten chased up a tree. Yore workin' yoreself in the ground. What's yore hurry, son?"

"Work's got to get done."

When Wes shook his head and stalked off, Tyler sighed and sipped godawful coffee. He hadn't remembered Wes's coffee being so bitter, or his meals so dang inedible. Since Lily left, nothing'd been the same.

There was no joy or laughter at the ranch. The ranch hands looked grim. Tyler knew he'd worked them hard, having them do double shifts to help get his house up and tend to his herd at the same time. He'd paid them for their trouble, but his paychecks couldn't stop their grumbling about missing Lily and the special care she took with them.

Tyler worked just as hard, pushing himself to the limit so that maybe, at night, exhaustion would claim his weary body. It was the only way for him to get any sleep. And not think about Lily.

"Papa, can I go into town to visit Miss Lily?"

The same question uttered every day for the last two weeks tore at his heart. "Not today, sweetcakes."

"But—"

"I've got too much work to do today. Now go on and tend to your chores."

"I already fed Pint-Size. There ain't no flowers left to garden."

Tyler's eyes immediately riveted to the garden Lily had tended with such loving hands. Everything had been destroyed. The sunflowers would never again peek up at the sun, vegetables didn't rise from the soil to prove Lily wrong about Bethann's willingness to eat them and flowers didn't spread their color to lift a spirit on a dreary day.

The destruction left Tyler empty. Losing Lily's garden was worse than smelling the ashes that had once been his family home. He could rebuild the house. But Lily would never be back to plant another garden.

Randy strode up to the table. Tyler looked up at the young smiling cowpuncher. Tyler was annoyed to see the man look so jubilant this early in the morning. And with both hands behind his back, it was obvious the man was hiding something. "Mornin', boss. Bethann."

They both grumbled a hello.

"I got in late last night after you sent me to town for supplies. Saw Miss Lily and her uncle."

Bethann's head popped up. Her smooth jade eyes fixed on Tyler's ranch hand.

"Actually, they were nice enough to invite me to dinner. Did you know her uncle has offered to take

Miss Lily to San Francisco so she could open a dress shop?''

Tyler's meal churned in the pit of his stomach.

"Papa, is San Acisco far from the ranch?''

Her pleading eyes tugged at him from every corner of his heart. "Yeah, sweetcakes, it's in California.''

Bethann put her head down.

"When's she going?'' Tyler asked, feigning a non-chalance he wasn't feeling.

"Don't rightly know. Maybe never. She's thinking on stayin' put right here in Sweet Springs and re-opening her father's mercantile. Her uncle's willin' to do whatever Miss Lily wants. But the train leaves day after tomorrow. Miss Lily hasn't made up her mind yet.''

Tyler grunted. "Just like a woman, doesn't know what she wants.''

Randy gave him a curious stare. "Jeez, boss, everybody knows what Miss Lily wants. Everybody but you, that is.''

Tyler twisted his mouth, then glanced at his daughter. Bethann gave him a hopeful look. Tyler glared off into the distance. Having Lily leave was one thing, but having her stay in town, just out of his reach, would test his willpower to the limit.

Tyler lifted the mug of coffee to his mouth. Bitter.

"While we were eatin' a fine meal at the hotel, Bud Henderson came up to pay his respects. Seems he's wantin' to court Miss Lily.''

Tyler spit the caustic brew out of his mouth. "Bud? Jim Henderson's boy?''

Randy scratched his head. "He ain't a boy anymore, boss. Bud's about the same age as Miss Lily, as I recall.''

"Humph." Tyler tossed the remaining coffee in his mug out. He watched the stream of liquid splash onto the ground. Blood pulsed up in his head, making it throb. Must be Wes's terrible coffee giving him a headache.

He cleared his mind as he made mental calculations, realizing Randy was right about Bud's age. An image of the handsome young blond-haired man he'd known for some time now flashed into his head. Bud Henderson and Lily? The throbbing in his head intensified. Angry, he shifted his body to view Randy directly. "Anything else you're wanting to report."

"Uh, report?" Randy looked puzzled. "Oh, yeah, I almost forgot. Miss Lily made this here doll up for Bethann."

He swung his arms around from his back to show her the doll. Bethann jumped for joy seeing the home-made doll that nearly resembled Miss Daisy. When he handed it to her, she clutched the doll to her chest.

"Oh, boy!" Bethann's face lit like a thousand candles. "Papa, lookee what Miss Lily made for me."

Randy added slowly, as if reciting from a book, "She says to treat the doll like a new member of the family. Not a replacement. She says you can love someone new, completely and wholly different from the way you loved the one you lost."

Tyler shot his head up to stare at his cowhand. Was that message meant for his daughter or for him?

Had he been unfairly comparing Lily to his deceased wife? Lizabeth couldn't abide living at the ranch. She wasn't cut out for it. Tyler had come to recognize that fact over the years. And the guilt he had felt at losing her in that stampede nearly destroyed him.

But Lily…was different. She adapted easily. She took to the ranch like a swan to a clear lake. Gracefully. She'd learned how to shoot, how to ride, and she'd saved his life on two separate occasions. Even when he'd told her not to, she'd holstered her gun and come to his defense against Muldoon. If she hadn't, perhaps both of them wouldn't have survived and Bethann would be at the mercy of a deranged man.

"Papa, now can we go into town so's I can thank her?"

Tyler still couldn't think past Lily almost losing her life because of him. "She's got her uncle now, Bethann. They're a family, just like you and me. It's best you remember that. We'll write her a note and I'll see that someone delivers it to her."

Tyler faced the miserable truth. He was no closer to getting over Lily than the day she'd left with her uncle. It had been weeks. And now the threat of her leaving, or worse, staying and being courted by the men in town, rankled. The thought brought searing pain to his gut.

Tyler was at a complete loss.

If he asked her to stay, as his wife, would she? She'd already refused his two other proposals. But he hoped this time would be different. He'd be asking her to stay for all the right reasons.

A wealthy uncle could offer Lily the world. All Tyler had was a small parcel of mud-entrenched grazing land, fly-stickin' cattle and a house only half built without a lick of furniture. Tyler got up from the table abruptly.

Damn it all.

He took a last look at his pouting daughter. "I've

got a ton of work to do today. Maybe by tonight, we'll be sleeping in our house again. Would you like that?''

Bethann's downcast expression was answer enough. His daughter learned a tough lesson at much too early an age.

Life wasn't always fair.

''I suppose,'' she said, keeping her eyes down. ''Won't be the same without Miss Lily, though.''

No, Tyler thought, nothing's the same without Lily.

Lily descended the stairs of the hotel slowly, recalling the last time she'd been here—when Tyler had dragged her up to a room to lecture her. He'd nearly destroyed her reputation that day, but none of it mattered now. She'd be leaving town soon, to start a whole new life.

The thought recoiled in her stomach with such commotion Lily rubbed the area reflectively. She met her uncle at the base of the stairs.

''Are you feeling poorly, Lily?'' He glanced at the hand protecting her stomach.

''No, I'm fine.'' She smiled and took his proffered arm as they walked into the dining room.

''You look very pretty this afternoon.''

Lily smoothed her green satin dress adorned with ecru lace then removed her gloves as Uncle Jasper helped her to a seat at the best table in the restaurant. ''Thank you.''

She made sure to smile often at her generous uncle. He'd been so kind, so loving. She didn't want him to know that her heart was slowly breaking. It wasn't his fault. He'd led as lonely a life as she had and now at least they had found each other.

He'd treated her to a whole new wardrobe, complete

with all the accessories. At one time in her life Lily would have been ecstatic having all these fineries. Little did her uncle know, she'd much rather be wearing simple cottons while cooking a meal in the Kincaide household than parading around in these exquisite clothes. She'd not tell her uncle how she felt. It had given him great pleasure to treat her to all these nice things.

"I've taken the liberty of inviting Joellen Withers to dinner tonight. I hope you don't mind?"

"Heavens, no. Joellen is the dearest woman I know. She has been a very good friend to me here."

"That's what I understand. I'm grateful for everyone who has helped you get by after Jonah's death. Including the handsome young rancher. It was a good thing, him hiring you." He quirked a graying eyebrow up.

Her uncle had been sweetly prodding her almost every day about her time with Tyler. Lily hadn't shared too much, but she surmised her uncle knew they'd had more than a business relationship.

"Yes. Bethann..." she said on a breath, remembering the child she held close to her heart. "Bethann is such a lovely child. Tyler needed some help out at the ranch with her and I needed a place to live."

"And that's all it was to you—a place to live?" Her uncle's expression seemed dubious. Lily couldn't explain to him what living with the Kincaides had meant to her.

The Circle K had been her home. She loved it there, but Tyler had made it very clear, it really wasn't her home. He'd discarded her the moment her uncle showed up. She'd had too much pride to plead with Tyler to let her stay. Lord knew, it was what she des-

perately wanted. The thought of him having to handle
Bethann, rebuild his home, take care of the ranch without her, brought knots to her insides.

What could she do but leave town? Tyler hadn't
given her any other option. She'd mulled over the idea
of staying, reopening the mercantile and competing
with the big emporium, but her heart wasn't in it. She
couldn't remain here and pretend casual friendship
with Tyler when the very sight of him would send her
into a tizzy.

Lily took a deep breath. She couldn't think about
Tyler anymore. She hadn't been sleeping or eating
well.

It was time to make a new life for herself. "I
worked for Tyler as nanny to his daughter. I was
the…housekeeper."

Her uncle nodded in understanding. "And now you
think it best to leave town?"

"Y-yes." Saying the words never got any easier.
"I don't want to stay on here. I've made up my mind.
If you'd still like to take me, I'd love to see San Fran-
cisco."

Uncle Jasper took her hand. "I told you I'd do
whatever it takes to make you happy. We can live
anywhere, Lily."

"Fine, then. I won't change my mind."

All this talk about leaving ruined Lily's appetite. It
was time to change the subject. "You seem to be enjoying Joellen's company lately." She smiled coyly at
her uncle, tilting her head.

He cleared his throat. "Yes, well, Joellen's been a
big help to me here. As you know, I came upon her
ranch first, and she helped me find Kincaide's spread.
I thought it only fitting to invite her to dinner."

Lily fidgeted with the silverware on the table. "You had lunch with her one day, as well. And didn't you bump into her at Wilbourne's Emporium a few days back?"

"Yes, yes, indeed. It was a pleasant encounter."

"Have you met her daughter, Letty Sue?"

The joy on her uncle's face vanished immediately. He frowned. "I did, indeed."

Lily chuckled, the sound feeling wonderful to her ears. She hadn't had a merry moment since leaving Tyler's ranch. "Not such a pleasant encounter."

He glanced around the restaurant and whispered, "No. That girl is terribly spoiled. Seems she needs a bit of straightening out."

"Joellen's had to raise her by herself. Her husband died unexpectedly when Letty Sue was a child."

"Hmm. I know. Joellen's such a fine woman."

"You admire her?"

Uncle Jasper blushed. "Well, yes. I do believe I do."

Lily bit back a grin. "You know, Uncle, I think I'll retire early tonight. Why don't you and Joellen have dinner without me? I have packing to do and some loose ends to tie up before we leave for San Francisco."

"Lily, are you sure? We'd both love your company."

"Oh, yes. I'm sure. Give Joellen my best."

Lily felt a sense of relief. They had only one day left in town. If her uncle found pleasure in Joellen's company, then she'd let them alone to enjoy their evening. Besides, as the time of her departure drew near, Lily's disposition grew increasingly more solemn. She'd not spoil her uncle's time this evening.

He nodded. "I shall. Well, then," he said opening the menu. "After we order lunch, I suppose I should tell you what I know of San Francisco. I believe it will be an exciting new experience for us both."

Lily sighed heavily and opened her menu. She didn't believe she would know another exciting day if she lived to be one hundred and one.

Chapter Twenty

"Papa, Papa, come quick."

Tyler woke to his daughter's excited voice. He'd lain awake most of the night struggling with thoughts of his future—a future without Lily. He must have finally slept in the early hours because he was usually the first one up and out of bed. Unlike most mornings, today the sun beat him in its rise.

Bethann tugged at his arm. "Whoa, hold on, sweetcakes. What's got you so excited?" He ran a hand through his unruly hair and squinted at his daughter.

Bethann had bedded down in the part of the house that was completed. Her room was the first one finished. Tyler chose to sleep in a room still devoid of walls. He found he needed the open air. It helped to clear his mind.

The sense of loss he felt not having Lily there, beside him in the night, seemed a bit easier to bear. He wondered how he'd feel when the walls went up and the roof was on. With the house completed, would it ever feel like home again?

"Papa, I got to show you somethin'. Hurry and get up."

Tyler scratched his head. "Okay, okay. I'm coming." He dressed quickly, throwing on a shirt, wondering what his daughter was so dang happy over.

She dragged him out of the makeshift house and into the front yard. "Look, Papa, look. Do you see it?"

Tyler's mouth dropped open. He couldn't believe what he was seeing. Amid the ashes on the side of the house he hadn't begun to reconstruct, next to a big pile of burnt smoky wood shavings, bloomed a stubborn, resistant, glorious flower. The purple-hued marvel lifted its face to the early morning sun.

"I think it's a lily," his daughter prodded. Tyler knew that it wasn't. But it was Lily, in all other respects. In all things that mattered.

"It's a miracle, Papa. Wes says so and so does Randy!"

"How'd you suppose…how on earth? I didn't think anything survived from Lily's garden."

"It's so pretty. The most beautiful flower I ever did see. Can we show Miss Lily, Papa? Can we?"

Stunned, Tyler continued to stare at the flower. "I, uh…" Dumbfounded, Tyler was speechless. If ever there was a sign, this had to be it. Thoughts filtered through, pleasing, hope-filled thoughts of the kind of life Tyler had always wanted. A life where he and the woman he loved could raise his daughter sharing the joys and challenges of ranch living.

He was struck hard and fast with the truth. This was Lily's home. He and Bethann were her family. On impulse and knowing in his heart what he was about to do was the right thing, he said, "Get dressed, little one. Make it quick, we have to go into town."

He had to get Lily back before it was too late. And

Tyler thought ruefully, he'd need luck and a whole lot of help from his friends to convince her to come back. "We're going to bring Lily home."

Lily knelt to place a bouquet of hand-picked wild-flowers between her parents' graves. Saying goodbye was not easy. But at least she'd done the one thing her father had asked of her—she'd located her uncle and was about to embark on a new life with him in San Francisco. The Lord's Prayer fell from her lips and as she stood, she wiped a tear from her eye.

Lily took a minute to take in a breath. There was another goodbye she'd have to make today. To Tyler and Bethann. Staying on in Sweet Springs would only tear at her heart, knowing how close she'd come to real happiness. She'd decided to make a clean break since Tyler had made his feelings clear by not inviting her back to the ranch.

She'd spent the past few weeks with her uncle. Getting to know him again had been a pleasure. He was a loving, dear man who enjoyed doting on her every whim. Even though Lily hadn't asked for much, just some clothes, since all she had had gone up in flames, Uncle Jasper had insisted on showering her with the finest gifts a woman could want.

Sighing deeply, Lily strode out the cemetery gate and secured the latch on the picket fence. A horse's snort made her turn quickly, glancing up the path. Stunned, Lily gasped. Tyler sat on Blaze, watching her.

He tipped his hat and shot her a dazzling smile. "Mornin', Miss Lily."

There were others on horses behind him, but she didn't notice who they were. Her gaze rested solely on the handsome rancher she had come to love. Her heart thrummed an erratic rhythm. "Hello, Tyler."

With a finger to his black felt hat, he shoved the brim up on his forehead, allowing Lily to see his face fully.

"You look beautiful, Lily."

Nervously, Lily brushed her prim white gloves along the creases of her sateen gown. Her plume hat nearly took flight from a strong breeze blowing by. With a hand to her head, she righted the lopsided hat. She felt self-conscious in the expensive clothes she wore. If Tyler bothered to ask, she would have told him great wealth didn't matter to her. Lily truly only wanted simple pleasures in life. Pleasures only he could give her.

But what had brought him out here? She wondered why he stared at her as though he'd never seen a woman before. She smiled softly. "Thank you."

Blaze shifted impatiently. Tyler leaned forward, resting a hand on the saddle horn. "I hear you're leaving town. Weren't you going to say goodbye?"

"I, uh, yes—of course. I wouldn't leave without saying goodbye. I was coming out to the ranch this afternoon."

"Can't let you do that." His solemn tone held conviction.

Lily's heart plummeted. Tyler still didn't want her at the ranch. Choked up, a small, "Oh" was all she managed.

"No. I can't let you leave."

Her eyes met his directly. "You c-can't?"

Another whisper of a breeze lifted her hat. She raised her hand to hold it in place.

"No, ma'am, I can't. Seems you still owe me. You promised to stay on at the ranch until the cattle drive."

That was all he wanted from her? Silly notions that should have gone up in smoke with the Kincaide ranch house brought a trembling to her lips. "Oh, I'm s-sure you'll h-have no t-trouble finding a replacement. My uncle and I have already made plans."

Uncle Jasper appeared from beyond a tree. His distinguished gray hair shone like a beacon in the bright light of day. "Lily, do whatever makes you happy, child. I'm beginning to like the town of Sweet Springs." His smile rested briefly on Joellen Withers, who stepped out from beyond the very same tree. The sweet-natured woman gave Lily a reassuring smile.

Joellen and Uncle Jasper? Lily knew he admired the woman, but as they stood side by side in front of the tall ironwood, she realized what a nice couple they made. Both had led lonely lives. Had they found solace in each other?

Tyler cleared his throat and Lily's attention once again focused on him. "No one could replace you, Lily."

When Lily didn't respond right away, Tyler went on. "Of course, we'd have to make it legal and all. I'm, uh, talking about getting married."

Lily dared not hope. She planted her hands on her hips. She wanted a real proposal from Tyler. Nothing else would do. "And why do you want to marry me *this* time?"

Tyler grinned. "The boys can't stand Wes's cooking."

Lily concealed a chuckle, noticing Wes several yards behind Tyler, grimacing. Randy gave him a playful jab in the arm. Was the whole town in on this?

"Not good enough, Mr. Kincaide."

Tyler rubbed his jaw. "My daughter cries every day for you."

Lily glanced around to see Bethann strapped into Pint-Size, pursing her lips in a pout, with tears in her eyes. Lily's heart bled for an instant, then she noticed Tyler giving his daughter a wink of approval.

"I'm still not sure," she hedged, but her deceitful heart began melting on the spot.

"There's a big beautiful flower in your garden waiting for you to tend."

Lily blinked back her surprise. This, she didn't expect. She could barely contain her joy. "I... don't...know."

Tyler dismounted, took off his hat, then approached her. His dark eyes held hers. In a rich powerful voice he declared, "Then know this, Miss Lily. I'm proposing marriage for the third and final time, because you're the damnedest best shot in the territory, because I don't want a day to go by without you by my side and because I love you with all of my heart."

Lily gave him her brightest smile. Inside she was turning cartwheels. "Could you say that last part again?"

"I love you, Lily," he said without pause.

Lily's heart cried out with joy. "I love you, too, Tyler." She stood there, staring into his handsome face, searching his love-filled eyes. On a winsome sigh she offered, "And I guess a woman could do much worse."

"But a man couldn't do any better, sweetheart."

He swept her up into an embrace. His lips took hers in a tantalizing kiss filled with pent-up passion and desire. Their eyes locked again. "Damn it, woman, I do love you."

Lily chuckled, pressing a soft kiss to his mouth. "Why, Mr. Kincaide, I do believe I'll have a lifetime to teach you not to swear."

Tyler cinched his hands around her waist, pulling her closer. "Then you'll marry me, sweet Lily?"

Lily tilted her head and gave him a sinful smile. "Hell, yes."

Epilogue

Lily knelt down, picking a perfect array of recently bloomed flowers from her spring garden. She held the bouquet in her hand, carefully checking the delicate petals.

"You forgot one, honey." Tyler crouched next to her, handing her one beautifully formed white lily. He cast her a big smile and Lily's heart hammered in her chest.

Darn the man.

One smile from her handsome husband had her acting like a foolish ninny. It would never change.

And she'd never been happier.

With hands together, they placed the last lily of the season in the center of the bouquet.

"I think Joellen will be pleased," she said.

Tyler stood and with both hands under her arms, gently helped her up. She felt cumbersome and awkward, but when her husband caressed her growing belly, Lily knew a moment of complete joy.

"It's a right fine bouquet, sweetheart, but I think Uncle Jasper is the one who's really pleased," Tyler said with a grin. "It isn't every day a man gets a new wife and a second chance at happiness." He kissed her cheek. "I should know."

Lily smiled. The baby rumbled inside, kicking and reminding her he'd be greeting her any day now. "I hope our child doesn't pick this exact moment to enter into the world. I really do want to attend Uncle Jasper's wedding."

"Anytime our baby decides to come is fine by me." Tyler cast her a somber look. "Are you worried, honey?"

Lily chuckled. "Heavens, no. I can't wait to have our baby, Tyler. It's more than a dream…it's a miracle."

"It's a miracle I got you to agree to marry me in the first place," he teased. Tyler never failed to remind her how she'd made him ask her three times before she said yes.

"I wanted your love," she said quietly.

"You have it, until the day I die."

He brought her close, carefully wrapping his arms around her. His lips took hers in a passionate kiss, then he set her away to look deeply into her eyes. "I suppose I shouldn't worry over you having our child. There isn't anything you don't do well."

It warmed Lily's heart that Tyler had such faith in her. Her husband sent her a thrilling smile and Lily might have melted right on the spot if Bethann hadn't come running out of the house.

"Bethann, you're all dressed!"

The little girl grinned, holding on to Miss Blossoms, the new doll Lily had made for her. "I took my own bath and everything," she beamed.

"Why, sweetie, how grown-up of you. You did a fine job with your hair, too." Bethann had managed to make two crooked braids in her hair. Lily had never seen anything quite so adorable.

"Papa says I have to help out more, because I'm going to have me a new sister soon."

"That's right, sweetcakes. And you've done me proud today," Tyler said.

"And me, too," Lily added, "but remember, you may be getting a brother instead of a sister. Only God knows for sure."

Bethann looked at her father then to Lily. "Don't matter none. Rhonda Mae loves her brother just fine."

Lily smiled and looked at the man she adored. "Love is most important of all, Bethann."

Tyler took Bethann's hand, then Lily's. He led them to the buckboard.

Lily stopped for a moment to take a look at the house that had become her home. Flowers bloomed from each and every corner of the yard. Her heart filled with immense joy.

"Couldn't be any prettier," Tyler whispered in her ear.

"I know, my garden." Lily sighed.

"The garden's nice enough, honey. I was talking about you."

Lily blushed and he kissed her quickly.

"You're the most beautiful flower I've ever seen."

* * * * *

CHARLENE SANDS

resides in sunny southern California with her husband Don and their two college-bound children, Jason and Nikki. Her love of the American West stems from early childhood memories of storytelling times with her imaginative father. There was always a "sheriff" who needed her help to save the day or a treasure hunt that would spill coins from her father's pocket. What fun it was for her to retrieve those "treasures."

When not writing, she enjoys all things romantic, including warm western nights, great coffee, to-die-for chocolate, Pacific Coast beaches and, of course, happy endings!

HH554

Travel back in time to America's past with wonderful Westerns from Harlequin Historicals

ON SALE MARCH 2001

LONGSHADOW'S WOMAN
by **Bronwyn Williams**
(The Carolinas, 1879)

LILY GETS HER MAN
by **Charlene Sands**
(Texas, 1880s)

ON SALE APRIL 2001

THE SEDUCTION OF SHAY DEVEREAUX
by **Carolyn Davidson**
(Louisiana, 1870)

NIGHT HAWK'S BRIDE
by **Jillian Hart**
(Wisconsin, 1840)

Silhouette
bestselling authors

KASEY MICHAELS

RUTH LANGAN

CAROLYN ZANE

welcome you to a world of family, privilege and power with three brand-new love stories about America's most beloved dynasty, the Coltons

Brides of Privilege

Available May 2001

Silhouette®
Where love comes alive™

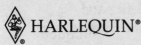

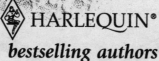
HARLEQUIN®

bestselling authors

Merline Lovelace
Deborah Simmons
Julia Justiss

*cordially invite you to enjoy three
brand-new stories of unexpected love*

The
Officer's
Bride

Available April 2001

HARLEQUIN®
Makes any time special®